It's Raining Cats And Dogs

Author
Norman JN Lobb

A USA Publishing Hub Book

Book Title: *It's Raining Cats and Dogs*
Author: Norman JN Lobb

Printed in the United States of America
Book Cover & Book Design by: USA Publishing Hub

This is a work of fiction. All names, characters, and incidents are either the product of the author's imagination or are used fictitiously. Any resemblance to actual persons, living or dead, business establishments, or other events or locales is entirely coincidental.

(Norman JN Lobb)

Contents

Chapter 1

RAINING CATS AND DOGS

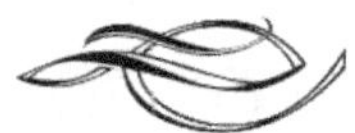

The High-Tech Facility

The Pet-link research lab stretched out in pristine, geometric precision beneath the harsh glow of white fluorescent lights. Sterile white walls met polished concrete floors, creating an environment that radiated a cold, clinical efficiency. Every line was straight, every surface immaculate. The hum of technology filled the space in a soft undercurrent, steady, controlled, precise. Along one side of the room, banks of computers blinked with rhythmic consistency, their monitors alive with real-time brainwave data displayed as looping neon graphs that pulsed like digital heartbeats.

In the center of the lab stood a ring of high-tech examination pods, sleek, metallic recliners outfitted with armrests bristling with sensors and fine-tipped electrodes. Each pod was flanked by a smaller adjacent platform, custom-designed for the comfort and monitoring of an animal companion. These paired stations stood like mirrored thrones of science, prepared to bridge the neurological divide between species.

Glass partitions framed the main lab, separating it from an adjacent observation area and a line of stainless-steel animal pens. The transparency allowed uninterrupted oversight without contaminating the sterile workspace. Every surface gleamed under the relentless lighting, there wasn't a fingerprint, smudge, or speck of dust anywhere. Even the air carried the unmistakable tang of medical-grade disinfectant and faint ozone, lending the illusion that even the very molecules had been sterilized.

Beyond the reinforced glass door at the far end of the lab, a specially designed walking yard extended outward. This indoor-outdoor enclosure, visible through a long horizontal window, was engineered as a small sanctuary for the facility's animal subjects. It featured artificial turf, carefully arranged shrub planters, and even a faux streetlamp, efforts meant to simulate a comforting, natural environment within the otherwise artificial context. The perimeter was ringed with tall chain-link fencing topped with sensors, and motion-activated floodlights flickered on as dusk began to settle. The entire facility echoed the aesthetic of ultramodern science: arcing steel beams overhead, embedded LED strips that mimicked the color temperature of daylight, and a barely perceptible white noise hum designed to reduce stress, for both humans and animals.

Despite its sophistication, the lab felt oddly devoid of life, like a silent spacecraft awaiting a mission launch. It was a temple of advanced medical research, yet its perfection seemed to repel emotion, leaving only anticipation in the sterile stillness.

The Volunteers and Their Pets

In stark contrast to the impersonal precision of the lab, ten volunteers and their cherished pets brought a necessary and touching warmth into the space. Gathered in a loose semicircle around the central pods, each person was accompanied by a dog or a cat, their presence breaking the cold symmetry of the room with softness, motion, and life. The low hum of conversation, occasional laughter, and scattered barks or meows created a gentle chaos, a living counterpoint to the mechanical drone of the equipment.

Some volunteers sat perched on the edge of their assigned chairs, hands constantly reaching to comfort their pets. Others stood, pacing or fidgeting, casting anxious glances between their companions and the technicians performing final checks on the Pet-link systems.

Victor Alvarez, a broad-shouldered former firefighter in his forties, stood with one hand resting gently on the neck of Max, his aging German Shepherd. Victor's calm, grounded presence lent a sense of stability to those around him. Max, ever loyal, sat obediently at Victor's side, though the dog's ears twitched with every strange sound. The tension in his posture revealed a deep attentiveness, he was alert, and perhaps a little wary.

Directly across from them, Serena Li cradled Tao, her sleek Siamese cat, like a fragile artifact. Serena, a wiry graduate student in neuroscience, wore her nerves close to the surface. Her eyes sparkled with intellectual curiosity even as she whispered reassurances to Tao in a barely audible tone. "It's a big adventure," she murmured, her voice soothing but tight. She wasn't just talking to the cat, she was talking herself through it, each word an anchor to keep her steady.

To Victor's left, Jamal King, who had been cracking jokes since the group arrived, was struggling to keep Peanut, his excitable pug, from wriggling off his lap. Jamal was tall, in his thirties, with a megawatt grin that usually lit up a room. Today, though, his smile faltered slightly, his hands trembling as he tried to calm his snorting companion. "Easy, little man," he chuckled, voice thinner than usual. "We're just going to become world-famous, no pressure."

Next to Jamal, Maria Sanchez, a gentle-eyed teacher in her fifties, rocked slightly as she held Luna, her plump tabby cat, in her arms. Her voice was barely more than a whisper as she hummed a Spanish lullaby, one she'd sung to her grandchildren and now instinctively used to soothe her anxious feline. Luna's tense body began to soften, her muscles loosening in rhythm with the familiar melody. As Luna calmed, so too did Daisy, the tension slowly draining from her shoulders.

At another station, Dr. Yusuf Khan was double-checking the delicate placement of electrodes on his cat Cleo's head. Yusuf, one of the lead neuroscientists on the project, had surprised many by volunteering himself and his beloved British Shorthair for the experiment. A man in his fifties with salt-and-pepper hair and eyes that held both intellect and kindness, he had insisted on going through the procedure firsthand. His sleeves rolled up, lab coat slightly askew, Yusuf knelt beside Cleo and gently scratched under her chin. "We'll be okay, girl," he whispered, voice heavy with a mix of resolve and guilt.

Nearby, Talia Chen, a young artist with streaks of purple in her hair, crouched beside her scruffy mutt, Picasso. Her bangles chimed softly as she patted the dog's patchwork fur. Picasso wore a rainbow-colored bandana, and Talia herself was a splash of color in the monochrome lab. "You're gonna be a superstar, Pic," she said, her tone bright despite the nervous tapping of her fingers.

Across the room, Rahul Patel, a software engineer in his late twenties, was preoccupied with checking the smart collar on Chai, his lively corgi. His leg bounced rhythmically, betraying his unease, and he muttered under his breath about data streams and signal fidelity. A fellow volunteer gently touched his shoulder, grounding him for a moment. Rahul offered a tight-lipped smile, adjusted his glasses, and turned his attention to petting Chai, trying to calm his own racing mind.

On the far side of the room, Ava Brooks stood immaculate in tailored slacks and a silk blouse, looking entirely out of place in the informal setting. A powerful corporate attorney by trade, Ava was used to maintaining control in every room she entered. But now, she sighed and knelt beside Winston, her fawn-colored French Bulldog, straightening the little sensor vest wrapped around his compact torso. "Just a little longer, champ," she said softly. Her voice wavered, ever so slightly. Winston tilted his head, sensing the uncertainty behind her polished exterior.

Toward the rear of the room, Kevin O'Neill, a nervous Columbia University student, was doing his best to manage Daisy, his exuberant Golden Retriever. Daisy's tail wagged like a turbine, knocking into equipment and nearly toppling a tray of sterilized instruments. A technician caught the tray just in time, chuckling. Kevin, face red, tugged Daisy gently and muttered, "Settle, girl... please." The embarrassment was clear on his face, but so was the deep bond between him and his joyful dog.

Near the entrance stood Taylor Morgan, an athletic ex-Marine in her thirties with short-cropped hair and sharp eyes. She held the leash of Titan, a towering Doberman with a physique that mirrored her own, disciplined, muscular, alert. Taylor's posture was rigid, every inch of her reflecting a lifetime of training and readiness. Titan, perfectly at heel, didn't move an inch unless she did. His eyes stayed locked on hers, as though silently awaiting instruction.

This collection of ten New Yorkers, diverse in age, background, race, and reason for volunteering, had come together for a shared goal. Some were motivated by a scientific spirit, others by financial need, and a few by the hope of deepening the unspoken bond between species. They traded nervous glances and quiet jokes, masking the swirl of anticipation that hung thick in the sterilized air. Each had offered up something deeply personal: their mind, and their most trusted companion.

Gathering Storm

Unnoticed by many in the lab, daylight had quietly surrendered to an eerie twilight. Through the tall windows, the Manhattan skyline disappeared behind a thick, swirling mass of clouds. Purple and charcoal layers twisted together, obscuring the last rays of the sun. The storm rolled in like a slow-moving predator, the first growl of thunder rumbling low and distant.

In the pet yard beyond the glass, the branches of the lone tree began to sway. A sudden gust of wind rustled the turf and caused the shrubbery to tremble. The lab's internal climate system kicked in with a subtle whirr, adjusting airflow in response to the sudden drop in barometric pressure.

Jamal was the first to comment. "Looks like Zeus is clocking in for overtime," he quipped, trying to lighten the mood with a shaky grin. Laughter flickered around the room, brief but welcome. Max whined softly at Titan's feet, ears folding back in discomfort. Luna gripped Maries's sweater more tightly, while Titan let out a low, cautious sound from deep in his chest.

Overhead, the fluorescent lights flickered once. The room collectively held its breath.

Dr. Yusuf glanced sharply at a technician, who immediately responded with a reassuring nod. "Backup generators will activate if there's a power loss," the tech called out clearly, trying to steady the growing anxiety.

But the tension had already taken root.

Thunder grew louder, each rumble closer, sharper. One technician tapped a command on a tablet, and a series of mechanical clicks echoed as automatic storm shutters began sliding down over the larger windows. Only narrow slits remained, framing flashes of lightning and the first sheets of heavy rain that now pelted the turf outside.

The rain patterns cast strange reflections through the window glass, shimmering across the lab floor in watery bands of light and Cleo. For a moment, the lab resembled an underwater vessel, suspended in a strange ocean of glass and storm.

Outside, nature gathered its fury. Inside, the humans braced themselves, for something new, untested, and extraordinary.

The Pet-link Procedure

"Alright everyone, it's time," came the steady voice of Dr. Nguyen over the lab intercom. The lead researcher's calm tone cut through the storm's growl, commanding attention.

The volunteers exchanged last glances with their pets, some hopeful, some anxious, then began guiding them into their designated stations. Chairs adjusted with a soft hydraulic hiss as participants settled in. The animals were coaxed gently onto the adjacent platforms, designed for their comfort and security.

Technicians moved with swift, silent efficiency. A fine mesh of electrodes was lowered onto each participant's head, a futuristic skullcap wired with tiny blinking sensors. Their pets received similar devices: dogs wore flexible collars embedded with neural sensors, while cats were fitted with delicate EEG caps that nestled between their ears. Cleo, never one to suffer indignities lightly, flicked her tail in protest.

Titan winced slightly as cold conductive gel touched his skin. Serena exhaled deeply and recited a silent mantra, eyes closed. Around the room, fiber-optic cables were plugged in one by one, connecting each human-animal pair to the central Pet-link system.

The monitors blinked to life. Across the room, ten paired graphs of human and animal brainwaves began to pulse in sync, their patterns fluctuating as the connection deepened. This was the heart of the experiment: an attempt to forge an empathic neural bridge, allowing both human and animal to glimpse one another's experience, if only briefly.

All participants had signed the necessary waivers. All had been warned that this was an early-stage trial, with unpredictable results. Most expected, at best, fleeting moments of shared emotion or sensory overlap. None could say what would actually happen next.

And outside, as lightning split the sky above the lab, something ancient stirred in the storm.

Inside the lab, the lights dimmed slightly to minimize distractions. A gentle whirring built in intensity as the Pet-link machines powered up, the sound echoing faintly beneath the hum of overhead vents.

"Beginning neural sync sequence in sixty seconds," announced a technician, his voice calm and professional over the intercom.

Heart rates quickened. Despite the cool, climate-controlled air, several participants felt sweat prickle on their palms. Taylor flexed her fingers around the armrests, offering a steadying glance toward Titan. The Doberman met her eyes, panting softly, his expression a question in itself, *Is this okay?*

Jamal cleared his throat, suddenly more solemn than he'd been all day. He leaned down and whispered to Peanut, his voice shaky but warm, "Let's become mind-meld buddies, okay, pal?"

His attempt at humor earned a faint smile from Rahul, though Rahul's own knuckles were white where he clutched Chai's tiny paw for reassurance.

The countdown timer on the wall ticked steadily downward. Thunder grumbled again outside, closer this time, like a warning. No one spoke now.

A symphony of soft beeps, whirrs, and escalating tones swelled within the lab as final calibrations finished. Overhead, the intercom chimed gently: Pet - Link initiating in... 3... 2... 1."

In that suspended moment, every volunteer inhaled together, a collective breath held like a diver's gasp before a plunge.

The machines engaged with a low thrum that vibrated through the floor. On nearby monitors, brainwave lines from each human and pet began to curve toward each other, frequencies gently syncing.

Some participants felt a tingling warmth spread across their scalps. Others experienced an uncanny clarity, like tuning into a frequency just barely within reach, a mental signal previously hidden in static.

Serena's eyes fluttered beneath closed lids. She focused on the rhythm of Tao's breathing, and with a jolt of recognition, realized she could feel it as vividly as her own.

Titan blinked rapidly. He could've sworn he tasted the peanut butter treat he'd given Max that morning, a phantom flavor blooming on his tongue, even though his mouth was empty.

Maria gasped, softly. A wave of affection hit her, so strong, so sudden, it brought tears to her eyes. It wasn't hers. It was Luna's love for her, reverberating back through the link like a feedback loop of warmth.

All around the lab, subtle reactions played across faces: awe, amusement, tears, the experiment was working. Human and animal minds were brushing up against one another, touching thoughts like fingertips through misted glass.

No one noticed that outside, the storm had grown fierce. Rain now fell in driving sheets, hammering the roof. The sky beyond the half-shuttered windows lit up with jagged pulses of lightning.

Inside, the building's power grid hummed under strain. Lights flickered once, then again.

The lab equipment, however, remained steady, cloaked in its own steady, blue glow.

Dr. Yusuf, both a participant and the proud architect of the Pet-link procedure, sat riveted in his chair, eyes wide as cascading streams of data poured across his monitor. Decades of theory were crystallizing into real-time phenomenon.

And then, in the microsecond a breathless instant, nature intervened.

A bolt of white-hot lightning speared down from the sky, targeting the building with uncanny precision.

It was as though the storm had been watching. As though it had decided to interfere.

Lightning Strikes

Without warning, the bolt struck. A searing spear of electricity slammed into the facility's roof with the sharp crack of a world tearing in two.

It hit the main power conduit, the artery feeding the lab, and overloaded the entire system in a blinding cascade of blue-white sparks.

Inside the lab, the overhead lights flared wildly, then, POP!

Several bulbs exploded overhead, raining tiny shards of glass across the polished floor.

Everything was briefly illuminated in stark, sterile white, Vision erased as though a giant flashbulb had detonated.

Then came the thunder: a deafening, bone-jarring CRACK-BOOM that piggybacked instantly on the lightning.

The floor shuddered.

Computers hissed, snapped, then died. Two monitors blew out in bursts of sparks and acrid smoke.

The room filled with the sharp scent of ozone and scorched plastic. Every hair on every head, human and animal alike, stood on end, a wave of static charge prickling across skin and fur.

Inside the Pet-link pods, something far more terrifying happened.

A surge of raw, unfiltered energy shot through the fiber-optic lines connecting human and pet.

Ten chairs rattled.

Ten human beings arched violently, backs stiff and eyes unseeing.

Ten animals convulsed on their platforms.

Time seemed to shudder. Reality paused.

For a fraction of a second, one impossible, stretched-out moment, blinding halos of light erupted around each human-pet pair. The metallic caps on human heads glowed in unison with the collars around their pets' necks, connected by pulses of rippling, liquid light.

It was like watching consciousness itself unzip.

Victor felt the floor vanish beneath his sense of self, like a trapdoor flung open under his soul. He heard Max yelp, not through his ears, but inside his skull.

Serena's world exploded in white. Sensations not her own slammed into her, chemical smells, ultrasonic whines, metallic hums too sharp for human ears.

Jamal saw stars. He also tasted peanut butter. Again. But this time it was richer, deeper, almost metallic, as though he were *inside* the flavor itself.

Daisy's heartbeat stumbled. Then a second heartbeat joined it, smaller, faster, and then took its place.

Each participant was engulfed in a surreal storm of shared sensation, a kaleidoscope of mental and physical overlap that defied logic or comprehension.

The light around each pair pulsed to a blinding climax,

And imploded.

With a final snap and fizzle, the Pet-link machines went dead.

The lab was thrown into darkness, broken only by the flickering red glow of emergency lights that blinked to life a second later.

The entire event had lasted no more than two seconds.

But nothing would ever be the same.

The Aftermath

Sparks dribbled from a scorched control panel. Smoke drifted lazily toward the ceiling.

Several technicians lay sprawled where they'd been thrown by the shockwave, unconscious or groaning.

Others staggered to their feet, ears ringing, shouting muffled through the aftermath haze.

The volunteers, ten of them, had slumped in their chairs or strained against their restraints, either unconscious or nearly so, their final moments of awareness tangled in confusion and pain.

Silence descended.

Only the drumming of rain and the far-off wail of an emergency siren broke it.

The Pet-link machines were dead. Their once-lively monitors were dark, cracked, and useless. Smoke coiled.

Nothing moved for several long, breathless moments.

And then,

A whimper.

From a human mouth that didn't quite sound human.

Followed by a howl, unmistakably canine, yet laced with something... not.

The silence shattered.

The real experiment had just begun.

Waking in the Wrong Body

Titan awoke to a world that made no sense.

Everything felt wrong.

The first thing he noticed was the smell, overwhelming, immediate, and impossibly sharp. He could distinguish the detergent used on the floor, the sweat of nearby technicians, the acrid sting of electrical fire, and something else: fear, rising like steam.

He blinked, no, not blinked. It was more like a shutter snapping. The world shifted, the edges too crisp, the colors too vibrant, the perspective too low. It was as though he were looking out through a wide-angle lens, his entire field of vision stretched into something both intimate and alien.

His limbs wouldn't move the way he wanted.

Victor as Max tried to speak, but the sound that escaped was not human. It was a bark.

A high, startled yelp.

No. That didn't come from me, he thought.

Except... it had.

That's when he looked down.

But it wasn't his chest rising and falling beneath him. It was Max's.

The lean, muscular body of his Doberman lay where Titan expected his own to be, his breathing quick, heart hammering. He tried to lift his hand, only to see a paw twitch instead.

A paw.

Titan whimpered, the sound escaping his throat before he could suppress it. It vibrated through the long, unfamiliar column of his neck, echoing inside his skull in a way that confirmed the impossible.

I'm in Max's body.

Panic surged. His heartbeat, Max's heartbeat, raced out of control.

Titan tried to sit up, but his new limbs didn't cooperate. His muscles jerked awkwardly, collapsing him onto his side. He whined involuntarily, the whimper low and trembling.

Across the room, another sound emerged, a choked gasp, followed by a strangled cough.

Daisy.

She was waking up too.

But the voice wasn't hers.

It was a low, anxious whine, Luna's.

Titan turned his head, far more easily this time, as instinct caught up with new biology, and saw Luna's small feline frame trembling in one of the restraint chairs.

Only now, the way she moved...

That was human panic in her eyes. Not canine confusion.

Luna looked back at him, no, *Daisy* looked back at him through Luna's body, and her gaze widened in recognition.

They knew.

They all knew.

Something had gone horribly wrong.

Something Wasn't Right

Dr. Harrow's voice cut sharply through the room, but Titan couldn't see her. His head turned too fast, overshooting the direction of the sound. His ears swiveled instinctively, *swiveled*, toward the noise before he could consciously process it.

"I need vitals! Where's my neurotech team?" she shouted.

A flurry of movement answered her. Footsteps, dozens of them, rushed in from the corridor, muffled only slightly by the soft rubber flooring. Monitors beeped wildly as technicians scrambled around the bodies of the human volunteers. Titan's, his *former*, body lay slumped in the chair, unresponsive.

He wanted to scream.

Instead, a deep, desperate growl welled up in his chest.

Two men in scrubs approached him with quiet caution, their voices barely above a whisper.

"He's in distress," one said. "Look at the eyes. He's tracking."

"But no human consciousness readings," the other muttered. "It's like the mind's relocated."

Titan barked, a sharp and deliberate sound that startled both men. Their eyes widened in realization.

"Is that... is that you, Taylor?" one asked, hesitantly.

Titan responded with a short, gruff bark.

The technician turned pale. "My god. It worked. But... not like it was supposed to."

Across the lab, another bark echoed, higher-pitched and frantic. Luna, was pacing in her seat, her tiny tabby body trembling uncontrollably as she tried to break free of the restraining straps.

Dr. Harrow moved in fast, her eyes wide with a strange mix of awe and horror. She wasn't yelling now. Her voice was low, intense.

"They've crossed the neural bridge," she whispered. "Completely."

She looked at the lead technician. "Are they stuck?"

"We don't know yet," he replied. "The system shut down mid-transfer. Lightning hit the backup conduit, fried the quantum interface."

"Is it reversible?"

He hesitated.

Titan caught the pause. Even through the haze of panic and unfamiliar instincts, he knew what it meant.

They didn't know.

Or worse, *they did.*

Trapped in Fur and Silence

The lab had fallen into a tense, organized chaos. Teams huddled around the unconscious human bodies, Taylor's included, hooking up monitors, scanning brainwaves, typing frantically into diagnostic tablets. But none of that helped Titan or Daisy now.

They were awake.

Alive.

And trapped.

Taylor shifted again in Max's body, attempting to stand. The action required immense concentration. His muscles responded on a delay, and his balance was off, his new legs longer than he expected, his center of gravity alien.

He managed to get upright on all fours, panting hard from the effort. Everything he did now triggered an onslaught of sensory input, scents, textures, vibrations in the floor, subtle changes in air pressure. It was overwhelming.

Titan turned and saw Luna's feline form still strapped to the chair, her body trembling as Daisy, still somewhere within, tried helplessly to work out how to move in this unfamiliar shape.

He trotted awkwardly toward her, his claws clicking against the lab floor.

A technician moved to intercept him, arms outstretched as though to block a rampaging beast.

Titan growled, not out of aggression, but frustration.

The technician froze. Then, slowly, he lowered his hands and backed off.

Dr. Harrow raised her voice again, this time addressing the entire room.

"We're not treating them like animals. That's still Taylor. That's still Kevin's. We follow protocol, but we treat them with dignity. Understand?"

Heads nodded all around, some more hesitantly than others.

A young woman approached Luna's chair with gentle hands, carefully loosening the restraints. Luna stumbled out, nearly falling, but Titan steadied her with his shoulder.

They stood like that for a moment: man and woman, now dog and cat, breathing the purefied electric air, both aware that the world they knew had irrevocably changed.

Titan's mind raced.

What if they couldn't go back?

What if their human bodies, those vessels lying unconscious just feet away, were nothing more than husks now?

His eyes met Luna's. Her ears were flat, her tail low, but her gaze was steady.

She was scared.

So was he.

But they weren't alone.

The facility staff were reeling, struggling to comprehend the scene unfolding before them. A nurse had rushed to Jamal's human body, assuming he was injured, only to have "Jamal" (really Peanut) lick her face in a panic. She screamed as the tall man, possessed by the mind of a terrified pug, nuzzled against her like an oversized puppy desperate for comfort.

Across the room, Dr. Nguyen stood frozen in disbelief Moments earlier, Dr. Yusuf had been a composed, dignified man in his fifties. Now, his cat body stood atop a chair, arms bent awkwardly, mouth open in a raw yowl of rage. Yusuf the human had taken over Cleo's body, and he was *confused*. His borrowed voice emerged not as words, but as wild, guttural cries, a symphony of fine indignation trapped in a human throat.

"This can't be happening..." a lab assistant gasped, backing away slowly from what looked like a scene from a horror-comedy film.

Just then, Taylor, driven by Titan's canine mind, lunged at the assistant with a low, feral growl, baring teeth. The assistant yelped, stumbling backward and knocking over an IV stand with a loud crash, *his* snarl was primal, teeth snapping inches from the man's arm.

It was pure chaos.

Red lights pulsed overhead. Alarms wailed through the corridors. Humans barked, yowled, hissed, and snarled, some crawling, some perched on furniture, some causing chaos. Meanwhile, the actual animals, now occupied by human minds, scrambled free from their stations, trembling with awareness.

But amid the pandemonium, something remarkable began to happen.

The displaced minds, Titan and the others, began to find each other.

Max, still disoriented, caught sight of Titan's Doberman body, crouched in a protective stance on the examination table. The dog's posture wasn't random, it was measured, alert, and deliberate. Titan recognized that fearless composure instantly.

That's Taylor.

Summoning his resolve, Titan let out a sharp series of barks, not words, but unmistakably a call. "Over here!"

Titan's ears perked at the sound. Taylor turned her head and gave a short, answering woof.

From beneath a nearby desk, Tao's Siamese form peeked out, drawn by the high-pitched panic bark of Rahul-in-corgi as he scrambled away from Ava-in-bulldog's accidental tangle. Despite the absurdity of the moment, Tao felt a flash of recognition, a *knowing*, in the corgi's wide, darting eyes. That chaotic energy? That had to be Rahul.

She crept out on silent paws.

One by one, the other animals, human minds trapped in furry bodies, began gravitating toward each other. Drawn by instinct, familiarity, or sheer desperation, they gathered at the center of the lab.

A German Shepherd. A Doberman. A Golden Retriever. A mutt. A pug. A French Bulldog. A corgi. And three cats: a Siamese, a tabby, and a shorthair.

They formed a rough, uncertain circle, facing outward as if bracing for a threat. It wasn't strategic, at least, not consciously, but it had the weight of instinct behind it.

They needed each other.

Eyes met across species, and understanding sparked. In the gentle brown gaze of the retriever, Titan saw Kevin's kindness. The pug's confused whimper could only be Jamal. Ava's trademark impatience burned in the Frenchie's squared stance. Talia's mutt paced restlessly, unable to stand still.

Barks, yips, meows, and whines filled the air, urgent and raw. To outside observers, it was noise. But inside that circle, the sounds carried meaning, fragmented but real. Tone and instinct filled the gaps where language failed.

Are you inside your pet? their expressions seemed to ask.

Yes... I think so.

What now?

The fear didn't vanish. But it became something they could share, *and sharing it made it lighter*. None of them was truly alone anymore. They could see it in each other's eyes: confusion, terror, disbelief, but also recognition.

Then, for a heartbeat, time seemed to slow.

Ten souls, still human at their core, regarded each other through the eyes of pets. Another flash of lightning lit the lab, illuminating the surreal circle they formed. For that brief instant, it was as if the universe had hit "pause," allowing them to witness the truth of what had happened.

They had no answers.

But they had *each other*.

And in that moment, an unspoken agreement passed between them: *We're in this together.*

Breaking Loose

"Secure the room! Get those animals under control!" Dr. Nguyen suddenly shouted, snapping out of his stunned silence.

His voice jolted the staff into action. The lab, already a scene of disorder, now surged with frantic energy. Somewhere, an alert klaxon blared louder, someone had triggered a facility-wide lockdown.

Two security guards burst into the lab. They weren't carrying rifles; just long poles tipped with nooses and holstered tranquilizer dart pistols.

They stopped short, overwhelmed by the madness in front of them.

To them, it looked like rabid chaos: human patients, snarling, or shrieking dogs and cats; scientists climbing trying to help humans, survive the electrocutions, to make matters worse, a pack of seemingly intelligent pets had gathered, watching with unnerving awareness.

"What the…?" one of the guards muttered, unable to decide where to aim his capture pole.

That moment of hesitation was all the opportunity Titan and the others needed.

Near the partially open lab door, the huddled group of animals sensed it at once: If they stayed, they'd be caught. Studied. Sedated. Or worse.

Titan-in-Max barked, a sharp, clear order. A command.

Run.

Taylor, now fully present in Titan's body, was already crouched by the exit. She didn't wait for further direction. Muscles tensed, she lunged through the gap in the door.

As one of the guards stepped forward, trying to loop the pug (Jamal) with his noose, Taylor bared her teeth and snapped, not to bite, but to distract. The guard recoiled, fumbling with the pole.

At the present time, Rahul-in-corgi darted low between the man's legs. Fast. Small. Impossible to catch.

A hiss of compressed air, *thwick!*, as the second guard fired a tranquilizer dart. It hit the doorframe just above Rahul's bouncing tail. The corgi yelped and bolted even faster.

Jamal, in Peanut's squat little body, followed, eyes wide with terror. Everything was too big, too loud. *Go go go go!* his mind screamed, stubby legs churning.

Another guard circled around, aiming to cut them off with a net. But Serena, inside Tao's Siamese form, moved like lightning. She leapt from a nearby table, landing squarely on the man's back. Her claws didn't break skin, but they startled him enough for her to spring away, sending papers and clipboards flying in her wake.

Daisy and Luna shot from beneath a chair her tabby form a blur. Talia's Picasso-mutt and Ava-bulldog followed, shoulder to shoulder in the race.

Kevin, in Daisy's golden retriever body, hesitated at the threshold. He turned back and caught a glimpse of his own body, *his*, as a technician plunged a syringe into the arm. Adrenaline.

Kevin O'Neill's human form sagged, limp, and was quickly hauled away by two lab workers.

Daisy whimpered. It was agony to leave himself behind. But there was no time.

With one last mournful look, he turned and ran.

In seconds, the lab's center was empty. The ragtag group of survivors had fled.

"They're loose! The animals!" shouted one of the guards into his radio, watching tails vanish around the corner.

Dr. Nguyen stood motionless in the center of the wreckage, bathed in strobing red light. Around him: ten unconscious or sedated human bodies, upended equipment, claw marks, scattered tools, overturned chairs.

Whatever had just happened, one thing was terrifyingly clear:

Their test subjects, or rather, their minds, were loose in the facility.

Breaking Into the Night

The hallway beyond the lab led toward the rear exits and the animal walking yards. Emergency lights flickered overhead, casting jagged shadows on the walls.

The pack ran hard, seven dogs, three cats, all human in mind, all desperate in body.

Claws skidded on tile. Tails streamed behind them.

"Sector C breach! They're heading toward the yards!" came the shout from somewhere behind.

Victor, in Max's German Shepherd body, saw it: the glowing EXIT sign. Beneath it, a door stood ajar, held open by a fallen trash bin, knocked over in the chaos.

Rain gleamed beyond, silver streaks illuminated by floodlights outside.

Taylor-in-Titan was the first through the door, her sleek Doberman form vanishing into the storm.

One by one, the rest followed, plunging out into the night.

Into the dark.

Into the unknown.

But, for the first time since waking in the wrong bodies, they weren't alone.

A wall of cool rain slammed into them, drenching fur in an instant and shocking their overheated senses. Taylor hardly flinched, the Dobermann's sleek coat was quickly soaked, but she forged ahead, driven by sheer determination and the need for distance. Jamal-pug was far less graceful; he hit a slick patch of patio concrete, and his tiny paws skidded out from under him, sending him tumbling rump over nose. He landed in a shallow puddle, dazed but unhurt, blinking in confusion until

Kevin-now the golden retriever bounded over and nudged him upright with the gentle push of a retriever snout. The pug gave a vigorous shake, sending droplets flying in every direction. If Jamal had lungs built for laughter, he would've cackled at how his wet, quivering body resembled a shivering gelatin mold.

Thunder cracked overhead, loud and sudden, as if spurring them on with nature's own urgency. Ava, trapped in Winston's stocky bulldog body, let out a startled yelp and instinctively tried to hide. In doing so, she dove beneath the nearest available "cover", which turned out to be Talia's mutt body. Talia yipped in surprise as the smaller bulldog attempted to wedge herself under her belly. The whole interaction would have been comical in any other context.

Just a few feet away, Maria, inhabiting Luna's stout tabby-cat form, made a be line for a bench beneath the partial shelter of a rusted awning. The cat, true to form, hated getting wet; Luna found herself hissing in disgust as cold rain plastered her fur against her sides. She leapt onto the bench with practiced agility and shook each paw with fastidious disdain, even as water dripped from her Tao. *I'm a woman in a cat's body, in a thunderstorm, Dios mío.* Even her inner monologue sounded incredulous.

Despite the danger, absurd little moments flashed amid the chaos. Rahul-corgi, adrenaline surging through his compact frame, couldn't help but bark furiously at a metal trash can that the wind had set rolling across the yard, exactly the kind of thing Chai, his corgi, used to do at home, and which Rahul had always scolded. And now here he was, barking without thought: *Woof! Woof! Stupid can, stop moving!* It was an irresistible corgi compulsion. Mortified, he clamped his jaw shut, silently scolding himself, even though no one could hear his thoughts.

A few yards away, Serena's Siamese body was faring no better. She recoiled at the sensation of being drenched, her every instinct recoiling. Tao's once-elegant cream fur was now a sodden, muddy beige. Shivering, Serena began frantically licking her foreleg, as if grooming could somehow undo the waterlogged misery. A bolt of lightning flashed across the sky, and she paused mid-lick, her ears back, her expression one of pure misery.

The group regrouped in the grassy central section of the yard. Mud was already forming, pawprints churned into the soggy turf. Titan, calm under pressure, quickly assessed the situation. The yard was a rectangular enclosure, surrounded by a high chain-link fence topped with an inward-leaning overhang. He sprinted along one side, splashing through puddles, eyes scanning for an exit. Titan, Taylor, in Doberman form, joined him, nose to the ground. Then they saw it: the gate. A double gate at the far end, likely leading to the outside or a parking area.

But as they reached it, their hope sank. The gates were padlocked shut with a thick metal chain. Titan growled and even bit at the chain, teeth clanking uselessly against cold steel. It was no use.

A flashlight beam suddenly sliced through the downpour, cutting across the yard from the direction of the building. "Over here! I see them!" a voice shouted from the doorway. The pursuit had resumed.

Taylor-Doberman barked twice in rapid succession, an urgent signal, then jerked her head toward a cluster of shrubs and a small maintenance shed in the dark, far corner of the yard. The pack understood: cover. They sprinted across the open lawn, mud flying beneath pounding paws, and dove behind the shed and overgrown bushes just as the flashlight beam swept over the spot they'd occupied moments earlier.

Panting, muddy, and soaked to the skin, they pressed low to the ground. A tranq dart hissed through the rain, narrowly missing Daisy-tabby and thunking into the soft bark of a cedar tree. Daisy flattened herself, ears slicked back against her skull. Serena, now beside her, fur plastered to her frame, looked like half-drowned wildlife. The Siamese pressed against the tabby in a silent gesture of solidarity, and Daisy found herself oddly comforted by the presence of another fChaine, despite knowing it was actually a friend inside that body.

At the yard's entrance, two silhouetted figures stood in the downpour. One kept the flashlight sweeping the yard while the other raised a capture pole. "Come on, come on…" one muttered, scanning for movement in the rain-drenched Cleos.

A bolt of lightning lit the sky, and for a split second, the entire yard was washed in blinding white. The guard thought he saw a jumble of forms near the shed, but in the Peanute flash came a crack of thunder, and the overhead lights flickered. In the strobing afterimage, the animals had vanished again. Now soaked and shivering themselves, the guards hesitated.

"Damn it… They're trapped in here anyway," one shouted over the roar of the rain. "We'll round them up when this lets up. Post two men at the door and watch them. They're not getting past that fence."

With that, the flashlight swung away, and the two figures retreated to the doorway awning's relative shelter. One guard tested the metal gate with a loud clank, still locked tight, before disappearing inside. The yard fell into silence once more, the rain the only sound aside from the breath of the huddled escapees behind the shed.

It wasn't true freedom, but it was a reprieve.

A Moment of Calm

Alone in the far corner of the yard, the ten soaked and frightened former humans realized they had won a small battle. They were outside the lab, beyond immediate reach, free, for now. Wind whipped through a nearby oak, spraying droplets onto their tight little group. They huddled closer beneath the eave of the maintenance shed, just enough cover to blunt the rain's full assault. Lightning still flashed, though less frequently, and thunder rolled farther away. In those brief illuminations, a strange scene emerged: dogs of various breeds and sizes resting in a loose circle, chests heaving, with three cats nestled among them. They looked like forgotten pets left out in a storm, but their eyes held a very human story. These weren't animals. They were survivors.

For a long while, none of them moved. They simply stayed close, flanks pressed together for warmth, the roar of rain on the shed's metal roof drowning out distant alarms and human voices. In that uneasy peace, each wrestled with the surreal reality in their own silent way. Ten pairs of eyes, blue, brown, green, golden, shimmered in the gloom with exhaustion, confusion, fear… and gratitude. Whatever nightmare had unfolded inside that lab, they were alive. Bruised, soaked, shaken to their very cores, but alive.

Victor-in-Max was the first to move. Tentatively, the big shepherd mix padded toward Jamal's tiny pug form, which was still shivering violently, more from shock than cold. Gently, Titan pressed his warm, sturdy shoulder against the smaller dog and nudged him with his nose, an instinctive gesture, like a mother dog comforting her pup. Jamal looked up, startled at first, then gave a feeble wag of his curled tail. That simple act of compassion, especially from the usually reserved firefighter, loosened something in all their chests.

One by one, the others followed Titan's lead. Physical instinct took over where words could not. Kevin-Daisy gave a low, soothing whine and began licking the rainwater from Daisy-retriever fur in long, gentle strokes. The retriever might have growled or fled under normal conditions, but Daisy leaned in, accepting the care. She even attempted a weak, raspy bark of thanks, eyes fluttering shut from the comfort of being cared for.

Nearby, the gray British Shorthair that now housed Dr. Yusuf's mind suddenly sneezed, Cleo's fine body protesting the chill. He shook himself vigorously, droplets flying from his plush coat. Reflexively, Yusuf tried to adjust the glasses that were no longer on his nose, and the absurdity of the motion made a deep, rumbling sound escape him, something between a chuckle and a confused purr. Soaked, disoriented, and burdened by the magnitude of what had occurred, he looked around at the others. This catastrophe was the unholy fruit of his life's work, a realization both sobering and humbling. In that moment, Yusuf-in-Cleo made a silent vow: if it was at all possible to set things right, he would find a way.

Their breathing slowed. Heartbeats gradually steadied, though it was hard to tell whether they beat in human rhythms or animal ones. Panic gave way to tentative hope. Though they couldn't speak, they found other ways to communicate, a comforting nuzzle or a paw rested gently on another's back, a glance that said *I'm here. You're here. We'll get through this.*

In that circle of soaked fur and quiet resolve, a new bond was forged. No longer just a collection of strangers and pets, they had become something more, survivors of a shared trauma, ten souls who quite literally knew what it meant to walk in each other's skin.

Winston, who prided herself on poise and elegance, sat miserably in the shape of a mud-splattered bulldog. Her fur clung to her stocky frame in wet clumps, and the cold crept into her bones. Yet even she had to admit, begrudgingly, that pressing her stout body against Peanuts' warm, fluffy mutt-side was infinitely better than sitting alone in the chill. With a sigh that escaped as a snort through Winston's flat snout, she surrendered to necessity.

Talia-in-Picasso welcomed her without hesitation, offering a soft wuff of acknowledgment and draping a shaggy tail over Luna's back like a blanket. The gesture was simple, instinctive, comforting.

Further down the huddle, Rahul-corgi finally stopped his anxious pacing. His little legs had churned up more mud than progress, and he conceded that no amount of frantic circling would carry him out of this predicament. With a reluctant grunt, he circled twice (a canine habit he simply couldn't fight) and plopped down beside Serena's small Siamese frame.

Cleo was diligently licking mud off one slender paw. She paused, mid-clean, and met Chai's gaze. The two had exchanged only brief hellos during the trial setup, cordial, distant, professional. But now, as cat and corgi, they shared a wordless moment of mutual exhaustion and quiet understanding. Serena gave a tiny, weary mrrp.

Chai chose to interpret it as, *We will be okay.*

He inched a little closer.

She didn't move away.

Despite the tension, the cold, and the looming unknown, a few of them found the corners of their mouths, beaks, muzzles, or otherwise, tugging upward in what almost resembled a smile. The absurdity of it all seeped in, slowly warming them from the inside out.

Peanut, crouched between Titan and Daisy for warmth, was the first to recognize the comedy of their situation. He was a pug now, his brain zapped by lightning into his dog's stocky little body, hiding in a high-tech kennel from men with guns. The irony was too much. *If my buddies could see me now...* he thought.

A chortle of laughter built in his chest, but what came out was a strange, chuffing grunt from Peanut's throat. Still, it was enough to make Daisy the golden retriever cock his head and blink at him curiously.

Jamal tried for a grin, which, on a pug, looked somewhere between smug and alarmed. The sound, the expression, whatever it was, it caught on. Others glanced his way, and although no one quite knew what he was laughing about, the tension eased by a notch. Tao twitched. A tail or two gave an idle wag. Something shifted.

Humor, however small, reminded them of their humanity.

Time stretched on in heavy breaths and the rhythmic beat of rain. Gradually, the worst of the storm began to pass. The thunder, once close and violent, now rumbled distantly, like an old beast wandering away. The downpour eased into a steady patter, droplets pinging off the tin roof of the shed with metronomic regularity.

A faint, bluish light crept in as the darkness thinned, perhaps it was morning, perhaps just a lull in the storm. Either way, the sharpest edge of the night had dulled.

Titan lifted his head. Ears perked, nose twitching, he scanned the ragtag group around him.

They were a mess, muddy, drenched, and visibly shaken, but they were alive. Together.

He saw resolve gleaming in their eyes: Taylor's Doberman gaze, sharp and alert even in stillness; Ava's bulldog scowl, edged now with grit; Jamal's pug eyes, anxious but trying for cheer; Daisy's gentle fine stare, full of quiet strength.

Titan felt pride swell in his chest, a very dog-like sensation, he noted with some detachment.

They had done the unthinkable.

Survived a lightning strike.

Endured a mind-swap.

Escaped containment.

Whatever came next, they would face it as one.

He let out a low, deliberate woof, just one. The sound cut through the rain, unmistakable in its clarity.

Heads turned.

Titan wasn't sure exactly what he meant by it, he wasn't a dog, after all, not really, but something old and instinctual translated it: *We've got this. Stay strong. I'm with you.*

Taylor stepped forward and pressed her Doberman shoulder to his in solidarity, offering a firm chuff in return. It was enough to trigger a chain reaction. Kevin-golden barked once. Rahul-corgi let out a high-pitched yip. Serena-cat gave a steady blink. Daisy-tabby added a quiet mew.

It was a ragged chorus. Wordless. Awkward.

But deeply, unmistakably *human.*

Under the light drizzle of a dying storm, ten animals made a pact, no contracts, no oaths, no speeches. Just presence. Just unity.

They would find a way. Together.

Huddled beneath the gray morning sky, the unlikely band of former humans found comfort in one another. Some leaned in closer, sharing body heat and the odd intimacy of survival. Others kept silent watch toward the glass building behind them, where clear silhouettes of staff still lingered behind reflective windows, too afraid or confused to intervene.

Beyond the fence, the sounds of a waking city filtered through the damp air. A distant siren. The hiss of wet tires rolling down asphalt. The impatient bleat of a car horn.

The world was going on, oblivious to the miracle, or perhaps the nightmare, that had unfolded in this isolated corner.

A new day had begun.

What it would hold for them, no one could guess. Rescue. Capture. Something else entirely.

But as they lifted their eyes toward the faint light breaking through thinning clouds, one thing was certain:

Whatever came next, they would meet it head-on, united by the bond forged in lightning and fear, in fur and fire.

They had started this night as ten strangers with pets.

They emerged from it as one pack, A family, made by fate. Ready to face the unknown future.

Together.

Chapter 2

THE EXPERIMENT

They couldn't rest.

"This way!" Titan barked.

He remembered seeing a street sign when they were brought in—Madison Avenue was west, just a block or two.

He led them down the alley. Paws splashed through puddles. The sun was bright, reflecting off concrete and windows. Kevin blinked. Cleo's eyes narrowed to slits.

At the alley mouth, they halted.

Noise hit them like a wave: horns, engines, voices. A delvery truck roared past. Pedestrians bustled along with coffees and briefcases. No one had noticed them yet.

They huddled behind a parked van, catching their breath. Titan peeked around the bumper. Across the street: a glass office tower and a hotel with an elegant awning. A doorman stood at attention.

If ten animals bolted into the open, someone would definitely notice.

Picasso's ears flattened as the full challenge hit him.

"Seven dogs and three cats loose together in Manhattan? We're gonna stick out like... like a dog in a cat show."

Jamal panted beside him.

"At least out here, we blend in better than in a lab. Plenty of city dogs around—though usually not bunched up like this."

Winston took a moment to assess the situation.

"We might need to break into smaller groups until we find a hiding spot. Too many of us at once will attract attention. We can regroup nearby."

"Central Park?" Daisy asked hopefully. Her terrier nose twitched as she caught the scent of greenery—maybe a pocket park or even a faint trace of Central Park's wide expanse on the breeze.

The aromas of hot dog stands and food carts threatened to overwhelm her senses, but that hint of grass and earth grounded her.

"That's quite a few blocks up," Kevin warned, his golden head tilting slightly. "Might be risky to split up on our first run."

"Let's at least get off this block," Titan said decisively. "Madison's too busy. Maybe we can slip into the next alley or side street. Stick to the quieter routes."

Cleo's tail gave a thoughtful swish.

"We'll also need food and some rest. I know we just ate kibble, but after that chase? I'm already starving again." She said it lightly, but the truth was they were all running on adrenaline and barely-sufficient rations.

Ava sniffed the air, her bulldog jowls wobbling slightly as she caught a strong aroma.

"There's a smell... oh wow, that smells amazing." Her tongue lolled out as she inhaled the scent of freshly baked bagels from a food cart. She gave herself a shake, snapping out of the trance. "Sorry. That was Luna's stomach talking."

Max gave a throaty chuckle.

"Don't apologize—we're all feeling it. I caught a whiff of a diner around the corner. My cat nose is having the time of its life."

"Focus, everyone," Winston said gently. "First, we find a safe spot to regroup. Then we can think about food."

"Agreed," Titan nodded. He peeked around the van. A small group of pedestrians had passed; the sidewalk was briefly clear.

"Now or never. Go!"

They slipped from behind the van, moving single file along the sidewalk, doing their best to appear like a group of pets out for a walk. The sight was something out of a surreal dream: a strange, mismatched pack of dogs with a couple of cats mixed in, weaving through morning foot traffic.

A businessman halted mid-step as Daisy darted past his ankles, followed closely by Picasso's tiny form.

"What the—?" he muttered, nearly spilling his coffee. But before he could react, Jamal and Titan flanked him, giving their best friendly dog grins. The man blinked and shook his head, assuming some hapless dog walker had lost control of a chaotic group, and moved on.

A little boy gasped and pointed.

"Mommy, look! Puppies and kitties!" He reached out to pet Kevin's golden fur as they passed. Kevin gave the boy a quick, gentle lick, tail wagging. The boy giggled. His mother looked puzzled but unconcerned—after all, they looked like normal, well-behaved pets.

The group made it down the block before any of the facility staff appeared at the lab's entrance. By that time, the animals had already turned onto a quieter side street.

Max, panting hard, slowed down.

"Guys... hold up... my cat cardio isn't built for this." His belly nearly skimmed the concrete as he struggled to keep pace. Dogs were built for endurance, but cats—especially overweight tabbies like Luna's body—were not made for sprints.

Cleo and Tao circled back to flank him.

"We'll slow down," Tao said gently, rubbing her head against Max's shoulder. The simple cat gesture of comfort settled his nerves. He gave a grateful smile.

Picasso's tiny nails clicked as he kept pace beside Winston's smooth stride.

"We actually did it. We're out!" he whispered, as if saying it too loudly might jinx their escape.

Winston let herself feel that small triumph. The sun on her fur, the heartbeat of the city in the distance—it was freedom.

"Yeah," she said. "We're out. Now we have to stay out... and figure out what's next."

They tucked themselves into a small alley behind a tall office building. Hidden by a dumpster, they were temporarily shielded from view. The smell was awful—old garbage, likely from a nearby restaurant—but it offered shelter.

Titan sniffed around and peeked out toward the street. No immediate pursuit.

"We're okay for now."

Jamal collapsed with a dramatic "oof," his tongue hanging out as he panted.

"I haven't run like that since the New York Marathon back in college," he joked, then winced. "Titan here probably could've kept going, but my heart's another story."

Ava sat heavily against the brick wall.

"Do you think... they'll try to track us down?" Her big brown eyes were full of concern. "From their perspective, ten animals just broke out of a lab. They might call animal control—or even the cops."

Tao nodded solemnly.

"We have to assume they'll be looking. If they find us, they'll bring us back. We can't let that happen."

"But they don't know we're us," Daisy said softly, ears perked. "To them, we're just pets. Our bodies—our human bodies..." Her voice faltered. "What about them? Are they just lying there?"

A heavy silence fell. Their human bodies—where were they? Still in the facility? A hospital? In comas, maybe. Or awake... but not with them inside.

Daisy stepped up and gently brushed his head against Daisy's shoulder.

"I'm sure they're being cared for. The staff are scientists—not monsters."

"And if our pets' minds are in our bodies... maybe it's for the best they're under observation," Victor added. The thought of Max inhabiting his human body—confused, scared—filled him with dread.

"We'll fix this. But we can't do it from a cage."

Cleo looked up at the narrow sky above the alley.

"Our poor pets. Imagine how terrified they must be, suddenly in strange, clumsy human bodies..." Her voice shook.

Skittles, her beloved Siamese, had never even left the apartment before this.

Max placed a tentative paw on her back—awkwardly, as cats aren't known for comforting gestures.

"Hey, at least they're safe. Probably confused, yeah. But safe. We'll get back to them. First, we keep ourselves safe. Then we figure out how to fix this."

Titan stood tall.

"Right. One problem at a time. First: survive out here without getting caught. We need food, water, shelter, and to stay low-profile."

Picasso sniffed at the base of the dumpster.

"Food might not be so hard. This city's a buffet—if you're not picky." He nudged a torn trash bag and out tumbled a chicken wing. Before his human instincts could kick in, his Chihuahua body snatched it up. He blinked, half in awe, half in horror.

"Uh… sorry. Instinct. Princess has zero shame about the five-second rule on street meat."

Jamal laughed.

"Better you than me. Though… I smell pizza." He turned his head, nose lifted. "There." He trotted toward a second bin.

Max followed, curiosity piqued despite himself. Together, they managed to tip over a smaller trash can, revealing a pizza box. Jamal flipped it open to reveal two half-eaten slices.

"Score," he grinned.

Max's Tao twitched.

"Oh, yes please." He tried to bite into a slice, but the cheese stuck. Jamal pinned it down helpfully, letting him tear a piece free.

One by one, the others began foraging. Winston found a mostly-wrapped blueberry muffin and took a careful bite, tail wagging unconsciously. Cleo and Tao unearthed a Chinese takeout container with rice and dumplings. Ava discovered a hot dog bun and shared it with a still-shaken Daisy, gently encouraging her to eat.

In less than fifteen minutes, they had assembled a ragtag meal. It wasn't glamorous—but it was food.

They toasted with crusts and chicken bones.

"Five stars," Max said with a burp. "Would dumpster dive again."

"Vintage pizza," Peanut added. "Aged at least overnight."

Laughter echoed through the alley—half-barks, half-meows. It was ridiculous. It was surreal. But it was also survival.

And yet, reality crept back in quickly.

As they finished, Titan's ears perked at the low growl of a motor. A white van marked Animal Control cruised past the alley entrance. He stiffened, watching every movement, breath held.

The van didn't stop.

They were safe—for now.

When everyone had eaten their fill—Max perhaps a bit more than his share—they gathered in a rough circle behind the dumpster. Some sat on their haunches; others sprawled on the ground. It was time to figure out the next steps.

"We've got food for now," Titan began, his tone measured, "and its still only mid-day. But we need a secure shelter for tonight. Somewhere safe. And we need to start thinking long-term—how to get back to our bodies or reverse this swap."

Winston nodded solemnly. "I'm convinced the answer lies with the Pet-Link equipment and Dr. Shen's team. This all started with their experiment—maybe it was accidental, but they might be working on a fix already."

"Or they could be trying to cover it up," Picasso growled, his ears flattening. He had always leaned toward skepticism. "What if they don't want the world to know they swapped people with their pets? They could just keep us locked up to study... and let the story disappear."

Ava whimpered at the thought. Titan pressed his large body gently against her side to comfort the trembling bulldog. "We don't know what their intentions are," he said carefully. "But Picasso's right—we can't trust them blindly. Not after they tossed us in cages without realizing who we were."

Tao licked a grain of rice from her paw, thinking. "Maybe we could reach out to someone on the outside. A family member, a friend... or even someone in academia. One of us must know someone who could help us. Someone who understands this kind of science."

Cleo's ears flicked up. "There's Dr. Nguyen at NYU. She was my mentor—she specializes in neural interfaces. If we could just get her attention... she might help. But how?" Her voice faltered. "I can't exactly waltz into her lab and start typing an email."

Jamal let out a quiet chuckle. "Can you imagine? 'Dear Professor, I'm a cat that used to be your student. Please help.' I'm sure that'd go over really well."

The laughter was brief but welcome. Still, they all knew the reality—they couldn't speak, couldn't type, couldn't use phones. Proving their intelligence while in animal bodies would be incredibly difficult. And trying might only get them captured.

Max scratched behind one ear with a hind paw, but froze mid-motion, his leg awkwardly suspended in the air.

"Guys... squirrel," he said, voice suddenly flat, far away.

Sure enough, a plump grey squirrel stood at the alley's mouth, sniffing toward the group. It twitched its tail and watched them, beady-eyed and bold.

A ripple of primal instinct surged through the group. Daisy's terrier brain zeroed in on the intruder. Her entire body trembled. Chase. Chase now. The instincts were strong!

Picasso's heart raced. His tiny Mutt body vibrated with the primordial need. Even Jamal, housed in a Pug body took a reflexive step forward.

"Don't..." Winston said sharply, teeth clenched. Her collie instincts screamed for pursuit. "Don't do it..."

The squirrel chirped and darted to the left, zigzagging toward the nearest lamppost.

And that was it.

Daisy barked once—sharp and high-pitched—then exploded into motion, a blur of white and tan.

"Daisy, no!" Titan barked, but it was already too late. Her Retriever body was in full sprint, legs flying, ears back, eyes locked on the squirrel.

With a chorus of groans, yips, and barks, the rest of the group charged after her. They couldn't stop her with words, so they'd have to catch her physically—before she caused a scene or got hurt.

It was chaos.

The squirrel raced along the sidewalk. Daisy was right behind it, determined and relentless. Behind her: six dogs and two cats in full pursuit. Pedestrians scattered in confusion, some laughing, some yelling.

"Get that squirrel!" Picasso barked, caught up in the excitement. He tore past Max, legs pumping furiously. Despite his human intellect, Picasso's instincts had completely taken over.

"Picasso, not you too…" Daisy groaned, running at a steady pace, trying to catch up without fully surrendering to the chase.

The squirrel veered sharply and darted across Madison Avenue.

Straight into traffic.

It narrowly avoided the wheels of a taxi and shot up a skinny sidewalk tree. Daisy bolted into the road after it, completely unaware of the danger.

A delivery bike swerved to miss her, the rider yelling. Horns honked. The scent of exhaust and rubber filled the air.

Titan, larger and more aware, skidded to a halt at the curb. He barked in a tone that was unmistakably commanding.

"DAISY, STOP!"

It came out as a deep, booming woof—but somehow, it cut through Daisy's tunnel vision. She paused, dazed, smack in the middle of the street.

Then she heard the bus.

A city bus was bearing down on her, brakes squealing.

Titan lunged.

His strong jaws clamped onto the scruff of Daisy's neck, and with every ounce of strength, he yanked her backward. The two tumbled together onto the sidewalk just as the bus whooshed past, missing them by inches. Heat and exhaust gusted over them in its wake.

Daisy lay trembling, stunned. "I—I'm sorry. I d-don't know what came over me," she stammered, voice shaking.

Titan released her scruff gently. His chest heaved. "It's okay," he said softly. "Instincts... they're hard to control. I'm just glad you're okay."

He gave her a comforting lick on the cheek—an automatic gesture that surprised them both. It was deeply canine, but the emotion behind it was human. Daisy offered a shaky smile, wiping her face with a paw.

They regrouped beneath the tree where the squirrel had vanished. It now sat safely on a high branch, tail flicking smugly, chittering down at them in Squirrel chatter.

Picasso barked once in frustration, but Winston nudged him with a shoulder. "Let it go, tough guy. We've made enough of a scene."

And indeed, several people had paused to watch. A couple of joggers, a vendor at a food cart, two businessmen near a hot dog stand—all stared, bemused.

One of the suited men laughed. "Must be a dog walker's worst day—lost all his dogs and cats at once."

His friend chuckled as they walked on.

New Yorkers had seen stranger.

But for the group, it was a sobering reminder: instinct was a real threat. Even more dangerous than being caught.

Cleo climbed halfway up the tree—cats being far more agile than the rest. From a low branch, she scanned the block.

Then she froze.

Coming out of a nearby office building were two familiar figures in white lab coats. Dr. Shen—head of the Pet-Link project—and his assistant. They stood on the sidewalk, talking animatedly. One held a tablet and was scanning the street.

Cleo's fur bristled. Her sharp Siamese ears zeroed in, catching fragments of their conversation through the hum of city noise.

"...escaped the holding area," Dr. Shen was saying, concern thick in his voice. "Have you alerted animal control and NYPD? Ten of them loose—it could be a disaster."

His assistant, a woman with her hair in a tight bun, nodded. "They're on alert. But what about the... human patients?"

Dr. Shen ran a hand over his bald head in frustration. "Still unconscious. Stable vitals, but no signs of waking. We need those animals back for testing, or we may never reverse this. And if this leaks to the press..."

He stopped mid-sentence as he scanned the block. His eyes landed briefly on the tree—and on the group beneath it.

Cleo didn't move. She held her breath, partially hidden by the leaves. But the others were out in the open.

Dr. Shen's gaze lingered. Something about the scene seemed to puzzle him.

Please, Cleo thought. Please just think we're strays. Please don't see us.

The assistant followed Dr. Shen's gaze. "Those... aren't those some of the animals? That looks like Kevin's golden retriever... and I think that's Peanut the Pug!"

Dr. Shen narrowed his eyes, squinting against the midday sun. "Yes... yes, I believe it is." A mixture of relief and confusion crossed his face. "How did they get this far so quickly? And why are they all still together? Cats and dogs, sticking in a pack..."

"We should call this in," the assistant said quietly, already reaching for her phone.

Up in the tree, Cleo fought to stay calm. She had to warn the others, but she couldn't act suspicious. Keeping up the ruse, she casually groomed her paw as if she were just a lazy cat lounging on a branch, indifferent to the humans below.

Down on the ground, Tao was the first to notice Cleo's alert expression. She tracked the Siamese cat's gaze to the two lab-coated figures down the block. Her voice low and urgent, she sidled closer to Winston and Max. "Guys. Problem at ten o'clock—lab people. It's Shen."

Instantly, the group shifted into performance mode, each animal adopting a relaxed or playful posture to avoid suspicion. They knew how important it was to look like ordinary strays.

Peanut sprang into a play bow and barked at Picasso. The smaller dog immediately caught on, yapping and spinning in playful circles like they were just a couple of dogs having fun. The rest of the group mimicked casual behavior: sniffing the grass, rolling over, stretching, or flopping lazily in the shade of the tree.

Titan lowered his head slightly and murmured to those nearest, "They recognize us. Don't stare. Move slowly, drift away. Don't draw attention."

But Dr. Shen and the assistant had already started walking toward them, their steps careful and deliberate. They weren't buying the casual act entirely—something about this scene was too coordinated, too intelligent.

Thinking quickly, Ava made her move. She shuffled forward in her bulldog body, head tilted and tongue lolling, wagging her tail in what she hoped looked like clueless friendliness. It was a risk, but she was the best bet—they wouldn't expect a slow, waddling bulldog to be a threat.

The assistant's face softened at the sight of Winston's familiar features. "Aww, Winston... hi there," she said gently, kneeling down and offering her hand.

Winston leaned into the role, giving the hand a big, slobbery lick. Her tail thumped lazily against the pavement, and she let her tongue hang out with exaggerated cheer. It wasn't all an act—Winston's sweet nature bled through, impossible to suppress entirely.

"She's such a sweetheart," the assistant cooed. "Doesn't seem stressed at all."

For a brief, shining moment, Winston had completely disarmed her.

But Dr. Shen remained wary. His hand slipped into his coat pocket, pulling out a soft nylon slip leash—the kind used in labs and shelters. He spoke gently, as if coaxing a scared animal. "Easy... let's get you safe."

Winston's heart pounded. If that loop slid over her head, it might be game over. She stood her ground, playing for time, tail still wagging and eyes wide with innocent curiosity.

Meanwhile, the rest of the group, taking advantage of the distraction, began slipping away one by one behind parked cars. Titan gave a subtle signal, and Cleo leapt from the tree to regroup with them, her landing silent as ever. She gave a quick nod—she'd explain everything later.

Just as the loop of the leash hovered inches from Winston's head, a sudden interruption saved her.

From up the block, the street cart vendor—the hot dog guy who'd seen them earlier—came jogging over, waving and calling, "Hey, doc! Yo!"

Dr. Shen turned, visibly annoyed. "Yes?"

The vendor, a middle-aged man with a genial face and an apron streaked with mustard, pointed to the animals slipping away behind a parked sedan. "Those your dogs and cats? They almost got flattened chasing a squirrel. You gotta keep 'em leashed, man—this city's no place for 'em to be running around."

The assistant looked up and immediately spotted the retreating group. "They're getting away—"

Her sudden exclamation startled Winston. Seizing the moment, she barked loudly and jumped back, just beyond the reach of the leash. She spun and bolted clumsily in the opposite direction, careening around the vendor's legs with surprising agility for a bulldog.

"Hey—!" the vendor exclaimed, trying to catch her, but Winston zigzagged past him like a pro.

She rejoined the group just as the others broke into a run. Now the whole pack was fleeing down Madison Avenue— seven dogs, three cats, sprinting together in a chaotic but determined blur of fur and tails.

"Stop them!" Dr. Shen shouted, breaking into a jog, but he wasn't fast enough. The assistant was already dialing backup on her phone, running behind him.

Sidewalk traffic scattered. Pedestrians gasped and jumped out of the way. A bike courier swerved and nearly wiped out.

A chorus of barks, yelps, and hissing accompanied the wild parade. People watched in stunned amazement as the animals tore down the block.

They didn't stop until they hit the next cross street. Titan led them around the corner and ducked down a side alley behind a hotel. Only once they were out of view did the group slow down, panting hard and heaving from the sprint.

"That was way too close," Winston gasped, sides heaving.

Winston was shaking slightly—adrenaline coursing through her—but Picasso nuzzled her shoulder. "That was badass. You deserve an Oscar for that performance."

Winston gave a tired, toothy grin I am just... really into people. I leaned into it."

Cleo spoke up, relaying what she had overheard. "They said our human bodies are still unconscious. Stable, but not waking up. They need us back to run more tests, or they might not figure out how to reverse this."

There was a flicker of hope in her voice—but also fear.

Peanut huffed. "That could be bait. Lure us back, then cage us again. I'm not risking that."

Titan nodded grimly. "He's right. We'll find our own way. If we ever deal with them again, it'll be by our rules. Not theirs."

He glanced around. The alley they'd stumbled into seemed promising. There were trash bins—of course—but also the comforting sounds and smells of hotel life: food, warm laundry, distant music. A few open service doors revealed glimpses of kitchens and supply rooms.

Beside one door sat a heap of discarded linens. Soft, clean, freshly laundered sheets—some slightly stained or torn, no longer fit for guest rooms. But to the ten tired souls staring at them, it looked like paradise.

"I think we found our hotel suite," Max quipped, padding over and pawing at the pile. The fabric smelled like detergent and warmth. A luxury compared to cold concrete and dumpsters.

Daisy nosed her way into the linens and gave a long, satisfied sigh. "It's not the Hilton, but I'll take it."

They made camp between the bins and the wall, burrowing into the linens to create a cozy nest. One by one, they collapsed. Jamal flopped onto his side, tongue lolling; Cleo curled into a tight ball; Max kneaded a pillow with fine precision before curling into it, purring softly despite himself.

Picasso circled three times before settling, pressed back-to-back with Daisy. Winston and Titan lingered a little longer, keeping watch near the alley's mouth. But the coast remained clear.

The sun dipped lower, casting long golden rays between the buildings. A warm, amber hush settled over the city. In their hidden corner, the group finally found a moment of peace.

Sore muscles, aching paws, swishing tails—they were adjusting to bodies they hadn't asked for. But they were alive. Together. And still free.

Winston finally let herself lie down, tucking her legs beneath her like a tired bulldog. Titan sat beside her, surveying the scene: his team—his strange, mismatched, determined team—safe for now.

He glanced at Winston. The way the fading light shimmered in her bulldog eyes reminded him of the woman beneath the fur—fierce, focused, full of heart. She caught him staring and smiled, weary but amused.

"Penny for your thoughts?" she asked softly.

Titan shrugged his furry shoulders. "Just... proud of everyone. Proud of us. And wondering what comes next."

Winston nodded, following his gaze over their makeshift camp of companions. Daisy was already dozing, her paws twitching—likely dreaming of chasing another squirrel, though hopefully under safer circumstances next time. Peanut and Max were bickering half-heartedly over who was hogging more of the linen sheet they shared, but their grumbling carried a tone of camaraderie, not conflict. Tao rested with her eyes closed, though her ears flicked now and then, as if her mind remained active even in the edge of sleep. Nearby, Chai and Picasso close in size if ever there were to long lost siblings had curled up beside one another. Picasso's t the Mutt's form was nestled against Winstons's warm, round bulldog belly, the two of them breathing in sync. The sight was sweet and unexpectedly heartwarming.

"It's crazy," Winston murmured. "We barely knew each other before yesterday. Some of us hadn't even met until... until this happened. And now..." She trailed off, voice thick with emotion.

"Now we're family?" Titan offered softly.

Winston's eyes shimmered—not just with unshed tears, but with something deeper: a quiet, genuine warmth. "Yeah. A weird, dysfunctional, furry family. But family." A small laugh escaped her, and the gentle wag of her tail betrayed her happiness more honestly than words could.

Taylor swallowed hard. A lump had formed in her throat. It had been years since she'd felt anything close to this—connection, belonging. Titan, her beloved dog, had been her only family for a long time. Now, wearing Titan's body, Taylor had somehow gained nine new friends who already felt more like kin than many humans ever had. Gently, she bumped her head against Winston's shoulder in a canine gesture of solidarity. "We'll get through this. Together."

She leaned into him with quiet gratitude. "Together," she echoed.

A peaceful silence settled over them, the kind that needed no filling. The soft sounds of the city reached them: distant car horns, the low hum of passing traffic, and the occasional muffled voice or clatter of pans from the hotel kitchen beyond the propped service door. Life went on out there, utterly ordinary. And yet, here they were—ten people inside the bodies of animals, hiding behind a hotel dumpster, huddled under discarded linens like war refugees from a sci-fi comedy.

Daisy raised his head, ever practical. "Let's set a watch rotation," she suggested in a low voice. "Just in case."

"I'll take first," Peanut volunteered with a wide yawn. "Got a second wind from that cat nap earlier." He smirked at his own pun.

Max groaned from beneath the sheet. "That was bad. Like, offensively bad."

Still, no one argued. Peanut would watch first, then Daisy, and if needed, Tao after that. With the rotation agreed upon, the others began to drift off again, one by one.

As the golden afternoon faded into dusky lavender, Peanut sat upright at the edge of their linen hideout, ears perked and nose twitching at every scent carried by the shifting wind. The city buzzed around them, oblivious to the bizarre turn his life—and the lives of his nine companions—had taken.

In a quiet moment, Peanut reflected on their strange journey. Just yesterday, he was volunteering for an experimental pet empathy project. Now he was guarding a bunch of strangers-turned-friends in a pug's body, running from the very lab that had promised understanding and progress. If this was fate's idea of a joke, it had a real sense of humor.

He let his eyes drift over each of them: all different ages, backgrounds, walks of life. Some probably never would've crossed paths in the real world. And yet, here they were, bound together by absurd circumstances and something far stronger—shared survival. Peanut felt it, deep in his chest. A kind of loyalty. A new pack, in every sense.

A soft scuffle behind the dumpster caught his attention. His muscles tensed—only to relax again when a rat darted past, vanishing into the alley's Cleo, Peanut chuckled silently. Good thing Max was asleep. He probably would've chased it on instinct—and possibly gotten stuck between a trash bin and a wall.

Above, the first stars peeked through the purple-gray haze of twilight, barely visible through the halo of city light. Peanut tilted his snout upward and let out a single, soft bark—not a warning, not a call, but a quiet burst of joy. They were alive. Free. Day one: survived.

Tomorrow would come with new problems. How to avoid being recaptured. Whether to reach out to loved ones. Where to go next. But those were problems for another day. Tonight, they had something far rarer—peace, connection, hope.

A pack. A clowder. A crew. Whatever you called them, they had become more than just victims of a freak accident. They were something whole.

Jamal's tail thumped the ground gently as he resumed his watch, feeling the weight of his duty, but also a growing optimism. They'd escaped the lab, navigated Manhattan's chaos, and even found comfort in a heap of hotel laundry. And maybe, just maybe, they were stronger for it.

Curling his lip in a canine approximation of a grin, Peanut thought, *Not a bad first day for a dog in New York.*

And so, beneath the murmur of the sleepless city, ten extraordinary souls found their first moment of real rest—not just as lost humans in animal skins, but as something new.

A team. A family. A story just beginning.

Chapter 3

THE WOLVES OF NEW YORK

Dawn's first light spilled across Central Park, washing the city in pale gold as the "Wolves of New York" huddled beneath the broad, protective boughs of an ancient oak. Just hours earlier, they had pulled off the impossible, a daring midnight raid on the Waldorf Hotel's kitchens, and emerged triumphant, bellies full of stolen delicacies. Now, ten figures, seven dogs and three cats, lay hidden among the park's early Cleos, panting softly from exertion and excitement alike.

There was a new glint in their eyes, a fragile but undeniable confidence. They might have been a ragtag collection of former humans trapped in the bodies of pets, but together they had become something greater: survivors, schemers, a family born of chaos.

Max, a sturdy German Shepherd with keen brown eyes, sat sentinel at the edge of the thicket. His posture was straight, every muscle taut as he peered through the leaves at the empty pathway beyond. In his former life, mornings meant polished shoes, briefing folders, and steaming cups of black coffee. Now, morning meant dew on his paws, scents of wet earth in his nose, and the weight of leadership pressing on his shoulders.

He was no longer a man, but a pack leader, and that role carried its own gravity.

Daisy, the golden retriever with a gentle face, stirred first. She lifted her head and yawned wide, her tongue curling as the faint sun lit the tips of her golden fur. Beside her, Peanut, a diminutive Pug with more attitude than height, sneezed at a bit of pollen and grumbled about the "dampness seeping into his old bones." Above them, Tao, a lithe Siamese, balanced gracefully on a low branch as if she had been born to treetops and twilight.

On the ground nearby, Cleo, a British short hair still in the throes of teenage awkwardness, stretched with exaggerated flair while Luna, a plump Tabby with steady green eyes, flexed her paws and blinked slowly in the dim light. Around them, the rest of the dogs shook themselves awake: Titan, the Dobermann, still wore the dazed expression of a man who couldn't quite believe last night's madness had succeeded. Max, the German Shepeard, wagged his tail furiously, the very picture of restless enthusiasm. Picasso, a Mutt, sat down heavily with a thump and scratched at a ear, while Titan, the sleek Doberman, paced with restless precision, radiating an air of impatient efficiency.

They had food in their stomachs, and even a name for their makeshift fraternity, the "Wolves of New York", christened amid the laughter of their Title. But now dawn brought cooler truths. Beyond the tree line, the city was waking. The park would soon be full of joggers, cyclists, and wandering tourists. They couldn't remain hidden here forever.

Max gave a low chuff, clearing his throat. "Alright, everyone," he began, his voice a curious blend of canine growl and human cadence. To one another, the words were clear. To any passing human, he would sound like just another dog muttering deep in his chest. "We did good last night."

"Good?" Max repeated, her tongue lolling in a grin. "We were awesome!" She let out a playful bark that echoed too loudly between the trees.

"Shh, dear, not so loud," Luna warned softly, her voice carrying the unhurried weight of someone who had seen too much life to waste it on unnecessary risk. "The last thing we need is a ranger stumbling across all of us."

Max's ears flattened in apology. "Right. Sorry."

Max nodded. "Luna's right. We need to keep quiet. We got lucky last night, luckier than we deserved."

"Speak for yourself," Peanut piped up, lifting his tiny head proudly. "I earned every bite of that feast. Did you see me navigating those table legs? Slick as a cat." He tossed a wink at Tao, who rolled her emerald eyes.

"Please," Tao purred, "you nearly toppled a chocolate cake. I had to catch the platter with my tail."

The group chuckled, the sound a mix of growls, barks, and purrs. They remembered the night's chaos all too clearly: Picasso's massive paws skidding on a ballroom rug, nearly collapsing a pyramid of fruit; Titan and Max wrestling a roast chicken off a counter while Daisy and Max distracted a cook by knocking over a trash can; Tao darting through silver trays while Cleo nearly singed his tail against a burner flame. Against all odds, they had escaped with treasures, roast meat, fine cheeses, even a wheel of bread, and somehow managed to smuggle it all in a monogrammed Waldorf tote bag.

Max's ears flicked toward the distant wail of a siren on Fifth Avenue. The city was stirring. Their window of safety was closing.

He lowered his voice. "We need a plan. We can't stay in New York. It's only a matter of time before someone notices."

The mood shifted instantly. Everyone knew what he meant. Ten pets acting far too intelligently, caught on surveillance cameras, fleeing the Waldorf with a bag of food, it wouldn't go unnoticed for long. And if the wrong people saw the footage, the chase would begin. The lab hadn't forgotten them.

Titan shuddered. "I keep seeing Dr. Smith's face when the system fried," he muttered. "One second we were strapped into those chairs, our pets across from us, and then..." His voice trailed, ears pinning back as though the memory itself could bite.

"...Then we were staring out of beady little eyes," Cleo finished, his tone forced-casual, though his claws worked at the grass. "Total Freaky Friday situation."

Daisy stepped closer, brushing Titan's shoulder with her golden muzzle. Her voice was quiet but firm. "At least we all found each other. Whatever went wrong, we didn't have to face it alone. I'm grateful for that."

Nods and murmurs of agreement circled the group. In the chaos of the failed experiment, they had stumbled together out of the lab's reach. Their human bodies were gone, or locked away somewhere, comatose and unreachable. But somehow, against all odds, they had survived and formed a new family.

Titan stopped pacing and sat, tail thumping once. His tone was brisk, clipped, carrying the authority of a man used to being obeyed. "Daisy's right. We stay together. But Max's also right, staying here is suicide. We need to move, and soon."

"Preferably somewhere warmer," Peanut muttered, tucking his tiny paws under himself. "This damp ground is murder on my joints. Carolina would be perfect. A sunny beach, a little sand, I'm set for life."

Picasso raised a massive paw in exaggerated ceremony. "I second the motion. The Carolinas, I don't care, anywhere with a breeze and no taxis honking at me." His deep voice took on a mock-regal flair. "Ideally with cabana service. Do they serve puppuccinos ocean-side?"

Tao gave a soft snort. "Sure, Picasso. I'll make us a reservation at the nearest pet-friendly resort."

Despite the tension, Max allowed himself a chuckle. Their banter was proof they still had hope left. "Actually, I was also thinking the Carolinas as a matter of fact," he said. "Far enough to vanish, warmer than here, and less likely the lab will track us that far."

Max perked up. "I, I think my cousin lives in North Carolina. Well, my human cousin did. I don't even know how to say it anymore." Her voice cracked slightly. Was she Max the firefighter, or Max the German Sheppard? Which self was real now?

Luna reached out a paw to touch her foreleg. "We are who we are, dear. The body doesn't change that."

Max's tail wagged faintly, encouraged. "Then yeah. The Carolinas could work. Rural enough that a few strays won't raise alarms. And no more dodging taxis, Cleo."

"Fine by me," Cleo said, flicking his tail. "Nearly lost it last night."

"Nearly?" Tao teased. "If I hadn't yanked you back, you'd have tire marks."

Cleo gave a sheepish grin. "Yeah, yeah. I owe you."

Max looked around the circle, catching every eye. "Then it's decided. We head south. We leave New York before it cages us again. The Carolinas will be our new home."

One by one, the pack nodded. As much as New York was familiar, it was no longer safe.

Daisy stepped forward, her golden tail sweeping the grass. "If we're really leaving," she said thoughtfully, "then we need to tie up our loose ends first."

Titan tilted his head, ears flicking. "Loose ends?"

Daisy glanced back toward the faint glow of the city skyline beyond the park's trees. Her golden eyes softened. "Our lives," she murmured. "Our old lives. We're about to leave them behind for good. I... I think we should say goodbye. Each of us."

A hush fell over the pack. In their daring escape and their frantic days of scavenging and hiding, none of them had given themselves time to grieve what had been lost. Homes. Families. Routines. Human hands that had once opened doors, poured morning coffee, and offered absentminded pats on the head. Bills, emails, and endless to-do lists, those, they would not miss. But the faces of loved ones, the places that had anchored them, the sense of belonging, those were much harder to release.

Max's ears dipped, his tail giving a slow, thoughtful twitch. He had fought not to dwell on the sharp ache that struck whenever he remembered the life he had left behind. Yet Daisy's words stirred something unspoken in him. Maybe she was right. Maybe a farewell was what they all needed, closure, before heading south with ghosts trailing behind them.

"That's... not a bad idea," Max admitted softly. "It could be dangerous, but if we're careful,"

"We'd have to be extremely careful," Titan cut in, his voice clipped. Ever the pragmatist, the sleek Dobermann stared at Daisy with a sharp, worried look. "Going back means being seen near the people who knew us. What if someone recognizes their pet and tries to catch us? Worse, what if the lab's watching our homes already, expecting us to come back?"

Titan whined at that thought, his Dobermann frame trembling slightly. "Would they really think we'd... go home?" His round eyes flickered with unease.

"People cling to the familiar in a crisis," Luna said gently, her Tabby tail wrapping around her paws. "It's a common enough instinct. But I doubt the lab is organized yet. Ten missing human test subjects, our human bodies, plus ten missing animals? They have chaos to deal with. Dr. Smith must be frantic." She sighed.

Cleo's fur bristled, his tail lashing. "Poor Dr. Smith? He's the one who zapped our brains out of our bodies!" The doctors voice faltered with the memory of terror still raw. Not entirely sure we need to start the blame game.

Luna shook her head, calm even in the face of his anger. "I'm not excusing him. I just... I remember his face. He looked horrified. I don't think he meant for any of this to happen."

"Regardless," Max interceded, his tone firm but gentle, "we can't assume we're safe. Titan's right, if we do this, it has to be quick and quiet. No lingering, no unnecessary risks. No being seen too closely." His eyes flicked to Cleo, who flattened his ears in guilty silence, and then to Peanut, who puffed his chest indignantly at the implication he might be reckless.

Daisy lifted her head, dawn catching in her eyes like fire. "I need it," she whispered. "I need to see my kids. Even if it's only from a distance. Just to know they're okay… to say goodbye, in my own way."

Picasso bent his scruffy head and gave her shoulder a tender lick. "Then you shall, darling," he said softly. "We all shall. One last tour of the city, a bittersweet farewell to the ghosts of our pasts! Tragic, poignant, with just the right touch of comic relief. A final act worth remembering." His theatrical attempt earned a few smiles, though his tone was weighted with sincerity.

Peanut puffed out his little chest and stood. "My old apartments in the Bronx. Lived there nearly seventeen years," he declared with mock gruffness. "If I don't check in and make sure no hoodlums trashed the place, I'll never sleep right again." His way of saying yes.

Tao leapt from her branch, landing with fine grace she still wasn't used to. Once, she had been clumsy in high heels. Now she landed like a gymnast, silent and sure. "I… I have someone to see too," she admitted in a low voice. She said nothing more, but the flicker of pain in her eyes silenced any questions.

One by one, every member of the pack either spoke or nodded. Ten souls, ten goodbyes.

Max felt the swell of emotion rise in his chest. His pack, his friends, were carrying unfinished stories inside them. A true leader would not ask them to bury those stories without closure.

"Alright," he said, resolve solidifying in his voice. "We do this. We each visit the place we need to see. We say our good-byes. Then we regroup, plan our escape, and head south. First train we can catch, or hitch, we take it."

"Understood," Titan said briskly. The others echoed agreement, tails wagging faintly with renewed hope.

Titan cocked his head thoughtfully. "So... what's the route? Manhattan, Brooklyn, Queens, Bronx... uh, anyone from Staten Island?"

Max hesitated, then lifted her paw slightly. "My parents' house is there. Staten Island. But I know it's... out of the way." His voice trembled; clearly he hated to burden the group.

"Nonsense," Picasso boomed kindly. "We'll plan around it. The ferry is always a delight." He gave her a wink.

"Awesome?" Tao muttered, licking her paw. "It's full of people. Maybe the bridge instead? How do we cross without a human or a car?"

"The Staten Island Ferry's free," Titan mused. "But animals need carriers. We'd have to stow away, or hide with the cars below deck."

Max flicked an ear. "Then we make it the last stop. From Staten Island we can head straight into New Jersey, then south."

The plan made sense. The Carolinas waited far beyond, and New Jersey was the first step toward freedom.

"So is it Manhattan first," Max continued. "Then Queens or the Bronx, depending on urgency. Then Brooklyn. Staten Island last."

Agreement rippled through the group. They rose from their makeshift camp, shaking off leaves and stretching stiff limbs. The air seemed heavier now with the weight of their task: a day and night of walking into their own pasts, one stop at a time.

Luna nudged the canvas tote of food they had stashed. "Bring this. No telling when we'll eat again. Might need to use it as bribery too." She smiled wryly at the memory of distracting a stray dog with a fillet the night before.

Cleo hopped onto a low stone wall, tail flicking eagerly. "I can help carry it." His wiry frame leaned down to grip one of the bag's handles in his teeth.

Titan took the other handle easily. "Got it," he mumbled through the canvas.

Max looked at them all and felt pride swell inside him. Who would have thought ten such different New Yorkers, once strangers, would end up like this, bound together by circumstance and loyalty? He gave a low chuff. "Wolves of New York," he said quietly, "let's go say our goodbyes."

Without another word, they slipped from beneath the oak into the waking city, hugging shadows, crossing lawns, and vanishing down side paths. Ten silhouettes moved together, one purpose carrying them forward.

Manhattan, Early Morning – Titan's Apartment Building

The Wolves padded through the still-sleeping streets of the Upper East Side, their paws silent on the pavement. Delivery trucks rumbled in the distance, and early commuters moved with coffee cups in hand, oblivious to the strange procession of animals hugging alley walls. The pack moved in careful formation: Max scouting ahead, Titan just behind him; Tao and Cleo slinking along the walls like wraiths; Daisy and Max flanking Peanut to keep the little Pug safe on his short legs; Titan and Picasso hauling the precious tote between them.

At last, Titan slowed, his sleek frame stiffening as he halted in the shadow of a bus stop. The others bunched behind him, following his gaze.

"There," he murmured.

Across the street, a gleaming high-rise towered upward, its facade of glass and steel glittering faintly in the early light. Inside, the lobby glowed warm gold against marble walls. A Christmas tree still sparkled in one corner, decorations that had survived the holiday season unremoved, though none of them had celebrated. Behind the desk sat a doorman in a tidy uniform, sipping coffee and glancing idly toward the door.

Titan sat on his haunches, staring. He could see every detail in his mind: the scent of polished brass, the sound of his own shoes on marble floors, the way he had hurried through this very lobby a hundred times, eyes glued to his phone, barely nodding to Reese, the doorman.

This morning, Reese looked bored. Then he reached under the desk and pulled out a stack of flyers. Crossing to the glass door, he taped one up carefully.

Titan's sharp canine eyes locked on it. From across the street, he could read the headline clearly:

MISSING.

Beneath it was a photo of a woman, clean-cut, mid-forties, dressed in a Marine Uniform, a faintly distant smile on her face.

Titan's own face.

He felt Max inhale sharply beside him.

"They're looking for you," Daisy whispered.

"For her," Titan corrected softly, his tone edged with quiet bitterness. "For that." He nodded toward the photo of her human self, the one who hadn't come home.

Peanut squinted at the flyer, scratching behind his ear. "Fancy place like this, of course they'll raise the alarm when a woman vanishes. There a reward on that thing, Vic?" He tried to make a joke of it, but his chuckle died in the air. No one laughed.

Titan's ears flattened, betraying irritation. "I'm sure my company insisted on the flyers. Missing CFO, all that bad press." She tried to sound detached, dismissive, as though it no longer mattered. Yet the restless flick of his tail gave him away.

She forced herself to scan the rest of the lobby, seeking distraction. Through the tall glass doors, the elevator was visible, gleaming in chrome, and beyond that, the mail area. In his mind, Titan traced the familiar path upward, to the 20th floor. To her penthouse suite, the one that looked out across the park. Once, she had loved that view, in the rare moments she had allowed himself to appreciate it.

A memory surfaced unbidden: late nights standing at the floor-to-ceiling window, the city sparkling beneath him like a sea of fireflies. He would stand there, whiskey neat in hand, gazing out as though he ruled it all. On top of the world, yet, beneath the polished surface, utterly alone. In those days, loneliness had seemed like a fair trade for success. After all, she had the corner office, the six-figure bonuses, the sleek sports car gathering dust in the garage, and an apartment that made her colleagues envious. Wasn't that supposed to be enough?

Now, the apartment was as lonely as she had been, perhaps more so. At least she had once breathed life into it; now it was nothing but a shell, a box of expensive furniture and cold silence.

From her vantage point across the street, Titan caught a flicker of movement on the 20th-floor balcony, his balcony. A flutter of fabric. Narrowing his eyes, he saw her: Elena, her housekeeper, watering the planters with her familiar careful touch. The elderly woman had been coming twice a week for years, steadfast and dependable. She must have a key. Maybe she tended the place still, hoping her employer would walk through the door one day. Loyal Elena, who always worried she wasn't eating properly, who left pots of stew in the fridge as though she were a mother fussing over a stubborn child.

Titan watched her fuss over the plants; her lined face creased with concern even at that distance. She paused, dabbing her eyes with a handkerchief, and then looked out across the city, as if willing her to appear from the crowd.

A lump rose in his throat. She remembered her voice once, months ago, soft but firm as she scolded her: *"you work too much. Life will pass you by."* She had only laughed, handing her a Christmas bonus as if money could erase her concern. *Life will pass you by.* How prophetic those words felt now.

"You okay?" Max's voice was soft at his side.

Titan blinked, realizing her eyes had misted. Embarrassed, she pawed at his snout. "Yeah. Fine."

No one pressed her. They simply waited, giving her the silence he needed. Around them, the city roused itself, the honk of a taxi, the clatter of a garbage truck, the hum of voices growing as the morning quickened. Titan gazed at the life she had left behind.

He had expected grief to hit her like a tidal wave. And yes, sadness was there, but to his surprise, so was relief. Seeing that flyer, seeing Elena's sorrow, thinking of Reese's worry, she regretted the pain she had caused them. Yet, she could not deny the liberation that stirred within. She would miss Elena's kindness. She would miss the quiet view of the park. But she would not miss the 80-hour weeks, the ulcer pangs of stress, or the avalanche of late-night emails that consumed her soul.

Who am I now, she wondered, *without that job? Without that life plan I clung to so tightly?* A dog, yes, but perhaps more than that. Perhaps someone with the chance to begin again. Maybe tragedy was also opportunity.

She drew in a deep breath. The crisp morning air filled his lungs, rich with scents her human self would never have noticed: pretzels sizzling on a corner cart, acrid exhaust fumes, the delicate perfume of a passerby hurrying a Yorkie across the street. Each smell layered itself upon the next, painting Manhattan in colors more vivid than sight alone ever had.

"It wasn't all bad, you know," Titan murmured at last, more to herself than to anyone. Daisy and Max perked their ears, listening. "I made some good memories there." Her gaze lingered on the tower. "But... I think it's time I moved on."

She rose to her feet, straightening with a quiet dignity. There was something solemn in the way she carried himself now, as though laying the past to rest. Her eyes roamed once more from the lobby with its missing poster and worried doorman, up the sleek glass tower, to the balcony where Elena had disappeared.

"Goodbye, old life," Titan whispered. The words were nearly lost to the wind, but in her heart, they carried weight. A silent thank you followed, for Elena, for those who had cared in their own ways. Gratitude, carried away on the morning breeze.

Then she turned back to her companions. "I'm done here," she said gently. "We can go."

No one questioned. With nods of respect, they began padding down the sidewalk, blending into the city's rhythm once again. Picasso fell into step beside Titan, the Mutt leaning his massive shoulder against him in quiet comfort.

"Proud of ya, Vic," Picasso said softly, without theatrics or flourish, just genuine sincerity. "Takes guts to walk away."

Titan exhaled a small huff of thanks, and together they left the high-rise, and the life it represented, behind.

Midtown Manhattan, Morning – Picasso's Old Apartment

As the sun climbed higher, the pack wound their way downtown. The city was waking in earnest now: more cars filled the avenues, early risers hurried with steaming cups of coffee, delivery bikes zipped between lanes. "The Wolves of New York" kept mostly to side streets, a silent procession of dogs and cats weaving through the metropolitan maze like shadows.

Picasso led them toward a neighborhood of brick tenements and warm brownstones, not far from the Theater District. At the corner of a narrow lane, a shop owner rattled open his shutters, releasing the rich smell of fresh bagels into the morning air. Several stomachs rumbled at once, despite last night's feast. Cleo crept toward a stray bagel that had rolled onto the sidewalk until Tao nudged him back with a smirk.

"Focus, kid," she whispered, amused.

Their destination soon came into view: a squat four-story building with a faded red door and a cracked stone stoop. A wrought-iron fire escape climbed its facade, and in one third-story window a rainbow flag fluttered proudly beside a Broadway poster.

Picasso stopped, gazing at it with a wistful half-smile. "Home sweet home," he murmured. In his mind's eye, he saw his human self, tall, gangly, bright-eyed, bounding up those steps two at a time, humming a show tune after a night's performance. How many times had he sat on that stoop, daydreaming about his name glowing on a marquee?

Now, in the body of a Mutt, he barely filled any of the sidewalk. Peanut and Titan set down the tote bag by a lamppost, giving Picasso room to move forward.

He padded slowly across the street toward the red door. The others remained behind, standing respectfully on the opposite curb.

At the stoop, Picasso lifted one paw and pressed it gently against the weathered wood, as though she could feel his old life vibrating within. The door was scuffed from years of use, each mark familiar in some forgotten way. On a whim, she nosed the mail slot open and peered inside.

Dust motes floated lazily in the sunbeam that cut through a rear window. The small lobby was quiet, lined with the blue battered mailboxes she used to fumble with after midnight. Her nose flared, catching layers of scents: lingering cooking oil,

Mrs. Greenberg's cats in 1B, incense from the yoga teacher upstairs in 2A, and faintest of all, the essence of her own third-floor apartment, stage makeup, detergent, and vanilla candles burned during late-night readings.

Her tail wagged once, slowly, as the memories returned. That cramped one-bedroom had been her sanctuary. She rehearsed monologues in the mirror there, patched thrift-shop costumes under the lamplight, hosted impromptu readings with friends who shared her hunger for the stage. It had been hand-to-mouth survival, but it had been alive.

And then, another memory stabbed deeper: the day she adopted Picasso, the Mutt puppy who would eventually become the body she now wore. It was after a small triumph, a part in an off-Broadway play, and she'd wanted someone to share the joy with. Picasso had been a handful in the tiny apartment, with the limited space, but Picasso had loved him fiercely. Picasso had charm, even a flair for the dramatic; he could steal applause with a single "play dead" routine.

A pang twisted Picasso's chest, had anyone noticed? Had the theater community cared for the confused "Picasso" wandering among them? Questions without answers. For now, all she could do was say goodbye.

Backing away, he sat heavily on the stoop, feeling the cool stone beneath him. The traffic hummed in the distance, but here the street was quiet. Her friends watched silently across the road as Picasso spoke, her deep voice tinged with reverence.

"Goodbye, 315 West 48th," she said softly, addressing the building by its number as though it were an old friend. "You've been a fine stage for this chapter of my life. From hopeful auditions to crushing rejections, from wild cast parties to lonely midnight karaoke, you saw it all."

Max and Daisy exchanged a glance but stayed quiet, letting her continue.

Picasso lifted his gaze toward the third-floor window where a Broadway poster still hung, perhaps left there in his absence, waiting. Her voice took on a note of theatrical gravitas, part farewell, part performance:

"I leave you now not in tragedy, but in triumph. For the world itself has become my stage, and I," she placed a small paw over her chest with mock drama, "I have a new role to play."

Peanut whispered to Titan, "Is she monologuing to a building?"

Titan hushed him gently with a soft nudge.

Picasso heard the whisper and couldn't suppress a tiny smile. Yes, she was being ridiculous, and she knew it. But she needed this little moment of theater; it was stitched into his very soul. Clearing her throat, she lifted her head and continued with a flourish:

"All the world's a stage, and all the men and women merely players. Well, this player has traded in her script and costume for fur and four paws."

The Mutt chuckled softly, the sound emerging more like a rumbling chuff. "And surprisingly, it's the role of a lifetime."

She drew a long, deliberate breath, steadying the quaver that threatened to overtake her voice. "I'll miss you, my quirky little apartment. I'll miss the leaky faucet in the kitchen that dripped in B-flat, and the radiator that clanked like a snare drum on winter nights. I'll miss the scent of takeout Thai drifting through the hallway, and the way the floorboards creaked hello when I came home late."

Her friends listened in silence. Some had watery eyes, others smiled through the lump in their throats. Max's tail wagged just slightly, a soft, reassuring rhythm that seemed to urge her on.

Picasso exhaled and straightened, drawing himself up with quiet dignity. "But like any great show... it must close, to make way for the next one."

She dipped her head in a graceful arc, bowing as if to an invisible audience. "Thank you," she whispered to the empty stoop, his voice thick with emotion. "Thank you for everything."

A single tear welled in her glowing eyes, and she swiped at it with a paw in a discreet, almost embarrassed gesture.

And with that, Picasso stepped off the stoop and crossed back to the waiting pack.

"That was beautiful, Picasso," Daisy said softly as she rejoined them.

"Bit long-winded for a goodbye," Peanut teased, trying to lighten the moment. "But hey, you always were one for soliloquies." Her own eyes, however, shimmered faintly.

Picasso gave an exaggerated shrug. "What can I say? I don't do half-measures." Then she sniffled, dropping character as she leaned down so tiny Peanut could pat his hairy foreleg consolingly.

Max pressed his nose briefly to Picasso's shoulder, offering silent solidarity. No words were needed. The pack closed in together, bodies brushing against one another, a fleeting circle of warmth and comfort.

Cleo, who had been uncharacteristically quiet through Picasso's speech, finally piped up. "That Shakespeare bit was actually kind of cool."

Picasso's lips curled in a broad grin, baring teeth in what was unmistakably a proud smile. "Stick with me, kid. I'll have you quoting the Bard by the time we hit Baltimore."

Tao flicked her tail. "Let's hope not," she said dryly, "or else we'll be the strangest-sounding strays in the South."

The quip earned a ripple of laughter, lightening the air and washing away the heavy ache that had lingered. With spirits steadied, the group prepared to move on. Picasso glanced back at his building one last time, his expression a mixture of grief and gratitude, then straightened with a deep breath.

"Where to next, chief?" he asked Max.

Max consulted the map etched in his mind. They had covered Manhattan. Four companions still needed closure: Peanut in the Bronx, Luna (and Cleo) in the Bronx as well, Titan and Tao in Queens, Daisy in Brooklyn, and Max in Staten Island. Winston was in Queens as well. His own name was missing from that list, but he shoved the thought aside. Getting the others through their farewells came first.

"We've done Manhattan," Max said. "Queens is next, then the Bronx, then Brooklyn, and finally Staten Island."

Winston nodded. "My place is in Queens."

"And mine," Tao added quietly. She hopped lightly back onto Max's broad back. The German Sheppard didn't mind; if anything, Max seemed comforted by the company. Max trotted ahead with his usual patience, Tao perched atop him like a small queen riding her steed.

Max turned to Luna, the tabby, who sat with calm composure, her tail curled neatly around her paws. "Luna, where would you like to go? We won't forget you."

Luna's gentle smile deepened the fine lines of age around her muzzle. "Bronx, dear. We can stop by on the way to Brooklyn. I'm in no rush."

Cleo raised a paw. "Me too – Bronx. Well, technically I lived in Harlem, north Manhattan, but it's basically on the way."

Max frowned slightly. Harlem wasn't the Bronx, but it was indeed enroute if they crossed uptown to head north. "Noted. We'll stop in Harlem, then into the Bronx for Peanut, Luna, and you Winston and, Cleo."

Agreement rippled through the group. They had a long road ahead, but direction gave them strength.

Titan and Cleo slipped the tote bag handles back into their grips. Together, the pack set off toward the 59th Street Bridge, their paws falling into rhythm. As they left Picasso's block behind, the German Sheppard held his head high despite the damp streaks on his muzzle. Like Titan before him, he had made his peace. One by one, each heart was untangling itself from the city's grip, preparing to be given to the horizon ahead.

Queens, Late Morning – Chai's Apartment

Crossing into Queens was an adventure in itself. The pack took the pedestrian path across the Queensboro Bridge, weaving between waves of joggers and cyclists. At one point, a passing cyclist nearly swerved into the railing when he caught sight of the improbable convoy trotting single-file. By the time he blinked and looked again, the animals had melted into a maintenance alcove, hearts pounding. If the man ever retold the story, who would believe him?

Queens unfolded beneath their paws: quieter residential blocks, brick buildings with corner stores tucked beneath, and streets buzzing less frantically than Manhattan's heart. A hazy winter sun pressed down through thin clouds, catching on windows and throwing pale gold across the pavement. Still, even here, they had to be cautious. A strange cluster of dogs and cats traveling together could spark unwanted attention.

Chai led them through a neighborhood of low-rise complexes, his breathing labored. He and Cleo had hauled the tote bag for most of the morning, but Max had stepped in to help when his strength flagged. His Shepard body was powerful, but the steady grind of distance travel was new to him, unlike pacing circles in a cramped apartment.

Finally, he stopped across from a nondescript brick building with a green awning shading its entrance. A faded welcome mat lay beneath it, declaring *Home Sweet Home* in both English and Hindi – a small nod to the community's roots. This was Titan's building.

His gaze rose to the second floor, to the dark window behind navy curtains his mother had once sent him as a housewarming gift. Had anyone touched them since?

A lump formed in his throat. As a man, Rahul had been shy, tucked away in his mid 30s, married more to his work than to people. He had friends, yes – online colleagues, Marines, a few drinking buddies – but day to day, his apartment had been both refuge and cage. He had coded late into the night, eaten takeout biryani by the glow of monitors, and talked to his Dobermann, Titan, about software bugs as though the dog were a coworker.

And he had taken that patient dog for granted. Chai would nap for hours beneath the desk, only pawing when it was time to walk. Sometimes Titan, buried in code, delayed longer than he should have. Yet Chai had never complained, only wagged his tail when Rahul finally surfaced.

Now, inhabiting Rahul's body, Chai understood. The restless need to move, the joy of air in the lungs, the demand for freedom in the muscles, it thrummed through him. Poor Chai had carried that playful hunger without words to voice it.

"I'm sorry, buddy," Rahul as Chai whispered to the empty air, hoping somehow his dog's spirit was listening. "I get it now."

Peanut nudged his leg gently with his tiny nose. "You're up, kid."

Chai blinked, pulled from his reverie. With a bracing breath, he trotted across the street and padded to the stoop. The front door, as expected, was locked, but through the glass he could glimpse the small lobby: a bulletin board cluttered with notices (a flyer for a long-past Diwali festival still tacked there), and a row of mailboxes.

Number 2C was crammed with letters and flyers, visible even through the little window. No one had touched it since he'd gone. He imagined packages stacked at his door upstairs, books and gadgets gathering dust. The mundanity of it hit him hardest: life in absentia marked not by headlines, but by unopened mail.

Just then, the door opened. Chai stiffened, ready to flee. An elderly woman shuffled out with a trash bag in hand – Mrs. Gupta from 1A. He remembered her wariness of Chai at first, the suspicion born from stereotypes, until one day Chai had licked her hand gently and won her over.

She passed him now without recognition, seeing only another stray dog in the neighborhood.

"Shoo," she said half-heartedly, waving her hand with more habit than conviction. But her voice carried warmth, not dismissal. She reached into her pocket and pulled out a crumpled napkin. From its folds, she extracted half a sweet sugar pastry slightly flattened but still fragrant with spices.

"Here, doggy. You look hungry," she murmured, tossing the morsel gently toward him.

Chai's stomach betrayed him with a loud, eager gurgle. He hadn't realized just how hungry he still was. Lowering his head, he devoured the spiced pastry in two grateful bites. The taste was more than food, it was kindness, seasoned with memory.

From across the street, Daisy whispered, "Aww," her voice hushed with tenderness as they watched the quiet act of charity unfold.

Mrs. Gupta gave a small, approving nod as Titan lifted his gaze, his eyes shimmering with gratitude. "Good boy," she said softly, as if replying to his unspoken thanks. With practiced effort, she hefted her trash bag and headed for the curb.

Chai knew he should hurry back to his friends now. But something held him in place, urging him to linger. He padded after Mrs. Gupta, watching as the elderly woman rubbed her knee wearily while setting down the bag. Acting on instinct more than thought, Titan moved to her side and gently pressed his muzzle against her free hand.

Startled, she gave a small laugh. "Friendly one, aren't you?" she said, her voice warm with amusement. Tentatively, she reached down and patted his head, right between his alert, perky corgi ears. Chai's tail wagged without his permission, betraying the swell of emotion inside him. This was the first time since becoming an animal that a human, any human outside of his fellow mind-swapped friends, had offered him such unguarded affection. It felt... achingly good.

Mrs. Gupta turned back toward her stoop, her slippers shuffling softly against the concrete. "Go on now, stray dog. Be careful out here," she mumbled with gentle concern before disappearing into her building.

Chai stepped back, his gaze fixed on the closing door. He realized he had gotten his wish he had said goodbye. Not with words, not directly, but in the only way he could. His neighbors would never know what became of Rahul Patel in 2C, the engineer with the loyal dog. Yet, in this fleeting exchange, he had found a final connection to the life he once knew. And somehow, it was enough.

When he rejoined the pack, he licked a few lingering crumbs of sweetness from his jowls. His eyes were shining, though whether it was from unshed emotion or the bite of spices making his nose run, even he could not tell.

"You, okay?" Max asked gently as they began moving again.

Chai nodded, his voice steadier than he felt. "Yeah. I think I am." A small, genuine smile tugged at his lips. "Mrs. Gupta gave me a sweet ball of delight."

Peanut let out a booming laugh. "Trust you to turn a farewell into a free meal, kid!"

Chai ducked his head sheepishly, though his grin betrayed him. "It was her way of saying goodbye, I think. Even if she didn't know it was me."

He felt lighter as they continued down the street. A chapter had closed, and the ache he expected had softened into something gentler. As his paws padded against the pavement, he realized something new: as a human, he had often felt invisible in the endless bustle of New York City. But strangely, as a dog, just another stray, he had been noticed. Seen. Cared for, if only for a brief, genuine moment. Ironically, he mused, sometimes humanity shows itself more clearly when you are no longer human at all.

Queens, Noon, Tao's Farewell

The journey to Tao's old home led them further east into Queens. By the time they reached her neighborhood, the sun was high, spilling gold across a quiet street lined with maple trees and neat single-family houses. This part of Queens carried a distinctly suburban calm: trimmed hedges, minivans parked neatly in driveways, and the faint sound of children's laughter drifting from a nearby schoolyard.

Tao, uncharacteristically silent during the trip, finally spoke as they climbed a gentle hill. Her voice was subdued but steady. "That's it. The blue house with the white fence."

They followed her gaze. The house was modest but welcoming, a two-story home with cheerful blue siding and a small front porch. Wind chimes tinkled in the breeze, their melody fragile and wistful. A silver sedan sat in the driveway, instantly recognizable to Tao. She had ridden in that car more times than she could count.

Sliding down from Max's broad back, the gray Siamese landed softly on the sidewalk. She seemed smaller now, shoulders hunched as though bracing herself. Max lifted a paw, motioning for the others to stay back beneath the shade of a wide maple tree. This was Tao's moment, and she deserved to face it alone.

Tao padded forward, crossing the street with hesitant steps. Her heart hammered in her chest. Unlike the others, she wasn't returning to an empty apartment or strangers' hands. Someone she loved deeply was inside, and the thought both thrilled her and split her with dread.

As she crept into the yard through a gap in the fence, her eyes caught the faint outline of drawn curtains. But the sheer veil over the bay window gave her a clear view inside.

On the couch sat a man, his face buried in his hands. Tao knew him instantly, Michael.

Her breath caught. The sight of her fiancé, shoulders slumped and spirit heavy, hit her like a blow. On the coffee table lay a small velvet box, open to reveal her engagement ring. She had removed it before the Pet-Link experiment, handing it to him with the promise: "Just for the day."

Now it gleamed like a lonely star, untouched and waiting.

Michael lifted his head. His face was drawn, unshaven, his eyes rimmed red from sleepless nights. He held a photograph in one hand, perhaps one of their engagement photos. Tenderly, he set it down beside the ring box.

Tao's vision blurred with tears. Every part of her ached to burst through the door, to tell him she was here, alive, though not as he knew her. But to him, she was gone. Missing. Possibly dead. And in a painful way, that was true.

Inside, Michael rose and paced, his hands pressing against his face as if to hold himself together. Tears glinted on his cheeks.

A small whimper escaped Tao before she could stop it.

Michael froze. His head snapped toward the window, brows furrowed. He stepped closer, searching.

Tao shrank back into the porch's Cleo, heart pounding. Too late. He had heard her.

He scanned the yard through the glass, but from her angle, she remained hidden. After a long pause, he sighed, rubbed his eyes, and turned away.

Tao let out the breath she'd been holding, chest aching with silent sobs. She crept forward again, back into the open yard, until she stood almost at the window. With trembling resolve, she placed one paw against the cool pane.

"Goodbye, Michael," she whispered, her words lost to the glass but etched in her soul. "Thank you for loving me. I'm sorry."

As if he had heard, Michael stirred. His gaze lifted, locking onto the window. For one agonizing instant, Tao thought he truly saw her. She didn't flee this time. She stayed.

Their eyes met, his grief-stricken, hers brimming with love disguised by fine form.

Michael approached, kneeling by the glass. "Hey there," he murmured softly, his voice muffled but tender. "You remind me of someone, kitty."

Tao blinked slowly, her fine smile, praying he understood the gesture.

Michael gave her the faintest smile in return, his first of the day. He lifted his palm against the window.

Tao aligned her paw to his hand, separated only by a thin pane of glass and an immeasurable gulf of fate. They stayed like that for a timeless moment, hand to paw, united in silence.

Tears streamed freely down Tao's cheeks, though no sound betrayed her. She wanted to scream her truth; to tell him she loved him. But instead, she etched the moment deep within her, her only goodbye.

Michael's eyes shimmered as well. Whether he truly sensed her or was simply comforted by the presence of a gentle creature, Tao could not know.

Summoning strength, she drew her paw back. His hand lingered a moment longer before falling away.

Tao retreated slowly, giving him one last longing glance before running, back across the yard, through the fence, and into the safety of her waiting friends.

Daisy was the first to meet her, the golden retriever pressing close as Tao collapsed into her fur. Shaking with sobs that broke into choked mewls, Tao buried herself there. Daisy said nothing, only licking the top of her head with quiet tenderness, a silent vow that she was not alone.

The others formed a protective circle, keeping vigilant eyes on the surroundings in case the scene at the blue house drew unwanted attention. But Michael never came out. He likely never realized that the cat he had glimpsed was anything more than just a stray.

After a few minutes, Tao's sobs quieted. She pulled back from Daisy, distress evident on her distinct features. "Sorry," she whispered, her voice thick with lingering tears.

"None of that," Luna said firmly, stepping forward to touch noses with Tao in quiet solidarity. The older cat's eyes gleamed with deep empathy. "There is no need to apologize for loving someone."

Tao nodded faintly, wiping her damp face with a paw. She drew in a deep, shuddering breath and glanced around at her friends, who stood in calm, patient silence. "Thank you... all of you... for letting me do that."

Max dipped his head with quiet conviction. "We've got your back," he said simply.

A tiny, fragile smile touched Tao's mouth. Her heart ached, but it also felt strangely whole. That brief connection with Michael, it was more than she had ever dared hope for. He was alive. He would heal in time. And she... she would carry his love with her as they journeyed on.

"Let's go," she said softly, her voice steadier now. "I'm okay."

The pack silently fell back into formation. They left the peaceful street with its blue house behind, moving onward toward their next destination. As they walked, Tao glanced back once over her shoulder. The wind chimes on the porch rang out a gentle, lingering melody. She imagined it as a final farewell song; one meant just for her.

As they walked away there was one dog that had made a hard decision. Winston decided that visiting her penthouse today was too just much. Now thinking like Ava, she decided that it was a better decision to skip the visit and move on. She did not have anyone there anyways. It was going to happen today. Maybe in the future but not today. The Wolves moved on and Max and Titan led the way.

Harlem and Onward, Afternoon – Cleo's Home

By early afternoon, the pack had made their way west-ward, crossing back through Manhattan's northern edge toward the Bronx. The winter daylight was already fading, a pale sun sinking reluctantly behind the city's skyline. Harlem's streets bustled with energy, vendors calling, buses groaning, people rushing past. Here, anonymity was paradoxical: easier because the sidewalks overflowed with life, no one sparing more than a glance at a few strays; harder because a pack of ten could still draw notice if they moved too closely together.

They chose caution, splitting into two clusters. Max led half the group through a narrow back alley, while Titan guided the others along a parallel street. They planned to meet at a small park ahead. Communication was minimal, quick glances, flicks of ears, soft barks, or the occasional mew. Through trial and error, they had become adept at moving as one, a make-shift army of strays bound by necessity.

Cleo padded down 128th Street, nerves tightening with each step. This was his neighborhood. His home. Or rather, his mother's apartment, the place where his human life had been lived. He hadn't shared much about it with the others, but now his tail flicked anxiously as familiar landmarks tugged at him: the corner bodega splashed with bright murals, the stoop where he and the neighborhood kids once skateboarded, the playground fence he had vaulted countless times despite the bold "No Trespassing After Dark" sign.

Max, reading his tension, gave a low chuff to gather the pack's attention. They regrouped in the alley behind Cleo's building, a weathered six-story tenement, its bricks painted with faded graffiti, laundry stiff with cold hanging between windows.

Cleo crept forward, his nose twitching. Then he froze. A scent, rich, unmistakable, drifted through the air. His mother's cooking. Stew, simmering with garlic and oregano.

The British Short Hair sat at the base of the fire escape, staring upward. The kitchen window above was cracked open, letting out steam. It was too high to reach from the ground, but Cleo had climbed that way countless times as a kitten, and now, as a cat, he had the intense determination. With a fluid leap, he landed on a closed dumpster, then scrambled up to a narrow ledge and the cold iron rungs of the fire escape ladder. The metal rattled faintly under his paws.

"Careful," Max whispered from below, her eyes brimming with concern.

Cleo gave a silent nod. This was his moment.

Step by step, he ascended to the second-floor landing. Through the window's small opening, he peered into the kitchen. It was exactly as he remembered, perhaps a little messier. A pot bubbled on the stove, filling the air with warmth. At the counter, chopping carrots with a distracted rhythm, was his mother.

Cleo's vision blurred. Ma. She wore her old pink housecoat; her hair tied in a scarf. An Afro-Cuban jazz tune crackled faintly from the radio, though she wasn't humming as she normally would. Her movements were mechanical, her eyes distant. Dark circles carved Cleos beneath them. She hadn't been sleeping well.

The kitchen door creaked, and a small girl entered, Tanya, Cleo's niece. She couldn't have been more than five, clutching a worn teddy bear. Her large eyes brimmed with worry. "Mommy, you think Cleo's cold out there?" she asked softly.

Their mother froze mid-chop. Slowly, she put the knife down and crouched to Tanya's height, gathering the child in her arms. "Baby, I... I don't know," she whispered, her voice breaking. "They're doing everything they can to find him. Your uncle... your uncle tough. He'll come back."

Tanya sniffled. "You promise?"

On the fire escape, Cleo pressed against the wall, fighting back tears. Tanya... He remembered teasing her about her ABCs just a week ago, how she'd thrown a crayon at him in retaliation. He had pretended annoyance, but in truth, he adored her.

Their mother stroked Tanya's hair. "I can't promise," she said gently, "but I have faith. We have to hold on to faith, okay? Remember what I said? Your uncle is like a stray cat, he always finds his way home." She let out a shaky laugh at her own bittersweet metaphor.

Tanya wiped her nose with her bear's ear. "Maybe he's with Cleo?" she asked innocently, naming their family cat, the very body Yusuf now inhabited. The thought twisted his stomach. If the swap had gone both ways, then Cleo was somewhere inside Yusufs's human body... the idea was too much to process.

"Maybe," their mother whispered. She kissed Tanya's forehead, then guided her toward the door. "Go wash up for dinner. I'll call you when it's ready."

As Tanya padded away, their mother lingered, leaning on the counter. For a long moment, she pressed a trembling hand to her mouth, holding in either a sob or a prayer, or both. Then, with visible effort, she straightened and resumed chopping, though her resolve looked thin as paper.

Cleo knew he had to leave. If he stayed any longer, the dam inside him might break. He backed away, descending the fire escape as silently as he had climbed.

When his paws touched the alley ground, Daisy and Max were there instantly, pressing close. He hadn't realized he was shaking until Daisy wrapped her golden body around him.

"I heard," Daisy whispered. Her ears had caught some of the conversation.

Cleo hiccupped, his voice breaking. "They're talking about me. Tanya thinks I'm with the cat. Well… I guess I am." He tried to laugh, but it came out cracked and wet.

Max stepped forward, resting a paw on the dumpster. His gaze was steady, his posture reassuring. "Your mom's right about one thing, kid. You're tough. You found us. And we'll make sure you're okay."

Cleo swiped at his eyes with a paw. "I never meant to put anyone through this," he murmured. "I snuck out that night to go to the lab. If I'd just… listened…" The bravado was, replaced by guilt.

Luna pressed gently against his other side. "We all made choices that brought us here," she said softly. "None of us could have known. But your mother's right about something else too."

Cleo lifted his gaze, eyes round and wet. "What's that?"

"You'll find a way home," Luna said simply. "Maybe not in the way she expects… but you have a family in us now. And one day… who knows? Life has its surprises. Keep faith."

Cleo sniffed and managed a faint smile. "Thanks." It wasn't okay, not yet, but with his friends, the weight was a little easier to bear.

Above them, the kitchen window creaked wider, releasing a wave of fragrant steam. The scent of beef stew drifted down into the alley, warm and rich.

Peanut's nose twitched, and he broke the silence with a quip. "No sense letting a good stew go to waste. Got any more acrobatics in you, kid?" He nodded toward the window with a sly grin.

Cleo gave a startled laugh. Trust Peanut to think with his stomach. "You want me to steal my mom's stew?" he whispered, half-scandalized.

"Steal?" Peanut feigned innocence. "I was thinking... a taste. A parting tribute to your old life's cuisine. We've got mouths to feed, and that smells like heaven."

Titan sneered. "Unbelievable."

Max sighed, though a reluctant grin tugged at his mouth. "We shouldn't... but yeah, that does smell good."

Mischief flickered in Cleo's eyes, the first spark of mischief and boldness returning. "Okay... one container for the road."

He sprang back up the dumpster, climbed swiftly, and disappeared into the kitchen window's crack. Minutes later, he reappeared, a small Tupperware clamped in his mouth. Inside sloshed a portion of stew, still steaming. He must have snatched it while his mother was out of the kitchen.

As he dropped down, the pack greeted him with hushed cheers, soft barks, muted purrs, a few playful paw-claps on the pavement.

Cleo's heart felt lighter. It was a silly act, but symbolic. He had carried a piece of home with him, something warm and real. And maybe, deep down, it was his way of promising: one day, he'd return for the rest.

They tucked the precious stew into their tote and slipped away before anyone in the building noticed the stray cat burglar. Cleo cast one last glance upward as they left the alley. He couldn't see his mother, only catch the drifting scent of her love lingering in the air.

"Bye, Ma. Bye, Tanya," he whispered. "I'll be okay."

The pack moved on.

Before long, they crossed a quiet bridge into the South Bronx. The cityscape shifted around them, Harlem's bustling streets gave way to industrial lots, elevated subway tracks, and clusters of aging apartment blocks. In the shadow of the tracks, they passed a small encampment of makeshift tents and shopping carts tucked beneath the concrete pillars.

A few figures stirred among the camp. A man in a ragged coat sat on an overturned bucket, softly strumming a weatherworn guitar. Another tended a barrel fire, coaxing warmth from its flames even though daylight still lingered.

The pack slowed, each instinctively sensing the solemnity of the place. A wiry woman bundled in scarves looked up as they passed, her own scruffy mutt growling at the unfamiliar animals encroaching on their tenuous territory.

Max signaled his friends with a soft woof to keep distance and show no threat. The pack gave the encampment a wide berth, but as they did, the guitarist paused mid-strum. Instead of alarm, a crooked smile spread across his weathered face.

"Well, I'll be damned," he murmured, just loud enough for Max's sharp ears to catch. "Look at that crew."

The woman's shoulders eased as she saw the pack keeping respectful distance. "Ten of 'em," she remarked in astonishment. "You ever seen so many together?"

The guitarist chuckled, resuming a gentle blues riff. "They got somewhere to be, that's for sure."

As the pack passed, the man tipped an imaginary hat toward them. In response, Picasso, ever the performer, dipped his head in a small, playful bow without breaking stride. The guitarist let out a delighted cackle, and even the mutt offered a begrudging wag of its tail.

Not all kindness came from the affluent and comfortable; sometimes, even those with little left found room for wonder, humor, and generosity. The scarf-wrapped woman called out hoarsely:

"Stay safe out there!"

It was hard to tell whether she was speaking to the animals or to any listening spirits, but either way, the blessing hung in the cold air. The pack carried it with them as they pressed deeper into the Bronx.

Bronx, Late Afternoon – Peanut's Neighborhood

The sun cast long, slanting shadows by the time Peanut led them into his old neighborhood. Narrow streets wove between rows of brick buildings, many adorned with rusting fire escapes and flags of Italy and Puerto Rico fluttering side by side, a patchwork mosaic of heritage and pride. Children played stickball in the road, their shouts bouncing off graffiti-splashed walls.

Daisy had to nudge Peanut to keep him from darting toward the game; his little legs were quick, and for a moment he looked ready to chase after the rubber ball rolling past.

"Don't blow our cover, short stuff," she teased.

Peanut harrumphed. "Who, me? Just testing my reflexes." But he smirked. In truth, the sight warmed him. These streets had once been his whole world. He'd grown up here, in an era when stickball, fire hydrant sprinklers, and summer stoop-sitting were the reigning joys.

They came to a particular brownstone walk-up. Peanut slowed, his cloudy eyes taking on a faraway gleam.

"That's my place," he said softly. "Second floor, with the green shutters."

A potted plant sat proudly on the windowsill, and the sash was cracked open despite the chill, likely to let in fresh air while someone cooked. The aroma of simmering tomato sauce drifted outward, unmistakable and comforting.

Max motioned for the others to hold back while Peanut advanced alone. The little Pug ambled forward, unnoticed by most of the street. A pair of teens leaned against a car, laughing over a phone. A mailman made his rounds. An old man sat on the neighboring stoop, rustling a newspaper. To them, Peanut was nothing more than another stray dog with somewhere to be.

The front door was propped open, as it often was during the day. Peanut could see the chipped foyer tile and the rickety staircase he had once climbed countless times. His paws hesitated at the threshold. Could he risk going inside, even for a moment?

Then he heard it: a voice from within.

"Shoo! ¡Vete, perro!"

Peanut's heart leapt. Carmen. His wife of forty years.

He edged closer, peering around the door. At the bottom of the stairs stood Carmen, wielding a broom against a mutt that had wandered in, perhaps a neighbor's pet following the scent of dinner. "Out you go," she scolded lightly, sweeping it back toward the street. The dog yelped and bolted past Peanut, vanishing down the block.

Peanut barked out a laugh. Carmen had always kept a strict household, no uninvited guests, not even four-legged ones.

She turned at the sound, expecting to see the Peanut mutt return. Instead, her eyes fell on Peanut.

His Pug body was distinctive, blue-fawn coat, white snout, one ear flopping, the other standing straight. It took only a moment before Carmen gasped, hand flying to her mouth.

"Dios mío... Peanut?" she whispered.

Peanut. The name of her missing dog. The very body Jamal now wore.

His throat tightened. He had vanished the same night Peanut did, his poor wife had lost them both.

Carmen's eyes brimmed with tears as she knelt, arms open. "Peanut... ven aquí, boy. Come here."

Peanut hesitated, torn between caution and longing. But this was Carmen, the love of his life. He couldn't deny her. He trotted forward, and she scooped him up, cradling him against her chest. She smelled of rosemary, laundry detergent, and the familiar perfume she had worn since 1985.

Peanut pressed his head against her heartbeat. He wanted to speak a thousand words, I'm here, I'm okay, I'm sorry, but all he could do was lick the tear from her cheek.

She laughed through her sobs. "Oh, Peanut, you gave me such a fright. Where have you been? I looked everywhere."

She stroked him, her smile softening years of worry. Then she carried him upstairs despite his gentle squirming. "Shh, it's okay. I'll get you some food, pronto."

Max's eyes followed from the street. Alarmed, he crept forward as if to intervene, but Peanut caught his gaze and gave the faintest shake of his head.

It's okay, his eyes seemed to say. Just give me this moment.

Max melted back into the Cleos, standing guard.

Carmen brought Peanut inside. The apartment looked unchanged, cozy clutter, familiar warmth, the scent of marinara sauce thick in the air. A TV murmured in the living room, a headline about missing persons flashing by before Peanut could catch more.

She set him down in the kitchen, fussing as she opened the fridge. Papers lay scattered on the table, flyers with Peanut's human face, crumpled and smoothed again in weary hands. His heart ached.

Carmen placed chicken on a dish before him. "Eat, eat," she urged, stroking his back.

He obeyed, savoring the familiar seasoning. When he looked up, she was smiling for the first time in what felt like ages.

"I prayed for a miracle," she whispered, voice trembling. "And here you are. Maybe... maybe he'll come home too, huh, chico?"

She meant her husband. Him.

Peanut padded over, resting his tiny paws on her knee. He barked softly, pouring all his love into the sound. If words could have formed, they would have said: *I am home, my love.*

Just not in the way either of us wished. But I will stay with you, however I can.

Carmen stroked his fur, grief washing over her. For one fleeting moment, Peanut let himself imagine this could last, that he could remain by her side as her loyal little dog, even if not as her husband. The thought tugged painfully at his heart.

Down below on the street, a car horn blared, and the familiar sounds of the neighborhood drifted through the open window. Life outside was moving steadily forward, indifferent to the struggles inside this small apartment. But Peanut had a mission, and with it, a responsibility to his pack. They depended on him just as much as he depended on them. In only a short time, they had become his family, and he couldn't turn his back on them now.

Nor could he bring himself to subject Carmen to another vanishing act. Not after the joy of their brief reunion, not after seeing her eyes light up with love and hope.

He forced himself to finish a few more bites of chicken while Carmen moved to fetch a small dog blanket. As she turned away, he knew it was the moment. The longer he stayed, the harder it would be to leave. He couldn't bear the thought of her returning only to find Peanut gone.

Summoning every ounce of willpower, so much that it nearly shattered his heart, Peanut sprang onto a chair and then leapt to the windowsill that opened onto the fire escape. The scrabble of claws against wood made Carmen whirl around in alarm.

"Peanut? What are you?" she began.

But before she could finish, Peanut gave her one last, soulful look. Then, with a deep breath, he hurled himself out through the open window.

The fire escape rattled beneath his paws, but he landed safely. Without hesitation, he bolted down the metal stairs. Behind him came Carmen's cry, raw and desperate:

"No! Come back!"

Her voice tore at him, nearly breaking his resolve. Every instinct screamed to turn around, to comfort her, to stay. Yet his little legs carried him onward, out through the alley, onto the street, and into the safety of Cleos where Max, Daisy, and the others were waiting in a tight, anxious cluster.

"Let's go," Peanut said hoarsely, not daring to look back. He couldn't.

They moved quickly, slipping down the block and around a corner. From above, Carmen's voice still carried: "Peanut! Peanut!" It grew fainter as the city swallowed the distance between them. Each cry pierced him like a dagger, leaving scars of guilt he knew would never fade.

At last, they stopped in a secluded driveway to catch their breath. Peanut sat trembling, his chest heaving. Max, ever gentle, nudged him with her nose in comfort.

"She thought I was... my dog," he murmured, voice breaking. "I couldn't stay."

No one rebuked him. No one questioned his choice. They all understood.

Picasso laid a broad, comforting paw across Peanut's back. "You gave her hope," he said softly. "Even if just for a moment."

Peanut closed his eyes, steadying himself as emotion caught in his throat. "Yeah," he managed. His voice was thick. "I... I did."

After a long pause, he forced himself upright, squaring his small shoulders with determination. "Alright," he said, clearing his throat, "we've got one more here, right? Luna?"

The Tabby, who had watched Peanut's ordeal with wise, sympathetic eyes, stepped forward. "Yes," she said. "I'm not far. Just a few blocks over, by the library."

Without another word, they resumed their march through the Bronx twilight.

Bronx, Early Evening – Luna's Apartment

Night had begun to fall by the time they reached Luna's Street. A streetlamp flickered to life overhead, spilling pale light across the cracked sidewalk. One by one, the apartment windows lit up as families settled into their evening routines.

Luna's building was a modest three-story walk-up perched above a bakery. The shop below, *Sullivan's Sweets*, had long since closed for the day, but the air was still heavy with the sweet trace of sugar and fresh bread. The scent made Titan's stomach growl audibly, earning a faint, rueful smile from the others.

"That one," Luna said softly, pointing to a second-floor window where lace curtains were drawn tight. Unlike its neighbors, the apartment was dark.

"I haven't been home much since... since my Harold passed," Luna admitted, her voice low. "I've been spending nights with my daughter sometimes, or staying late at the library when I volunteer. No one will be in there now."

Her daughter, who lived upstate, had begged her countless times to move in permanently. But Luna had resisted, clinging to her independence and to this little Bronx apartment filled with memories. Deep down, though, she knew that fate had already made the decision for her.

The bakery's security gate was locked tight, blocking the front entrance. Without hesitation, Luna led them down a narrow alley to the side of the building. In true fine fashion, she leapt atop a closed dumpster with grace that belayed her years. Her sharp eyes scanned the fire escape ladder above, too high for the dogs, but not for her.

With an elegant bound, she launched onto a drainpipe, then scrambled effortlessly onto the iron stairs. Even in old age, she moved with agility that surprised the others.

"Show-off," Cleo muttered with a teasing grin, earning himself a playful swat on the head from Tao. Under different circumstances, she would have rushed, the climb herself.

"I'll only be a few minutes," Luna called down softly. "Just… cover me."

"Take your time," Max said firmly, gesturing for the others to form a loose perimeter. They stationed themselves around the alley, watchful for curious passersby.

Luna reached her window. It was locked, but Harold had once rigged a trick latch. With a practiced tug at the frame, the window clicked open. She slipped silently inside.

The apartment was cold and dim. Furniture loomed like quiet sentinels, familiar even in the half-light. The floral couch she and Harold had bought decades ago. The Afghan draped across its back one she had knitted when their first grandchild was born. Bookshelves crammed with romance novels and history texts alike. A cross-stitch and reading *Home Sweet Home*, now more ironic than comforting.

Her tail flicked with emotion as she padded softly through the silence. Dust stirred beneath her paws. How empty it felt without Harold's laughter, without the kettle whistling on the stove.

She paused at the cabinet where her photo albums were stored. With delicate precision, she nudged one open with her nose. Pages turned, revealing snapshots of a full life: her cradling her infant daughter; Harold in uniform; herself in a librarian's cardigan surrounded by children at story hour; countless holiday gatherings filled with joy; and, most recently, a picture of her at a charity bake, Maria smiling proudly beside a towering cake. Even after Harold's passing, she had filled her days with service and community, trying to soften the sharp edges of grief.

"I did all right, my love," she whispered to the empty room. "I wasn't done yet."

With care, she closed the album and padded toward the bedroom. On the dresser rested a jewelry box. She pushed it open to reveal what she had come for: a single locket on a broken chain. Inside was a miniature photo of her and Harold on their wedding day. She had worn it faithfully until the chain had snapped. She had meant to repair it, but never did.

She picked it up gently in her mouth. It tasted of metal and memory.

Before leaving, she paused to take in one last look. This little place had been her refuge and her joy. But even if she had remained human, she knew she would have had to leave soon, whether to her daughter's home or to an assisted living flat. Change was already inevitable.

She caught her reflection in the dresser mirror: a calico cat with green eyes, a twinkle of gold chain dangling from her jaw. "Not what you imagined for me, eh, Harold?" she murmured with a wry chuckle. "Me neither."

Still, she recognized herself in that gaze. A survivor. Adaptable. Steady.

"Alright then," she whispered. "Time to go."

She slipped back out the window and closed it as best she could. With careful steps, she descended the fire escape, hopped back to the dumpster, and landed softly on the ground.

When she rejoined the pack, Tao immediately noticed the locket. "What's that?" she asked, though her voice carried knowing warmth.

"Something to remember my husband by," Luna said, setting it at her paws. "And my life here."

Titan eyed the delicate piece. "Good idea," he said with a nod. More than one of them looked wistful, silently wishing they had retrieved their own keepsakes.

Max offered a small smile. "We carry plenty of memories without objects... but I'm glad you got that, Luna."

With Max's help, the chain was looped twice around Luna's neck and tied securely. The locket now rested snug against her calico fur.

"There," Max said proudly. "Wear it. Don't just carry it."

Luna purred softly in gratitude as the others offered approving looks.

It was done. All their farewells, save one, were complete.

Night had fully fallen now, bringing with it a biting wind that rattled trash in the gutters and stung through their fur. Seeking shelter, the pack huddled together in the recessed doorway of a closed laundromat. Ten pairs of eyes met in the darkness.

Exhaustion was written in every line of their bodies. They had walked miles, both in distance and in memory. Yet in the shared silence, there was also a sense of peace. Together, they had faced their pasts, said their goodbyes, and survived.

Daisy, who had been quiet since their departure, finally spoke. "I don't know about all of you," she said slowly, "but I feel... lighter."

Tao gave a small nod, her eyes still red from earlier tears. "Me too. It hurts, but... I think I can move forward now."

Titan managed a faint smile. "I realized I haven't really been living for a long time. Not until now. Funny it took becoming a dog to finally wake me up."

"That *is* funny," Cleo said with a short laugh. "I thought being a doctor was rough. Try being a cat doctor on the streets. But I also think I... grew up a little today." He straightened his back with pride. "Never thought I'd say it, but I actually appreciate all the stuff my family did for me. All the things I had."

Titan sat tall, the neon glow outlining his Doberman frame. "I built a life that looked perfect on the outside but left me empty. Now, stripped of all that, no money, no title, no penthouse, I feel freer than I ever did."

Picasso, sprawled out on the cold concrete, raised a dramatic paw. "Hear, hear. No rent, no critics, no waiting tables to pay for auditions. Just all of you, the open road ahead, and an endless stage called life."

He winked, but there was real sincerity beneath the jest.

Max was curled up against Daisy for warmth, her golden tail wagging lazily against the floor.

"I won't miss my physics exams, that's for sure," she joked, her voice carrying a note of forced cheer. Then, more softly, she admitted, "I think… I think I was always anxious as a human. Always worrying about my future, about making everyone happy. Now I'm oddly… calm. Like I'm just living in the moment. Dogs are good at that. It's teaching me something."

Luna's voice entered, low and steady, carrying the weight of years:

"When you reach my age, well, my old age, you realize life is nothing but change. You can either spend it fearing what's next, or you can adapt and find the beauty in what's new. I choose the beauty. Even in this." She gestured with a paw at herself, then at the others, a half-smile curling her muzzle.

Max listened, his chest swelling with something that was equal parts pride and affection. He had been a man of duty and service his whole life, always the one who put others first. And here he was still, guiding, protecting, keeping watch. Yet something had shifted inside him. As silence stretched before he spoke, the truth settled on him: for the first time since his army days, maybe even before, back in his police academy years, he felt like he truly belonged to a brotherhood again. A brotherhood, and a sisterhood. A Wolf Pack.

"I'm proud of you all," he said simply. "This was maybe the hardest thing we've done, and we got through it. Together."

A ripple of sound moved through them, soft growls, murmurs, and whines of agreement, as they pressed closer. Ten creatures huddled together in a doorway, drawing warmth and comfort from one another. They were no longer just strays or anomalies. They were a family.

After a quiet moment, Daisy broke the silence. "There's just me and Max left, right?" she asked. Her tone was calm, but the quiver beneath betrayed the anticipation.

Max nodded. "Brooklyn for you, Daisy. Staten Island for Max."

Daisy inhaled deeply, steadying herself. "Then we better get to it. The night's not getting any younger, and we have a train to catch after." She tried to smile, though her brow furrowed with worry for her children.

"Whenever you're ready," Max said softly.

Daisy nodded, though hesitation flickered in her eyes. Max leaned in with a reassuring nudge.

"We're all with you," the fire fighter-turned-dog promised.

Daisy's gaze softened as she looked around at the pack. Gratitude warmed her face. "I know. Thank you."

With renewed determination, they slipped out of the doorway and set off into the night once more, bound for Brooklyn, and the final chapters of their New York story.

Brooklyn, Night – Daisy's Family

The journey into Brooklyn was swift, shielded by the cover of darkness. At a subway entrance, they caught a rare moment of luck: when a pair of late-night commuters swiped through and pushed the gate, Max whistled, and the entire pack darted in behind them like ghosts.

An almost empty F-line train carried them across the East River, a rattling metal chariot with graffiti-scratched walls and buzzing fluorescent lights. Ten animals sat close together on the plastic seats, mostly unnoticed except by a drowsy passenger who blinked twice and decided he was dreaming.

They disembarked in Brooklyn and wound through streets Daisy knew well. Her pace slowed as they drew nearer to her neighborhood, a middle-class enclave of neat row houses with narrow yards, not far from Prospect Park. Here Kevin had lived his life: even played fetch with the golden retriever whose body she now inhabited.

Turning a corner, Daisy halted beneath a sprawling oak tree. "That's my house," Daisy whispered.

It was a modest brick duplex with a tiny patch of lawn. In the upstairs window, a faint glow leaked from a night-light with a lampshade of clouds and stars, the one in her children's bedroom. Downstairs, the larger living room window still glowed, light spilling against the curtains.

From their hiding place across the street, they saw silhouettes: a woman pacing, his wife, Alanis, and two smaller figures curled together on the couch. The flicker of a TV painted the walls with bursts of color.

Daisy stepped forward, tail low and wagging timidly. She needed to be closer.

Picasso and Max flanked her as far as the fence, then stopped, standing watch. Daisy nosed open the gate, it had never been locked; the neighborhood was that kind of place, and crept into the yard.

The smells of home rushed over her like a crashing wave: detergent, the lavender bush by the steps, the faint sweetness of crayons and cookies. Her eyes stung, but she forced back tears.

She rose onto her front paws to peer through the living room window. Alanis was pacing with a phone pressed to her ear, her voice taut with strain. On the couch, six-year-old Lucas and nine-year-old Sofia huddled under a blanket, the TV flickering before them. Neither seemed to care about the movie; Sofia's eyes were red-rimmed from crying, and Lucas kept glancing toward the hallway, as though expecting their father to appear at any moment.

Alanis ran a hand through his hair, still gripping the phone. "...I know, Mom. I'm trying to hold it together for the kids. No, no news yet. The police say they have a lead, but who knows. I just," Her voice cracked. "I just want him back."

The sound of her breaking nearly undid Daisy. She pressed her forehead to the glass, wishing with every fiber of her being that she could speak, that she could tell her she was right here. Her golden retriever eyes looked in helplessly.

Lucas noticed first. His gaze shifted from the screen to the window, locking on Daisy's face. His eyes widened. "Doggy!" he shouted, pointing.

Sofia turned, startled, and Alan froze mid-step before following their gaze.

Daisy ducked down instantly, heart hammering. Too late. They had seen her silhouette.

Through the glass, Sofia's muffled voice carried. "It looked like Goldie!"

Goldie. The retriever's name. The body Daisy now wore. Their family dog for three years.

Alanis moved toward the window, cautious. Daisy pressed herself flat to the ground beneath the sill, praying the reflection and shadows would conceal her.

Moments later, the front door opened with a creak. Alanis stepped onto the stoop, scanning the yard. Daisy crouched low, out of sight, but she could smell him, her perfume mixed with the sharp tang of stress in her sweat.

"Diasy?" Alanis called softly. "Here, girl!"

Daisy nearly whimpered in answer. Of course, she thought the family dog had returned. How could she imagine otherwise?

She hesitated. If she revealed herself, he might take her inside. She could be near them again, even if only as the family pet. The thought was intoxicating. But reality struck hard: she couldn't explain the truth, couldn't protect them if danger came. Eventually, she'd vanish again, leaving them doubly wounded. No, she couldn't do that.

Summoning strength, Daisy slinked along the side of the house, slipping behind a shrub. Alanis came down the steps, eyes searching. Lucas and Sofia stood in the doorway in their pajamas, peering out with hopeful faces.

"Goldie! Come here, girl!" Alanis coaxed again, his voice breaking with both hope and dread.

Daisy held her breath, refusing to move.

At last, Alanis sighed, shoulders slumping. "I'm not sure, kids. Maybe it was just a stray. Goldie's... Goldie's gone, honey." The last word dropped heavy.

Sofia sniffled. "Gone like Daddy?"

Daisy's chest tightened so fiercely it hurt.

Alanis quickly ushered them back inside. "No, sweetie. Daddy isn't gone. We just... haven't found him yet. And Goldie... maybe Goldie's with Daddy. Maybe they're together, and they'll both come back."

She was reaching for any comfort she could give.

Lucas's voice was small. "You really think so?"

Alanis crouched, pulling them into his arms right on the doorstep. "I hope so. We have to hope."

Daisy crept closer around the side of the house for one last glimpse. His family stood there in the doorway light, Alanis holding their children close. He ached to throw himself into that embrace, to be their Father and Daddy again.

Instead, she offered the only gift she could. From her throat came a soft, wavering sound, almost a whine, but shaped into something more. She hummed the lullaby she had sung to her children every night.

The tune floated toward the porch: a fragile thread of memory carried on a dog's voice.

Lucas's eyes widened. "Mommy... did you hear that? It sounds like... music."

Alanis froze, frowning, searching the night. Daisy fell silent. She hadn't meant for them to hear, only to feel.

For the briefest of moments, the connection bridged the impossible gap: father and children, hearts straining toward each other across the divide.

Sofia leaned into her mother, her voice weary. "I miss him."

Alanis kissed the tops of their heads. "Me too. Every second."

She gathered them inside and shut the door. The porch light clicked off, and the yard fell into darkness once more.

Daisy lingered in the yard a while longer, seated beneath the window. Through the glass she could see Alanis shepherding the children toward their bedroom, though she suspected she would let them fall asleep on the couch again, another "campout" night by her side. The sight tightened her chest with equal parts sorrow and gratitude.

She drew a slow, deliberate breath and committed the scene to memory: his brave wife, her beautiful children, all safe for the night in a warm home. Whatever storms the future carried toward them, she would carry that image like a talisman against despair.

"I love you," he whispered, forming the words silently with his lips, for sound had betrayed him once already. "Be strong. I'll be with you… somehow."

When at last she crept back to the street, Picasso draped a massive paw across her shoulders, steadying her as they walked away from the house. Daisy's cheeks were streaked with tears, but she held her chin high.

"They'll be alright," she murmured, her voice more a reassurance to herself than a statement of fact. "Alanis is a good mother. She'll take care of them."

"And you'll take care of you," Titan said gently. "So that one day, who knows…"

Daisy gave a small nod. Hope. She had to cling to that slender thread.

Now, only one farewell remained: Max's. And it required crossing the water.

Midnight Ride – The Staten Island Ferry

At Manhattan's southern tip, the city glowed like a jeweled crown against the black horizon. The pack gathered at the edge of Battery Park, gazing across the harbor where the Staten Island Ferry sat docked. Its unmistakable orange hull gleamed beneath the floodlights as a handful of late-night passengers trickled aboard.

"Boat time," Peanut muttered, his ear twitching nervously. Water, in his view, was no friend of Pugs.

Tao leapt nimbly onto Max's broad back, her balance effortless. "I'll scout," she volunteered, tail flicking with confidence. A lone cat slipping aboard was less suspicious than an entire pack of canines and cats.

Max crouched near the railing, and Tao sprang from his shoulders with amazing speed, landing soundlessly on the ferry's ramp. She wove among the night's travelers, weary shift workers, a pair of restless teenagers, an elderly woman tugging a cart, her nonchalance perfect camouflage. To human eyes, she was nothing more than a stray on her own midnight errand.

The crew paid her no mind, too absorbed in their chatter and rope work. When Tao's tail flicked in a subtle *all clear*, the others moved. One by one, they slipped across the gap.

Picasso and Titan melted into Cleo near a stack of life vests. Peanut and Titan wriggled under a bench. Max and Daisy pressed low behind a maintenance cart. Max and Cleo hugged the cover of a column.

To any casual glance, they were merely strays, not a clandestine band of wolves and companions with the weight of a city on their backs.

The ferry's engines roared, and the vessel churned away from Manhattan. The group exhaled in unison, tension bleeding into cautious relief.

They gathered along a quiet side deck where no passengers wandered. The skyline stretched behind them, ablaze with a million lights like stars scattered upon the earth.

Luna sat primly, her locket catching stray reflections. "Would you look at that," she murmured. "Beautiful."

"It really is," Max agreed, propping her forepaws on the railing as the wind teased her black-and-white coat. Beyond her, the Statue of Liberty loomed, torch lifted high.

"For all its hardships," Picasso said, voice low, "New York is a sight to behold. What a final image to carry with us."

Max stood apart, gaze locked on the retreating skyline. The city had shaped him, its streets, its cases, its people. Now, as the distance grew, he felt something unexpected: not relief, but a bittersweet release. Gratitude for what the city had given. Sorrow for what he was forced to leave undone.

He bowed his head, offering New York a silent farewell. His burdens, the regrets, the ghosts, seemed to scatter with the night wind over the dark waters.

A light touch pulled him back. Tao, sidled close, brushed her head against his shoulder in a gesture she'd never confess was affection. "We'll come back someday," she whispered, eyes tracing the skyline. "When it's safe."

Max nodded. Maybe. Whether or not their paws returned to its streets, New York would remain in them. They were, and always would be, the Wolves of New York.

The ferry ride was mercifully short. As the St. George terminal neared, the pack regrouped near the exit. Tao slipped out first, bypassing a distracted guard glued to his phone. The others followed in staggered bursts. A port worker spotted Picasso's diminutive outline in the shadows but dismissed it with a mutter of, "I need coffee."

They were in Staten Island now. Only one walk remained, the hardest of them all.

Staten Island, Late Night – Max's Parents

Staten Island slept differently from Manhattan. The streets were tree-lined, and hushed, single-family homes tucked into neat rows. It felt more suburban dream than city grit. The pack moved carefully, their paws soundless on the quiet pavement.

Max led with certainty, her nose catching faint traces of memory. There, the corner candy store where his allowance disappeared in sweet bursts; the yard where the neighbor's beagle had once barked nightly like clockwork. He almost expected him still. But the night was still.

His home appeared at the cul-de-sac's end: a modest Cape Cod with a tended lawn and an aging swing set swaying faintly in the breeze. The lights still burned. Nearly 1 AM., but Max knew his parents hadn't slept since she vanished.

Through the curtains she glimpsed his father, hunched on the couch with papers strewn, maps, reports, desperate notes. Her mother, upright, pacing with a phone pressed to her ear.

"...I don't care if it's late, Detective! My son has been missing for five days!" His mother's furious voice cracked through the night air.

Max winced. His mother's rage was familiar, but this time sharpened by terror.

Inside, Mrs. Alvaraz slammed the phone down, voice breaking. "How can a man and his dog just vanish into thin air?"

Frank pulled her close, weary but gentle. "We have to trust he's okay. Victor is very smart. And Max's with him..."

Max swallowed hard. They assumed her German Sheppard was at his side. In a sense, they weren't wrong.

His mother whispered, "I'd give up anything, if he'd just come home safe."

Max's throat tightened. Flaws and all, his parents' love was fierce, desperate, unconditional.

A playful impulse sparked. On the porch, his old toy basket sat forgotten. One tennis ball had rolled inside.

Slipping through the half-open door, he crept into the vestibule. His paw nudged the ball gently across the hardwood. *Thump.*

Frank noticed first. "Did that ball just move?"

A soft claw scrape followed. Mrs. Alvaraz froze. "Max?"

Max eased just enough of her white-tipped tail into view before retreating into the night.

His mother's breath caught. She yanked the door open.

And there, at the bottom of the steps, slipping into darkness, was a German Shepard.

"Max!" Frank cried, astonished.

The Shepard paused in the street, glanced back for a fleeting moment, and gave a single bark, neither sad nor fearful, but almost cheerful, as though to say, *"I'm okay!"*

Under the amber glow of the streetlights, the Alvaraz's could clearly make out their dog's familiar form. Max's tail wagged faintly before he slipped around the corner of a hedge and out of sight.

They did not give chase; the shock of the moment and the lateness of the hour held them rooted in place.

"He was here... did you see that?" Linda whispered, clutching her husband's arm tightly. Her voice trembled, but not from fear. "If Max's here... maybe, maybe Victor really is out there somewhere, alive." For the first time in days, genuine hope crept into her words.

Frank drew her close, his arm steady around her shoulders, his eyes lingering on the darkness where Max had vanished. A bemused smile softened his face. "Our boy's a survivor, Linda. I think, yes, I think he might just find his way back to us."

Beyond the hedge, Max regrouped with her friends, who had witnessed the emotional exchange from a careful distance. He was panting, his chest rising and falling with the adrenaline rush, yet his expression brimmed with satisfaction.

"You risky rascal," Peanut teased, a chuckle rumbling out as he wagged his stubby tail. "Almost gave your folks a heart attack, huh?"

Max shook her head. "They thought I was just the dog," she explained. "And… it gave them hope. That's what I wanted."

Daisy pressed against his side affectionately. "Clever move. Now they'll really believe you're out there with Victor, watching out for each other."

"Which isn't far from the truth," Max added warmly, his eyes glowing with pride. "You're out here, and you're not alone."

Max exhaled deeply, as if a weight had lifted from her chest. "Yeah. I have you guys."

And with that, the circle felt complete: almost ten farewells, ten hearts made heavier yet lighter all at once, ten companions bound tighter than ever before.

Now, all that remained was to leave.

The Rail Yard Escape

Staten Island held a modest freight yard not far from the ferry terminal, where shipments were transferred onto trains bound for New Jersey and beyond. Max guided the pack there, relying on both old instincts for navigation and scraps of intelligence he'd picked up in Manhattan about how goods slipped out of the city.

It was well past midnight when they arrived. The yard sprawled before them in muted light, illuminated only by a handful of floodlamps. Long rows of freight cars stretched into the darkness, some idling, some coupled to locomotives that hummed with a low mechanical growl. The still night air carried the metallic squeal of shifting wheels and the distant clank of cars being shunted into place.

A chain-link fence ringed the perimeter. The main gate stood locked, with a dimly lit booth beside it, but further down the fence sagged just enough to leave a narrow gap at the base. For humans, it was nothing. For determined dogs and cats, it was a doorway.

Max pointed the gap out with a silent nod. One by one, they squeezed under. Titan, the largest, had the hardest time; he exhaled forcefully, his paws digging furrows in the dirt as the others tugged at his hind legs. With a muffled grunt and a final push, he popped through, tail nearly pinched in the process. He swallowed his yelp, his dignity mostly intact.

They were in.

Immediately, they dropped low behind a stack of pallets. Up ahead, a lone worker strode along a track, flashlight beam swaying as he checked couplings. Off to the right, another shape prowled the darkness near a parked boxcar, a German Shepherd, broad-shouldered and confident, the very security dog they had anticipated.

Max signaled with a flick of his ears. Instinctively, the group split: dogs one way, cats another. Words were unnecessary now; they trusted one another's cues.

Tao and Cleo slipped right, Cleo wanted to appear in the dog's sight line, angling to pull the shepherd's attention. Meanwhile, Max, Daisy, Titan, and the rest crept left, toward a string of cars attached to a locomotive that hissed with building steam. If they could board unnoticed before it departed, freedom was within reach.

But first, the distractions.

The Sheppard spotted Cleo and the chase was on. Under cars and through gaps they bolted and eventually this had to end so Peanut and Picasso came to the rescue. Creating a second distraction in another part of the yard. The Sheppard could not decide. Finally, the seven dogs and three cats were all in view. The Sheppard spooked when the pack attacked and ran off in the other. It was a quick and battle and victory. The so-called guard dog ran away with it's tail between his legs, in the other direction never to be seen again. The pack had used numbers to make the difference, now they all had a story, that were like proverbial fish stories. The big one, that got away.

Peanut broke the silence with a hearty laugh, his sides shaking. "Did you see the look on that guy's face?" he wheezed.

Picasso snorted, puffing out his chest. "I gave him my best tongue-out performance. I do hope it haunts his dreams."

Cleo, still buzzing with adrenaline, chimed in. "That dog nearly got us. Tao, you were epic! Pow!" He mimed her swat with exaggerated flair, causing Tao to purr with pride and lift her chin a little higher.

"I'm just glad none of us got left behind," Tao said, brushing her tail against Max's side with quiet affection.

Max gave a soft, affirming woof. "Everyone accounted for. And great work, team. Couldn't have asked for a smoother escape… whistles aside." His tone carried both relief and pride, though his eyes still flicked toward the door with caution.

They peered out through a narrow gap in the boxcar door. The city lights were fading now, swallowed by distance, replaced by the dark outline of trees and the scattered shapes of industrial outskirts. The rumble of the train seemed louder here, as if urging them onward.

Luna gazed at the vanishing skyline, her paw reaching instinctively to the locket around her neck. "Goodbye, New York," she whispered, her voice trembling just slightly.

Daisy leaned into Max, the Dobermann pressing close to share her warmth. "Goodbye," Daisy echoed softly, though her heart ached with thoughts of her family still somewhere beyond those lights.

One by one, the others added their quiet farewells, some whispered, some silent, each carrying their own memories. They were leaving behind not just streets and buildings, but pieces of themselves: the lives they had known, the struggles that had shaped them, and the fragments of human love or cruelty they had once endured.

But as the train thundered onward, the weight of sorrow began to mingle with something else, an undercurrent of excitement, of fragile but undeniable hope.

Titan cleared his throat, breaking the silence. "So… Carolinas, huh? Any idea what we'll do when we get there?"

"Find a beach for Peanut," Max teased, nudging the bulldog with a grin.

"Open a bed and breakfast for stray animals," Tao mused with a dreamy flick of her tail.

"Start a street performance troupe?" Picasso offered grandly, puffing himself up like an actor on stage. The others chuckled at the image, laughter echoing lightly over the rattling of the train.

Max listened quietly, a smile tugging at the corners of his muzzle. These suggestions were half-jokes, thrown into the air like leaves on the wind, but beneath the humor lay a truth he felt deep in his bones: they would figure it out together. That was all that mattered.

He moved toward the narrow sliver of the door, pressing close enough to feel the wind sting his face. For a long moment, he looked out at the faint glow on the horizon where New York still shimmered far behind. Then he tilted his head back and let out a long, soulful howl, part farewell, part promise.

One by one, the others joined him. A chorus of howls, yowls, and barks rose above the clatter of the train, blending into a wild, untamed anthem. It was a song of release, of tribute, of determination. Ten voices united in a cry only they understood, mournful and joyful all at once.

"The Wolves of New York" were on the move.

As their howls faded, the night reclaimed its rhythm: the steady beat of iron wheels on tracks, carrying them deeper into the unknown.

In the darkness of the boxcar, they settled together in a furry heap for warmth and comfort. The air was cold, heavy with the scent of wood and metal, but their hearts were warm with each other's presence.

Tao curled against Max's side, her steady purring vibrating softly against him. Peanut got closer to Picasso's broad back, and Picasso did not complain, even shifting to give him more room. Luna tucked in beside Titan, who lay protectively near the door as if keeping watch. Max and Daisy pressed back-to-back, eyes half-closed but still watching the moonrise through the gap. Titan and Cleo sprawled belly-up, limbs askew, their goofy positions sparking a round of tired chuckles. Winston and Chai were off in the corner of the box car sound asleep already.

"Get some sleep, everyone," Max murmured, his voice low but full of affection as his eyes swept over the pack. The look in them was as deep as any member of his family. "We've got a long ride ahead... and an adventure waiting at the end of it."

One by one, eyes drifted shut, lulled by the rhythm of the rails. Tomorrow, worries would come, about food, about finding the Carolinas, about countless uncertainties they hadn't yet faced. But tonight, none of that mattered. They had each other, and that was enough.

The train roared on through the night, a steel serpent cutting its way south, ferrying ten brave souls away from one life and toward another. Inside the boxcar, the Wolves of New York slept soundly, their dreams rich with visions of open fields, southern breezes, and the unbreakable bond of a pack that had chosen one another against all odds.

Chapter 4

FLIGHT FROM THE CITY

Night fell like a heavy blanket over the freight train as it thundered southward, pulling away from the sprawl of New York City. Inside a rattling boxcar, ten figures huddled in the darkness, creatures who had once walked upright on two legs, but now padded uneasily on four. The air carried the cool bite of evening, thick with the scents of old wood, rust, and engine grease that seeped from every crack of the steel walls.

Max pressed his face close to a narrow gap in the sliding door. Through it, the city lights glittered like broken glass, twinkling as they shrank into the distance, bright memories dissolving into the dark. Beside him, Winston, had woken up , lifted her muzzle to the crack as well. His ears were perked forward, alert and restless.

Behind them, perched high atop a stack of wooden pallets, Peanut the Pug moved his short tail lazily, though his sharp eyes missed nothing. Below him, Tao, a sleek Siamese with a coat that caught what little light there was, licked her paw with deliberate indifference, grooming as if the rocking of the boxcar posed no inconvenience at all.

"It's really gone, isn't it?" Winston murmured, his voice low, almost carried away by the hum of wheels on track. Her brown eyes lingered on the final glimmer of Manhattan fading along the horizon. That had been home once, when they had been human.

Max gave a soft, canine whine, his tail stilling. "Yeah... bye-bye, Big Apple." He tried for cheer, but the words cracked with a tremor he couldn't mask. "Never thought I'd literally leave on a midnight train, as a dog, no less."

Up on the pallets, Peanut let out a dry, raspy chuckle. "At least you got the window seat," he said, stretching his back in an elegant arch. "I'm up here in the cheap seats." He gave the stack of pallets beneath him a dismissive nod. Dust motes, disturbed by his stretch, drifted lazily in the pale moonlight that trickled through the slats.

Tao paused mid-lick, her icy blue eyes catching the glow. "First class, this is not," she purred with her usual refined sarcasm. "No meal service, drafty cabin, and my seat cushion appears to be... nonexistent." With a dainty hop, she leapt down from the floorboards and landed with the poise only a cat could manage. "One star. Would not recommend."

That drew a small laugh from Winston, brittle though it was. Humor, even faint, dulled the edge of fear. Hours earlier they had been sprinting through alleyways and slipping past rail-yard shadows, desperate to flee the city that had turned on them. Now they were stowaways in a steel box, fugitives with fur, running into a future none of them could yet imagine.

Max shook out his coat, sending a light spray of straw scattering across the floorboards. The remnants of whatever cargo had last filled the car crackled faintly under his paws. "Could be worse," he said with a grin, tail giving a hopeful wag. "At least we've got a roof tonight, even if it's one that moves at sixty miles an hour."

Peanut sprang lightly down from his perch, landing without a sound. "True," he admitted. "Better than that alley behind the fish market, with rats thinking I was their new roommate." He shivered, his Tao twitching at the memory.

Tao's ears flicked, amusement rippling across her face. "I don't know... the fish market wasn't so bad." Her voice dipped into mock innocence. "Midnight sushi, anyone?"

Max shot her a look, his tone mock-stern. "You would say that, cat."

Tao stuck out her pink tongue in reply. "Jealousy doesn't suit you, dog. Just admit it, you're bitter that I can slip through cracks you can only sniff at."

"Oh, here we go again..." Winston groaned, though her tail thumped once against the floor. She circled twice, and settled, paws tucked neatly beneath her chest. "Cat versus dog, round twenty. Can't we save it for daylight?"

Max flopped down beside her with a huff, the vibrations of the train carrying up through his ribcage. "She started it," he muttered.

"Did not," Tao fired back immediately, hopping onto an overturned crate with queenly authority. From there she looked down at the dogs, tail curled in smug grace. "And besides, you're the one drooling about pizza earlier. Dumpster pizza, no less."

At the word pizza, Winston's ears perked, betraying her hunger. "Don't remind me," she groaned. Her stomach growled loud enough for all of them to hear. "I smelled that pepperoni place when we were waiting near the tracks... If only we'd had time to grab a slice."

Max's nose twitched at the memory. His sharpened canine senses had catalogued every scent, grease, bread, old French fries, the faint tang of hot dogs drifting from a cart on the street beyond the rail yard fence. It was overwhelming, maddening, and mouthwatering all at once.

"You know what I miss?" Peanut mused, tail wrapping neatly around his paws as he sat. "Fish and chips. Real fish, golden and crispy, with lemon on the side. Not... fish guts out of a trash bin."

"I miss coffee," Winston said wistfully. "A big latte with hazelnut syrup. Just the smell of it... Can't exactly get that out here."

Max tilted his head. "Would coffee even taste good now? Dogs aren't supposed to touch caffeine."

"I know," Winston admitted with a small laugh, nudging him playfully. "But it's not about the taste. It's about the memory, holding that warm mug between my hands. It's strange, remembering what hands felt like."

Tao gave an exaggerated sniff. "Forget coffee. I'd kill for chocolate right now. A chocolate bar. The irony of craving what could literally kill me now is not lost on me." She flexed her claws against the crate lid, a cat's instinct overlaying the ghost of a human habit.

Peanut licked his lips theatrically. "At this point, I'd even take those sad little crackers they give you on airplanes."

Tao rolled her eyes. "Airplane crackers, the pinnacle of fine dining." She hopped down again, slinking to the crack in the door where the night air whistled through. In the silver glow, her sleek coat shimmered like quicksilver. "Well, no crackers here. No pizza, no coffee, no chocolate. I suppose fasting it is."

Max padded over to join her, careful not to push the door too wide. Even the smallest clang echoed into the night like a warning. "We'll find something," he said with stubborn hope. "These trains haul goods. Somewhere there's got to be food, grain, produce, canned beans, anything."

At the word grain, Peanut's ears twitched. "Actually... I saw a line of covered hoppers near the back when we climbed aboard. If this train's headed south, it could be carrying grain shipments. There might be spillage on the platforms."

"Grain isn't exactly appetizing," Winston admitted, lifting her head.

"Better than starving," Max said, tail wagging faintly. He nudged at the heavy door with his shoulder, muscles straining. It scraped forward barely an inch before catching, secured from the outside.

"Move," Tao insisted. She slipped into the narrow opening, bracing her paws against the frame. With surprising force, she wrenched and clawed. The metal screeched grudgingly, sliding just wide enough to breathe cool night air into the car.

The wind rushed around them, bringing with it the scents of fields, pine, and wild grass. The city's grit and smoke were far behind now. The air smelled like freedom.

Max pressed his shoulder into the door again, shoving until it grudgingly widened enough for a slim body to slip through. Panting, he glanced at the others with a toothy grin. "Ladies and gentlemen, mind your step."

Winston rose quickly, peering out at the blur of moonlit trees and the occasional glimmer of rooftops rushing past. The train had slowed on a gentle curve, but it was still fast enough to make her hesitate. "We have to be careful," she warned. "One wrong step and…" She trailed off. No one needed the reminder of what falling would mean.

Luna, pragmatic as always, padded forward with his tail swishing in balance. "I can make it across to the next car," he said, eyes locked on the narrow platform and metal coupling ahead. The car before them was a tanker, its cylindrical body gliding through the night.

"You cat's and your balance," Max muttered, half admiring, half worried. "Just, don't get cocky."

Luna smirked over her shoulder. "Please. I was walking rooftops while you were still figuring out how to lift a leg to pee."

That drew a chuckle from Tao and even a soft laugh from Winston. Max groaned, shaking his head. "One day I'll get used to you trash-talking me, Luna. But tonight is not that day."

Luna gave an exaggerated high five with one paw, then timed his movements with the rhythm of the swaying cars. In a blur of Tabby power, she leapt across the yawning gap. For an instant, her body hung against the night sky, fur lit silver by moonlight, before she landed silently on the narrow steel platform at the end of the tanker car. It was so smooth, so precise, it almost looked choreographed.

"Show-off," Tao murmured affectionately. Her Tao twitched as if daring herself to match him. With a sleek coil of muscle, she sprang forward, a pale blur against the dark, and landed neatly beside Luna. The two cats now stood tall and sure on the platform, tails flicking high in the air.

Max's heart lurched into his throat. His mind knew they were capable, felines with balance wired into their bones, but his instincts screamed otherwise. They weren't just cats. They were his friends, once human like him. Losing them wasn't an option.

Winston sucked in a breath, then launched himself forward. For one terrifying heartbeat he was suspended over nothing, the silver rails and gravel a dizzy blur beneath her. His front paws struck the platform edge, but her back legs flailed, searching for purchase. Luna lunged and caught his scruff, hauling up with all her might. Max then shoved from behind with his snout, practically lifting his hindquarters over the gap.

Together, they pulled her up. Winston collapsed onto the platform, panting hard. "Thanks," he managed between breaths, giving Luna a grateful nod and flashing Max a shaky smile from across the divide. "Guess my aim was a little off."

Now it was Titan's turn. Being heavier than Winston and bulkier than the cats, the risk was greatest for him. He stepped back inside the boxcar, paws clattering faintly on the wooden boards. His chest heaved as the train's rhythm clack-clacked in time with his pulse.

"All right, Titan, your turn!" Tao called, voice raised over the wind. She tried for lightheartedness, but concern edged her tone.

Titan exhaled sharply, then broke into a loping run. The gap loomed before him, and then he was airborne. For a fleeting second the rush of wind and the sensation of flying filled him with wild exhilaration. But gravity pulled quickly. He hit the platform with his forepaws, chest slamming against the metal rim. His hind legs slid, scrabbling desperately, paws screeching against steel.

Before he could fall back, Winston lunged forward and clamped her teeth around his foreleg, anchoring him. Tao leaned in to brace her weight behind Winston, while Luna grabbed Titan by the scruff with surprising ferocity. With a united heave, the three hauled him over the ledge.

Titan sprawled awkwardly on the narrow platform, sides heaving, heart hammering so hard it rattled in his chest. For a long beat, they all simply panted together, the night wind roaring around them.

Finally, Titan barked out a shaky laugh. "Well... that was fun. Let's not make a habit of it."

Winston butted her head against his shoulder, relief softening her features. "You scared the life out of me, you big oaf."

He licked her ear apologetically, tail thumping once. "Sorry. And thanks, all of you. Teamwork for the win."

Tao sat primly and began licking dirt from her coat. Her fur still stood slightly on end, though she tried to disguise it with casual grooming. "Dogs," she muttered. "Always leaping before they look."

Luna flicked her tail, ears twitching toward the wind. "We should keep moving. We're too exposed out here."

She was right. Out on the platform, the full force of the night rushed at them, chilling and relentless. The train had picked up speed again after the curve, and the tanker beneath their paws hummed with the weight of liquid cargo, oil or chemicals, judging by the sharp tang. Useless to them, but a necessary bridge.

A ladder clung to the tanker's side; its rungs narrow and cold. Tao and Luna scrambled up with feline ease, claws clinking faintly on metal. Winston followed with care, paws slipping once before catching again. Max went last, gripping each rung carefully, wrapping his toes for purchase until he hauled himself over the top. Titan stood guard.

One by one, they emerged onto the rounded roof. It was wide enough along the central ridge to walk safely, though the wind tugged at their fur. A nearly full moon hung bright above, painting the scene in silver. Ahead and behind, an endless line of freight cars stretched, curving like a vast steel serpent across the landscape.

"Wow," Winston breathed. Her eyes shone as she stood steady against the breeze. "I've never seen anything like this."

Max too paused, awestruck. To one side, pine forest unrolled like a black ocean, alive with the faint chorus of crickets and frogs. To the other, an open field shimmered faintly under moonlight. The train's relentless rhythm, clack-clack, clack-clack, was strangely soothing, like the heartbeat of the earth itself.

Tao closed her eyes, Tao blown back by the wind. "It feels like a dream," she murmured. "Riding a train at midnight... as a cat. If anyone told me this a month ago, I'd have laughed in their face."

Luna gave a dry chuckle. "A month ago, I was working overtime, no vacation in sight. Now here I am. King of the boxcars."

Max caught the pain behind his humor. "Do you miss it? Your old life?"

Luna didn't answer right away. She hopped nimbly over a gap to the next car, a covered hopper. The others followed in turn, paws clinking softly. Finally, she said, "Yes and no. I miss people, my sister, my friends. I miss hot showers. I miss wasting hours on video games. But I don't miss deadlines, or traffic, or bosses yelling in my ear."

"I miss my phone," Tao admitted with a self-conscious meow of laughter as she trotted gracefully across the hopper's roof. "Texting, scrolling dumb videos at night... all of it. But now..." She glanced around at the rolling countryside, the wide-open sky. "Now I feel like I'm actually here. Like every second counts. Especially when slipping off means being ground under a train wheel."

Max exchanged a glance with Winston. He nodded. "She's right. It's terrifying. But there's a kind of freedom in it too. No rent, no jobs, no alarms or calendars, just survival."

Winston's ears pinned back slightly as she stepped over a raised hatch on the hopper roof. "Maybe. But freedom doesn't feel so free when you don't know if you'll make it to tomorrow. Or if we'll ever be human again." Her voice trembled faintly.

Max brushed his shoulder against hers in reassurance. "We'll figure it out. At least we've got each other."

Her tense features softened into a smile. "Yeah. I'm glad we're in this together."

"Save the group hug," Luna called softly. "I think we've found something."

They had reached the center of the grain hopper. Several circular hatches dotted the roof, sealed tight with metal lids. Luna sniffed one and pawed at it. "Definitely grain. Smells like starch."

Tao padded to a vent along the edge, pressing her nose against the grate. Her tail twitched. "Corn, maybe wheat. Definitely food."

Max eyed the heavy hatch. "If only we could pry this open..."

"Not happening with bare paws," Winston said. "Even a human would need tools."

Luna prowled further. "Maybe there's a spill chute. Or a gap somewhere along the side."

Then Tao froze, ears flicking. "Wait... do you hear that?"

They all stilled. Beneath the rush of wind and wheels came a faint scratching, scuttling, something alive ahead.

Max lifted his muzzle, sniffing. A musky scent drifted toward him. Familiar, but wild.

Before he could place it, a silhouette rose on the next car forward, a boxcar taller than the hopper they stood on. The figure's ringed tail swayed in the moonlight. A pointed snout tilted toward them.

"Well, what have we here?" came a chittering voice.

Winston instinctively edged closer to Max. Tao arched her back, fur bristling faintly.

The shape stepped forward into clearer light: a raccoon, large, scruffy, with a ragged coat. A strip of cloth, an old bandana, hung knotted around his neck like a scarf. His black eyes gleamed, masklike face tilted in wary curiosity.

Luna was the first to speak, voice calm, diplomatic. "Just passing through," She knew raccoons could be fiercely territorial.

The raccoon adjusted the bandana with a paw, his voice gravelly but not overtly hostile. "You folks aren't from around here, are you?"

Max stepped forward slightly, careful to keep a respectful distance across the gap between the two cars. His voice carried a mixture of honesty and caution. "We're, uh... new to the rail," he admitted.

The raccoon sniffed the air, Tao twitching as though testing their scent. "Dogs and cats riding together," he mused, shaking his head with a low chitter. "Now I've seen everything. Must be a full moon or something." He scratched behind an ear in a leisurely fashion, as if the danger of balancing on a moving train didn't apply to him.

Tao eased just a fraction, sensing that this raccoon wasn't immediately aggressive, at least not yet. "We're just trying to get south," she offered, her tone even. "We don't want trouble."

"South, eh?" The raccoon tilted his head, studying them more keenly now. "Running away from something? Or running to something?"

Luna's tail flicked, sharp as a whip crack. "What's it to you?"

The raccoon raised both forepaws in mock surrender, his voice raspy but almost playful. "Easy there, kitty. Just making conversation." His eyes gleamed in the moonlight. "Name's Rusty. I've been riding these rails for years. Know 'em better than any human hobo does."

Max exchanged a glance with Winston. The name fit, the reddish tint in the raccoon's scruffy fur showed even beneath his torn bandana. He carried the aura of someone who had scraped through many nights like this and lived to tell the tales.

"Maybe you could help us, then," Max said, trying for diplomacy. "We're looking for food. Anything at all. You wouldn't happen to know if there's... I don't know, a refrigerated car with meat, or a grain car with open access on this train?"

Rusty settled back on his haunches, perfectly at ease despite the rocking beneath his paws. "This train's hauling plenty of goodies, sure. The trick is whether you can get at them. He scratched his chin thoughtfully. "Smelled produce a few cars up. Likely a refrigerated car, but those are sealed tighter than a banker's vault. Trust me, I tried once. Nearly froze my tail off and all I got for it was a nibble of half-thawed broccoli."

Winston's mouth watered embarrassingly at the mention of broccoli, of all things. Hunger twisted perspective; right now, even soggy vegetables sounded like a feast. "What about grain? We think this is a hopper, but it's sealed."

Rusty's nose twitched knowingly. "Corn or wheat in there, yeah. Not easy unless you've got wings."

As if summoned, a flurry of wings burst from the dark and shadowy end of the next boxcar. Two sparrows darted upward from the dark gap between cars, scattering into the night sky with startled cries.

Rusty chuckled. "See? Birds always know. Peck at the tiniest cracks and dine like kings while the rest of us scrape by."

Luna let out a disgruntled growl. "Great. Everyone's eating except us."

Rusty narrowed his eyes, as if turning over an idea. "Actually... there might be something." He rose smoothly to all fours and padded toward the far end of his boxcar. "Follow me. Careful on the crossing, the latch on that hopper's sharp."

Without hesitation, the raccoon swung himself down the ladder at the boxcar's side and disappeared from view, moving like he'd done it a thousand times.

Max hesitated only a heartbeat before leading the others across. One by one they hopped the short divide, landing on the flatter roof of Rusty's boxcar. Moments later, Rusty's striped head popped back up from below, nodding for them to descend.

The sight of two dogs and two cats clambering backward down a steel ladder would have looked comical to any onlooker. But the group managed, gripping with forepaws, hindquarters trembling with the strain of holding balance on a moving train.

Max landed on the narrow platform first. Rusty was already there, prying the heavy boxcar door open with practiced paws. It wasn't locked, and with Max's bulk adding leverage, the door creaked just enough for them to slip inside.

The interior smelled faintly of hay and something sweetly musty. Moonlight filtered through slats, revealing stacked crates at the far end and loose straw scattered across the floor. It felt abandoned, perhaps once used for produce or livestock feed.

Rusty wasted no time. He scurried toward a corner, muttering as he dug behind a tipped bucket. "Knew I stashed it somewhere..."

Tao and Luna vaulted lightly atop a crate, out of the straw, while Winston and Max remained on the floor.

"Ah, here we go!" Rusty tugged free a small cloth bundle tied with twine. With nimble paws, he loosened it to reveal a humble treasure: a half-eaten granola bar, a bruised apple, and a single wrapped slice of processed cheese.

Winston's tail thumped uncontrollably. "Is... is that cheddar?" she asked, nearly drooling.

Rusty winked, sliding the cheese toward them. "Good nose. Snagged it out of a picnic trash can in Newark. Was saving it, but you folks look like you need it more."

Max blinked at the generosity. "Thank you, Rusty. Are you sure? What about you?"

The raccoon popped some crumbs from the granola into his mouth, shrugging. "Eh, I'll find more. I always do. Got contacts all up and down the line. Cats in Philly, watchdogs in D.C., even a crow or two who owes me favors. You learn to trade."

They shared the meager banquet reverently. Max carefully peeled the cheese slice's wrapper with his teeth, portioning strips for everyone. Tao daintily nibbled the apple before passing it on, while Max and Winston crushed the rest with eager jaws. Luna crunched granola bits, savoring every bite.

For a few quiet minutes, hunger gave way to contentment. The rattling boxcar walls faded beneath the warmth of shared food and company.

Rusty chewed on an apple seed, watching them with a grin. "So, tell me, how'd a bunch of house pets end up hopping trains? You said you're not from around here..."

The four exchanged uneasy glances. Telling the truth, we used to be human, felt dangerous, even absurd. Still, Max decided on a half-truth. "We come from the city. Something... happened to us. We're on the run from people who wouldn't understand."

Rusty raised an eyebrow but didn't press. "Mysterious lot, aren't you?"

Luna stretched and hopped down. "What about you, Rusty? How long you been at this?"

Rusty brightened instantly, puffing his chest. "Oh, years. Learned the ropes as a pup. My ma taught me how to pop a boxcar latch before I even knew how to wash my dinner. By now, I know every major line." His grin widened. "This one here's headed straight south. Philly, Baltimore, Richmond, then the Carolinas."

Tao's ears perked. "The Carolinas? That's where we're heading!"

Rusty nodded, all-knowing. "Figured as much. Lot of critters migrate that way when winter comes. You're early, but maybe that's good. Less competition." His eyes sharpened. "Got kin down there?"

"Something like that," Winston said softly. In truth, they had no kin, only rumors of help further south.

Rusty, mercifully, let it lie. He bundled the cloth again and tucked it away. "Well, then, maybe you stick with me awhile. I'll guide you. But..." His voice dropped low, ears flicking toward the door. "You got to, be cautious. Humans aren't as blind as you think. Some are dangerous."

Max stiffened. "You mean conductors? Security?"

Rusty's tone hardened. "Railroad bulls. Guards, yard workers, even other riders. Some'll toss you out, some'll do worse. Not everyone's friendly on the rails."

Winston's tail curled tight with unease. "We'll be careful."

Tao glanced through the cracked door, eyes narrowing. "We saw a man at the yard when we hopped on. He almost caught us. We barely made it."

Rusty nodded. Beyond the gap, the train rolled past city lights, Philadelphia's outskirts. "We'll be hitting the yard soon. Best find a hiding place and keep still. Bulls don't take kindly to strays."

Luna flicked her tail with resolve. "We can handle that. Hide-and-seek's become our specialty."

But Max wasn't done. "Rusty... you mentioned symbols, codes. How do you stay in touch with your contacts?"

Rusty's eyes gleamed, clearly enjoying the chance to share secrets. "We got our own language. Scent marks. Scratches. Signs. Just like the old hoboes, only we've made it our own."

Rusty lifted a paw and pointed toward the inside wall of the boxcar. In the dim, shifting light, Max noticed scratches he hadn't seen before. They weren't random; they looked deliberate. One was a crude carving that resembled a cat's face, while another mark formed two interlocking circles.

"I didn't even see those before," Winston said, moving closer to sniff. Her ears quivered. "What do they mean?"

Rusty's grin spread wide. "That one's a cat symbol. When you see it in a yard, it usually means 'safe spot' or 'food source nearby.' The circles? That's a warning, 'beware of humans.' Two eyes watching."

Tao's ears pinned back. "Spooky. But smart."

Rusty shrugged as though it were obvious. "It pays to be organized. Humans think we're just scavengers, but we've got ourselves a little network. Rats in the city subways, birds on the power lines, we all pass messages. Word can travel fast if you know how to read it." He tapped his nose with satisfaction. "Still, nothing beats a sharp nose and good ears on the ground."

For the first time in a while, Max felt his tail flick with excitement. Despite the fear and the grief, they carried, there was something thrilling about being part of this hidden code, this underground society. "Well, Rusty," he said, smiling faintly, "count us as part of the network now."

The raccoon bared a mischievous grin. "Stick with me, and you'll be veterans by the time we hit the Carolinas."

Before Max could answer, the train horn blew, a long, piercing blast that rattled the walls. Everyone jumped. Rusty peeked out through a crack. "Yup, nearing a city. Time to hide. You lot should scoot back into the grain car if you can, or stay in this one but keep that door just cracked. I'll head to my usual spot."

"Where's that?" Peanut asked.

Rusty pointed upward. "This car's near empty, but up in the rafters there's a little nook, just big enough for me. You'd be better off in the grain car. Philly yard workers sometimes shine lights into empties like this."

Max understood instantly. One gleam of a flashlight on a pair of canine eyes could ruin everything. "Alright. Thanks for everything, Rusty. We'll see you after we're moving again?"

"You bet," Rusty replied, already climbing up the wooden slats toward the roof. "Keep on keeping on, friends."

Tao offered a polite "meow" in farewell as the four slipped back out.

The train was slowing now. They hurried across the coupling to the covered hopper car, reasoning that cargo made a better disguise than an empty box screaming "stowaway."

On top of the hopper, they scanned quickly for options. Inside? No, the hopper was sealed. Between cars? Too risky. Max's eyes landed on a rolled tarp strapped to the side, likely for covering loads. "What about behind that tarp?" he suggested.

Winston gave it a quick assessment. It was bulky enough to hide them if they stayed close. "Worth a try."

They scrambled onto the end platform and wedged themselves behind the tarp roll, pressing flat. It was tight, too tight. They ended up piled in a heap. Tao, squished beneath Max's foreleg, let out a muted hiss. "Sorry," he whispered.

The train groaned as it entered the Philadelphia yard. Through cracks in the tarp, fluorescent light spilled in. Voices echoed: workers shouting, couplers clanging. Diesel fumes and the sharp tang of hot metal filled the air.

A flashlight beam swept across their car. All four froze.

From their cramped hide, Max's nose caught a sharp mix of scents, Rusty somewhere above, faint but present. And something else: the musky, unmistakable smell of another dog. Not one of them. A patrol dog.

Before he could process, footsteps rang on the platform. A gruff voice muttered, "...swear I heard something..."

The beam of a flashlight swept overhead. Winston trembled against Max. Luna's claws dug nervously into the tarp fabric.

A figure stepped onto their car. Keys jingled. And then the soft, steady panting confirmed it: the man had a dog.

Max's stomach turned cold. If they were discovered now, what then? A fight? Capture?

The sniffing came next. The patrol dog had caught their scent. Max risked a glance at Tao. Her wide blue eyes shone with fear, but also fire. If it came to it, even the cats would fight.

The guard's voice cut sharply: "What is it, boy? Something in there?" The flashlight beam angled dangerously close, illuminating the gap where they hid.

And then, Luna acted. Quick, reckless, brilliant. She let out a piercing "Hisss!" that echoed like a feral banshee. Tao joined in with a yowl so wild and furious it rattled the siding.

The effect was instant. The German Shepherd barked furiously, lunging on the leash in bewilderment. The unholy shrieks had thrown it off balance.

"Damn cats and dogs," the guard muttered, irritation heavy in his voice. "Always fighting with each other."

He smacked the siding with his flashlight. "Git! Get out of here!"

Max, seizing the moment, added a guttural snarl, half dog, half raccoon growl, that reverberated like something dangerous. The racket drove the Shepherd into a frenzy, barking and whining, torn between aggression and unease.

The guard tugged his dog away with a curse. "Not worth it. Just some critters." His boots clanged down the steps, the beam of light fading as he moved to another car.

The group stayed rigid in their hiding place, hearts hammering. At last, Luna answered softly. "I always wanted to be an actor."

Winston licked his cheek in relief. "That was brilliant. You too, Tao. I think you burst my eardrum with that screech."

Tao smoothed her fur, still puffed with adrenaline. "Desperate times. Ever hear alley cats fight at two in the morning? I just channeled that."

Max let out the breath he'd been holding. "That was too close."

They remained hidden for what felt like forever, though it was only twenty minutes. Finally, the train lurched and began rolling again, slowly at first, then faster as it left the Philadelphia yard.

When the coast felt clear, they crept from behind the tarp. Rusty's striped face peered down from a boxcar roof. "Y'all okay? I heard the ruckus."

"We had to scare off a security guard," Max admitted, still shaky.

Rusty chuckled. "Wish I'd seen that. Told you, stick with me and you'll be pros." He scrambled down to join them.

The eastern sky was streaked with pink and orange. Dawn was here. They had made it through another night.

"I'd say that calls for a celebration," Rusty announced, producing a crumpled packet from his bandana. With great ceremony, he revealed a single pepperoni stick.

Tao's eyes widened. Is that?

"Hot and spicy," Rusty confirmed with a wink. He cracked it in half. "Best I got. Share, share."

They savored the small bite of spicy meat, the hitting like a memory of simpler days. Max's eyes stung unexpectedly.

Soon, Rusty guided them to a fresh boxcar loaded with lumber. The sharp scent of pine surrounded them as they nestled between stacks of wood. For once, there was calm. The sun rose higher, painting the fields in gold. They would have to go back and reunite with Daisy, Picasso and Peanut. Some how they had to find food to bring back to the rest of the wolf pack.

"You know," Winston said, licking a crumb from her Tao, "we still haven't done our joke-of-the-day competition." Her tail wagged hopefully.

Rusty tilted his head. "Joke-of-the-day?"

Max chuckled, remembering. "Yeah. We thought we'd start a tradition. Each day, one of us tells a joke. Best joke wins. Originally, the prize was first dibs on the best food we find."

Rusty slapped his knee with a raspy laugh. "I like it! Count me in. I know some terrible jokes."

Tao giggled, the sound light and chiming. "Oh dear. What have we unleashed? Raccoons telling jokes now."

Luna stretched out languidly, his paws kneading the air like biscuits. "We could certainly use the laughs. Last night was... intense."

And so, as the freight train clattered on through the pale morning, crossing into Delaware and Maryland, a makeshift comedy club was born in car number who-knows-what on Train 457.

Winston volunteered to start them off. She cleared her throat, an endearing little "ahem" that came out as a whine through her muzzle. "Okay, I've got one. What do you call a dog who can do magic tricks?"

Max tilted his head, pretending to puzzle it out. "Hmm, what?"

Winston held the pause just long enough for suspense, then barked triumphantly, "An abracadabra-dog!"

For a beat, there was silence. Then Rusty exploded in laughter, nearly toppling backward off his wooden perch. Tao slapped her paw to her forehead but was grinning despite herself. Peanut groaned, his Tao twitching. "That's awful," he muttered, though a growl slipped out. "Utterly awful."

"Thank you, thank you, I'll be here all week," Winston said with a dramatic bow.

Rusty was still wiping his eyes when he offered to go next. "Alright, my turn, critters. Prepare yourselves for the pinnacle of humor." He wiggled his striped tail like a drumroll. "Why do raccoons never get invited to parties?"

"Why?" Tao asked, playing along.

"Because we tend to get trashed!" Rusty crowed, flashing a toothy grin.

Max and Luna both burst into laughter at the pun, while Tao rolled her eyes, though even she was smiling now. "That's on brand, alright," Luna wheezed between chuckles.

Rusty and Winston smacked paws together in a triumphant high-five, or high-paw.

Tao rose gracefully, tail coiling around her paws like a ribbon. "I've got one," she purred, eyes sparkling. "What's a cat's favorite subject in school?"

No one answered, waiting for the reveal.

"Hisssstory!" Tao announced with a flourish; paw raised like a lecturer.

Groans and laughter collided. "Terrible!" Winston yipped. "Absolutely dreadful, and I love it," Max added. Luna gave an approving nod at the cleverness.

Finally Luna raised a paw. "Alright, one more for the road. Since we have such a cultured audience." He winked at Max. "Why do dogs run in circles?"

Max played along. "Why?"

"Well, it's hard to run in squares," Peanut deadpanned.

It was so absurd it was brilliant. Max barked with laughter until his sides hurt, and the others joined in. The jokes wouldn't have earned applause in a human comedy club, but here, in the belly of a rumbling freight train, each one was priceless because it made them forget the fear for a few fleeting minutes.

When the laughter finally faded, the "judging" began. Rusty stroked his chin theatrically. "Hmm, tough call. I gotta say, I liked that abracadabra door one. But I'm biased, I like dogs."

Winston wagged her tail proudly. "Thank you, thank you."

Tao stretched like a queen and said slyly, "I think Luna's feral cat impression last night might actually take the prize, even if it wasn't strictly a joke."

Luna bowed low, Tao twitching. "Thank you, thank you, survival performance art, at your service."

Max looked around at them, yes, friends now, not just companions, and felt a rush of affection. This strange little fellowship: two dogs, two cats, and a raccoon, laughing together as dawn broke. It was absurd, yet it was also one of the most genuine moments of belonging he had ever known.

"You know what I vote?" Max said, stepping into their circle. "I vote we all win. Because we're alive, we're fed, kind of, and we've got each other. That's the real prize."

Winston whined softly in agreement and nuzzled against his cheek. Tao jumped down and brushed against both of them, while Luna purred quietly and pressed close. Rusty waddled over, laying a paw in the center like a teammate in a huddle.

"Group hug, I can work with that," the raccoon said cheerfully.

For a moment they stayed like that, pressed together, sharing warmth that had nothing to do with the rising sun outside.

Then a horn blast shattered the peace, making them all jump. The train was nearing another crossing, and in the distance, the faint skyline of Washington, D.C. appeared, the Capitol dome glinting like a pale crown on the horizon.

Rusty squinted through a knothole in the boxcar wall. "D.C. already? We're makin' good time. They'll probably swap engines or crews here. We'd better lay low again."

They only had a half-hour more to savor the golden morning before the train slowed into the capital's freight yard. Just as Rusty predicted, it was time for a crew change.

"All right, time for me to get off," Rusty announced, hopping down from the lumber stack. "Got some pals here I need to visit. Besides, I prefer city dumpsters to country ones," he added with a wink.

The others looked crestfallen at his sudden departure, but they understood. Each offered farewells and thanks. Tao touched her nose gently to Rusty's. "Take care of yourself, you rascal."

Rusty tipped an imaginary hat. "And you lot take care too. Remember what I showed you. Maybe I'll catch you further down the line. Funny thing about the rails, they always find ways to bring folks back together."

With that, he scampered to the doorway, then paused, looking back one last time with a crooked grin. "Oh, and watch out. Some humans 'round here aren't as nice as that Philly guard. Eyes open."

Then he was gone, melting into the darkness as the train ground to a halt.

Max felt a hollow pang. They had known Rusty for only a short while, but it felt like saying goodbye to an old comrade.

"Down! Hide!" Luna hissed. Through cracks in the lumber, they saw men in orange vests on the yard platform. Now they had to find the other three companions as they assumed they made the train on a car behind them. They were right and the team reunited. Winston, Chai, Titan, Max, Daisy, Picasso and Peanut were all back together and the three cats Luna, Cleo, and last but not least Tao. They did not have time to be social and find out about each others struggles to get here.

The ten animals squeezed into a recess between the stacked beams, the sharp scent of fresh pine filling their noses. Through a narrow gap, Max watched as the outgoing crew climbed down from the engine and the new crew took their places. The yard bustled with life, though not chaotically.

Bootsteps echoed nearer, crossing the length of their car. A Cleo filled the doorway. A middle-aged man leaned in, wearing a railroad-logo cap and a kindly, weathered face beneath a gray mustache.

Max's heart pounded like a drum. They froze in the Shadows, but the man's eyes adjusted, and widened. He had seen them. Ten pairs of eyes glowing from the dim recess.

"Well, I'll be," the conductor murmured softly, more curious than alarmed. He stepped inside, one hand resting on the frame. "What're you fellas doing' in here?"

Winston whimpered, inching forward in appeasement. Max's tail wagged faintly, a silent plea for peace. The cats crouched tight, poised to flee if danger came. They were already to charge the exit and run for their lives.

The man glanced over his shoulder, making sure no one else was watching. Then he reached slowly into his coverall pocket. "Hungry, are ya?" he said quietly.

He drew out a crumpled wax-paper bundle and opened it to reveal a half-eaten ham-and-cheese sandwich. He tore it into smaller chunks and crouched, extending his hand with a morsel.

"It's okay, I won't hurt ya," he whispered.

The aroma of smoked ham hit them like a tidal wave. Max inched forward, unable to resist, and gently took the piece from the man's fingers. The sweet meat and mustard burst across his tongue, comfort and kindness wrapped in bread. Winston followed, nibbling at a bit of cheese. Tao and Luna crept forward more warily, so the man placed pieces of bread and ham on the floor for them. One by one, they ate.

"There ya go," the conductor murmured. "Poor things musta been ridin' all night. Dogs and cats together, huh? Not somethin' you see every day. Now, you stay quiet and keep outta sight."

He reached out once more and stroked Max's head gently. Max closed his eyes at the touch, a kind human touch, something he thought he might never feel again after becoming a dog. His tail thumped the floor in gratitude.

Suddenly, a distant shout from another worker made the conductor straighten up. "Alright, that's my cue. You critters take care, y'hear?" He rose and shuffled back to the door.

Before slipping out, he drew the heavy panel nearly shut, leaving only a narrow crack so air could flow inside.

Max caught his parting whisper: *"Safe travels, little ones."*

And then he was gone.

For a long moment, the four remained frozen, ears pricked and eyes wide, absorbing what had just taken place. The train jolted and began to pull from the yard, but they barely registered the motion over the tide of emotion swelling in their chests.

"He... he was kind to us," Winston murmured, almost incredulous. She licked a crumb from her Tao, as if trying to prove the memory was real. "He actually helped us."

Tao's eyes glistened, not only from the sunlight streaming through the narrow crack in the door, but from something deeper. "I forgot what that felt like," she whispered. "A human being gentle. Taking care of us."

Peanut dipped his head in a slow nod. "Restores your faith a bit, doesn't it?"

Max swallowed against a tightness in his throat that had nothing to do with the sandwich he'd eaten. That man's small act of compassion sent warmth coursing through him. It reminded him of the days when *he* had been human, how he would've tossed scraps to a stray, offered kindness if he could. The roles were reversed now, but the spark of humanity was still universal.

Silence stretched between them as the train gathered speed, rolling south out of Washington. Each was lost in private thoughts, gratitude, relief, and perhaps a sharp pang of homesickness for the human lives they had left behind.

Eventually, the steady rhythm of the rails coaxed them back into the present. The ten nestled among the lumber stacks, the closed door lending a sense of safety. The midday sun pressed heat into the metal walls, turning the car warm and drowsy. Their bellies were full, and exhaustion pulled gently at their eyelids.

But Max's ears twitched suddenly. A new sound threaded through the hum of the train, a faint *shuffling* from the far end of the car. He lifted his head, nose working the air. A smell reached him then, human, sharp and unwashed, sour with old sweat.

Winston was dozing lightly at his side. Luna and Tao were curled together atop a plank of wood, oblivious. Max stood slowly, hackles prickling, just as a figure stepped from the shadow behind the stacks.

It was a man. His face was grim, his hair greasy under a tattered beanie. He must have slipped aboard earlier, while they were preoccupied with hiding from officials, or during the conductor's visit. None of them had thought to suspect another stowaway.

"Well, looky here," the stranger drawled, baring yellowed teeth in a grin that was anything but kind. "What do we got? A couple of dogs... and some cats? Strays on the train, huh?"

The unfamiliar voice snapped the others awake. Luna's back arched in an instant, a growl ripping from his throat. Winston scrambled upright, putting herself between Tao and the man. Tao leapt down to stand beside her, ears flat, tail lashing.

Max padded forward, lips peeled back in a low, steady growl. The difference between this man and the conductor was stark, the stench of sweat and cheap liquor rolled off him, and his eyes gleamed with a predator's hunger.

The man chuckled, utterly unfazed by their defiance. He reached behind his back and pulled out a frayed loop of rope, a crude noose. "Here, doggy, doggy," he crooned in mock sweetness. "Be a good pup and come to papa." He advanced a step. Titan was not impressed; he bristled and growled.

Max snapped out a bark, sharp and commanding, teeth flashing. Winston's growl joined his, but Max could smell her fear. They were trapped in a moving boxcar, no escape, no way around this man.

The stranger's eyes flicked to Winston, sizing him up. "Pretty little mutt," he muttered. "Bet someone'd pay good money for you... or maybe I could use a new friend." His cracked lips curled as he lunged, rope arcing through the air.

It looped around Winston's neck in a flash. He yelped as the man jerked hard, dragging him toward him. Her paws scrabbled helplessly on the wood, breath choking in the tight snare.

Max's vision went red. With a furious snarl, he launched himself at the man's legs, teeth sinking deep into his calf. The stranger roared, kicking savagely, his boot slamming into Max's ribs and knocking him sprawling.

But Luna and Tao were already in motion. Luna sprang onto the man's back, paws raking down his shoulders as he yowled like a banshee. Tao darted low and sank her teeth into the wrist that held the rope.

"Argh!" The man bellowed, thrashing. He released the rope to grab at the cat clawing his back. Winston stumbled free, hacking and gasping for air, then threw herself at his other leg, jaws clamping down in desperate fury.

It became a blur of fur and violence. The intruder staggered under the combined assault, stumbling toward the boxcar door that still hung slightly ajar. He swung blindly, managing to fling Luna off his back and delivered a vicious backhand that sent Tao tumbling aside with a hiss of pain.

Max shook off the blow to his ribs and lunged again, teeth snapping at the man's ankle. Bleeding from scratches and bites, face streaked with red, the intruder's bravado crumbled. With a wild, fearful snarl, he hurled himself through the door, tumbling out into the dust and weeds along the trackside.

The ten animals crowded at the doorway, panting, hearts hammering. They watched the man roll, bounce, then stagger to his feet limping. He shook a bloody fist at the retreating train, shouting curses that quickly faded behind them as the rails carried the boxcar onward.

Max stood at the threshold, chest heaving. Winston collapsed back on her haunches, trembling, the rope still dangling from her neck. Luna's tail was puffed like a bottlebrush. Tao spat once into the wind. "Good riddance."

"That... was close," Winston whispered, her voice shaking. She pawed at the rope, and Max leaned in, gnawing it apart with careful teeth until it fell away.

"He was going to take you," Max growled, anger still burning hot. "Not on my watch."

"Not on any of ours," Luna agreed, licking the scratch above his eye. His tone carried both pride and lingering adrenaline.

Tao pressed close to Winston, grooming her face with gentle licks like a mother soothing a kitten. "Are you alright?"

"I... I think so," Winston murmured, leaning into her. "Just shaken."

They all were. The boxcar rocked steadily on, indifferent to the battle that had raged inside it.

Max's voice cut through the silence, low and grim. "That guy... he didn't see us for who we are. To him we were just animals. Property to catch. Tools to use."

Peanut's green eyes darkened. "Some humans are like that. They see a stray and think 'pest' or 'profit.' Not a living being."

Tao lowered her gaze. "When I was human, I never thought much about strays either. I'd feel pity, maybe offer food, but I never imagined what it was like to *be* one. Not until now."

Winston shivered. "When he threw that rope over me... I pulled so hard. It felt like I was losing everything. My freedom, my breath, my... self. To him, I was nothing but a dog to leash."

Max pressed his muzzle gently to her cheek. "But you're not just a dog. None of us are. We know who we are inside."

Winston's eyes stayed on the fields rushing past the crack in the door. "But he didn't. He couldn't see it."

A heavy silence fell, Cleo by the realization that to most of the world, their human identities were gone. They were only animals now.

And yet, not an hour before, another man had treated them with warmth, with compassion, without ever knowing their secret. Two faces of humanity revealed in a single day.

"People can be cruel," Peanut said at last, softer now. "But people can also be kind. We've seen both."

Tao flicked her tail thoughtfully. "Like two sides of a coin."

Winston mustered a shaky smile. "At least we gave that sidewinder a run for his money. Did you see his face when Luna went all ninja-kitty on him?"

That broke the tension. Laughter, weak, weary, but real, spread among them.

Max turned back to the horizon. The train chugged southward, the sun now sliding into afternoon. The landscape had shifted, green fields stretched wider, buildings thinning. A highway ran parallel for a time, and Max caught sight of a sign whipping past: *Richmond – 20 miles.*

They were in Virginia now. Together but still uncertain about the destination and their future prospects.

He looked back at his friends. "I guess the world's always going to have people like that guy... and people like that conductor. We just have to stay alert, and stick together."

Luna leapt onto a stack of lumber, striking a mock-heroic pose. "Hear, hear! I say we dub ourselves the *Boxcar Battalion*, defenders of freedom and devourers of donated sandwiches!"

Tao giggled. Winston barked softly in amusement. Max shook his head with a wry smile. "That's the spirit."

They slid the door mostly shut, leaving just enough of a gap to peek at the passing world. The adrenaline ebbed, replaced by exhaustion and a strange, renewed bond. Their conversation drifted back to lighter things, the clatter of the rails steady beneath them as the train carried them further south. Then the story of the other six Wolves of New York came out. As it turns out they had no issues while on the train and they slept most of the trip.

"I've been thinking," Tao said at last, breaking the thoughtful silence that had settled as they rested. Her Tao twitched with mischief. "About a juicy T-bone steak."

Winston's ears perked. "Oh no, here we go, favorite foods again?" she asked with a pretend groan, though her wagging tail betrayed her amusement.

Tao grinned, flashing sharp little teeth. "Why not? It beats thinking about rope traps and creepy men with nooses. Let's imagine our dream dinners. If we were human tonight and could have anything in the world, what would it be?"

"Ooo, good one," Peanut said, rolling lazily onto his back atop the lumber, paws sticking up like antennae. "Alright, I'll start. If I were human? I'd hit the best sushi spot in D.C. Order a whole boat of sashimi and just... not share a single bite." His eyes half-closed in bliss, and he gave a loud, exaggerated *purr* at the thought.

Tao licked her lips approvingly. "Fresh fish, excellent choice. How about you, Winston?"

Winston's eyes softened, a warm glow of memory in them. "Honestly? I'd keep it simple. A cheeseburger, fully loaded. Double patty, cheddar melting everywhere, tomato, lettuce, mayo, with a side of crispy golden fries. And a strawberry milkshake to wash it down."

Max's stomach rumbled in sympathy. "You paint a picture, Winston."

She laughed, ears flicking back with nostalgia. "It was my Friday ritual after work. There was this little diner near my apartment... I swear, I can almost taste it still."

Max turned to Tao. "So you mentioned steak?"

"Indeed," Tao said, stretching her lean body like a queen in her court. "A thick, juicy, medium-rare T-bone. Dripping with garlic butter. Roasted potatoes on the side. And I'd eat it with..." she paused dramatically, "my *hands*!" She broke into laughter at the scandalous declaration.

Peanut shared. "Terrible table manners, Miss Tao. But considering we're animals now, I suppose it fits."

They turned to Max expectantly. He tapped his chin with mock seriousness. "Well, since we already have burgers, sushi, and steak covered... I'll claim the giant New York-style pepperoni pizza. Extra cheese, grease dripping down. And I'd fold the slices in half, let it run all over, and not use a single napkin."

The others groaned in mock horror.

"No napkin?" Winston teased. "Truly embracing your inner dog there."

Max shrugged, unrepentant. "As a human, I was all prim and proper with my fork and knife. But now? I just want to dive face-first into a pizza and not care if I get sauce on my snout."

Their laughter filled the boxcar, bright and genuine this time. Tao set her paw lightly on Max's knee. "You know... when, if, we ever do become human again, we're going out for a massive feast. Together. And we'll eat however we like. No judgment."

"Deal," Peanut said immediately, reaching out his paw. One by one, they placed theirs atop his, a silent pact sealed without need for words.

Their stomachs might have been emptying again, but their hearts were full.

The sun began to dip toward late afternoon, casting a warm orange light through the crack in the door. The train's horn blared, echoing across wide stretches of land. Soon they caught sight of a sign flashing by the tracks: *"Now leaving Virginia, Come back soon!"* Not long after, another: *"Welcome to North Carolina."*

"We're really doing it," Winston said, her voice trembling with a mixture of relief and excitement. "We made it out of the Northeast. North Carolina... it feels like a new chapter."

Max nodded with a grin. "A new chapter for "The Wolves of New York" but maybe our new moniker might be "The Strays of Carolina, huh?"

Peanut groaned loudly at the switch from being a Wolf to become a Stray, rolling his eyes. Tao snorted. "Lions of Carolina," she said, she was smiling. She was becoming the Lioness.

Evening crept in as the sky shifted from blue to pink-orange, fading gradually into violet. The train showed no sign of stopping, likely pressing toward a major yard somewhere deep in the Carolinas before nightfall. Challenges still lay ahead, but for now, they were content, tired, scraped, but together.

Max peeked through the narrow gap in the door one last time as daylight waned. Pine forests swept past on either side, their needles dark silhouettes against the glowing sky. The air smelled different here, earthier, fresher, tinged with resin and warm Carolina soil.

Winston rested her head on Max's shoulder with a sigh, while Peanut and Tao curled close against his other side. Together, they gazed out at the blur of the passing world.

"Today was one for the books," Tao murmured drowsily.

"No kidding," Peanut said, stretching his paws. "I think we've officially earned our stripes as boxcar animals."

Winston yawned wide, her eyes sliding shut. "Wake me if you spot a steak tree or a burger bush."

Max chuckled under his breath, then grew quiet again, his gaze fixed on the horizon. His mind wandered to tomorrow, and the day after that. The uncertainty was still there, but so was something steadier, hope.

They had survived a night and a day on the rails. They had forged friendships, in each other, and in unexpected allies. They had faced danger and come out stronger.

Humor and heart, paw in paw, Max thought. Maybe that was how they'd make it through this strange new life.

As dusk settled fully, Max let his eyes drift shut, the rhythmic clack of the rails lulling him toward rest. The freight train carried them deeper into the Carolinas, bearing not just their bodies, but their dreams, fears, and unbreakable bond. Whatever tomorrow brought, they would face it together, former humans, current animals, and a true pack on the journey of a lifetime.

Chapter 5

THE FAST AND THE FURRIEST

A Plan for a Lifetime of Kibble

It was well past midnight in the abandoned shed the fugitive animals had claimed as their temporary home. The summer night in North Carolina was heavy with humidity, pressing down on the land like a damp blanket. A chorus of crickets droned steadily outside, their voices weaving into the stillness as if serenading the ragtag group huddled in the dark.

Near the doorway, a lanky-legged Dobermann paced restlessly. His ribs showed through his short fur, and every step betrayed his gnawing hunger. Titan, as the others called him, couldn't keep still. His stomach growled audibly, echoing in the shed and drawing a long-suffering groan from Tao, the Siamese cat perched regally on a torn-up armchair cushion.

"We know, we know," Tao sighed, her tail flicking with theatrical annoyance. "We're all hungry, Titan. But pacing isn't going to make kibble magically rain from the sky."

Titan paused mid-step, his ears drooping in apology. "Sorry. I can't help it," he said quietly, careful to keep his voice low even here in the dark shadows. "It's been two days since

158

we had a real meal. I'm starting to look at those crickets out there like they're hors d'oeuvres."

A shiver ran through Max, the German Shepard lounging against the wall. His lips curled in distaste. "Ugh, please don't. I'm desperate, but I'm not that desperate, at least not yet." He rolled onto his back, exposing his belly and stretching his legs toward the air. "Though if Tao keeps complaining, I might start considering cat for dinner," he teased, flashing a crooked grin.

Tao narrowed his green eyes, her voice dropping into a silken purr edged with mock sweetness. "Try it and see what nine lives gets you." He arched his back slightly, adding, "Besides, I doubt I'd pair well with your palate. Too much sarcasm in my diet."

The others chuckled softly, their laughter like small sparks in the gloom. Even in dire straits, the banter gave them a thread of normalcy.

In the corner, Cleo, sleek, and unnervingly quiet, was rummaging through their pitiful stash of supplies. He nudged aside an old blanket, a flashlight whose battery wheezed on its last bit of power, and a dog-eared map of North Carolina. From beneath the pile, he drew out a crumpled flyer scavenged from town. "If only we could waltz into a grocery store," he muttered, eyes narrowing. "But every time we risk being seen, we risk them catching us."

At the mention of *them*, silence swept through the shed like a cold wind. They didn't need to say the name: Pet-link. The research facility that had stolen their human lives and trapped them in these animal bodies.

Titan's paw drifted to the back of his neck, where a small scar from the implant still lingered, a scar that pulsed with memory. Neural experiments, wires, tests, commands. He swallowed hard. Weeks had passed since their escape, but the fear still lived in his bones. They'd been running ever since, hiding in the urban forests and abandoned buildings, scavenging for scraps, doing whatever it took to survive. And survival was only getting harder.

Max broke the silence with a grunt, rolling back to his feet. "We can't keep this up much longer. We're getting weaker every day. We need food." His voice was steady, but the weight behind it pressed on everyone. He gestured at the half-empty can of cold baked beans sitting nearby, yesterday's spoils. "And I don't mean this. I mean *real* food."

Tao stretched leisurely, though his eyes betrayed fatigue. A sliver of moonlight slipped through a crack in the shed wall, catching the faint stripes in his fur. "Suggestions, then? Shall we become farmers? Old MacDonald's secret farm, with a moo-moo here and an oink-oink there..." His sarcasm drew another ripple of half-hearted laughter.

Titan couldn't help but chuckle softly. Tao always had a way of twisting the moment, even if only to lighten their dread. He resumed pacing, careful not to step on Cleo's tail. "Maybe tomorrow night we raid behind the diner on Maple Street again. Last time we scored a sack of stale burger buns. Not gourmet, but at least it was something."

Before anyone could reply, Cleo let out a sharp yowl. His golden eyes gleamed as he smoothed the flyer flat with a paw. "Hold on. Look at this."

The group gathered closer, curiosity stirring. Cleo pressed the paper against the wall so the moonlight could illuminate it. Titan squinted, then read aloud the bold heading:

"Raleigh Pet Expo – Annual Dog Talent Show."

Max blinked. "Dog... what now?" He padded closer, head cocked.

Cleo's claw tapped the text. "This weekend. A dog talent show. There's even an agility obstacle course competition."

Tao hopped down from his perch, his Tao twitching with interest. "Agility course? The whole tunnels, ramps, weave poles ordeal?" He gave a wistful sigh. "I used to watch those at the fair. Back when I had Netflix and opposable thumbs."

Titan's tail began to wag, slowly at first, then with growing excitement. His eyes caught on a line at the bottom of the flyer, printed in bold red. His heart skipped. "Guys... the grand prize is a *lifetime supply of dog food* from Pet Paradise in Raleigh."

For a moment, silence reigned. Then Max's jaw dropped open, his tongue lolling in disbelief. "A lifetime supply? Endless food? Are they *serious*?"

Cleo's eyes glowed with something between hunger and hope. "That's what it says. Probably some publicity stunt, but still."

Titan felt his chest swell with a fragile surge of hope. The thought of regular meals, not scavenged but theirs by right, was almost overwhelming. He imagined crunchy kibble, savory canned stew, maybe even treats. Dog food had never sounded so heavenly.

Tao quickly deflated the moment with a sharp tone. "Don't start drooling yet. Did you forget we're fugitives? Walking into a dog show in front of humans is suicide. We might as well send Pet-link our coordinates."

The fragile spark dimmed, reality pressing back in. Titan bit his lip, frustration simmering. Tao was right.

But Max spoke up, hesitant but firm. "What if we *can* pull it off? Think about it, hundreds of dogs, their owners, a noisy crowd. We'd blend in. Titan just needs an owner for the day."

"And if that 'owner' happens to have the fastest dog in the competition," Cleo added smoothly, "we walk away with the food before anyone suspects a thing."

Tao' tail lashed. "You're all insane. If something goes wrong,"

Titan interrupted softly, "We're out of options. Do you have a better idea? Something that doesn't involve starving, or crawling back to Pet-link?"

Tao bristled but had no retort. Finally, he sighed, shoulders slumping. "I hate that you're right."

Titan gave him a small, almost sheepish smile. "We limit the risk. Only one of us competes. The rest stay hidden and help from the Cleos."

Cleo dipped his head. "Fitting."

Max grinned. "And Titan is the obvious choice. He's built for speed."

Titan shifted uneasily under their eyes. Before the experiments, he'd been a human sprinter, racing on his college track team. Now fate had locked him into a Dobermann body that seemed almost designed for the course. "I... I can try," he murmured. Running was the only time he felt like himself again.

Tao gave a reluctant nod. "Titan it is. But he'll need an owner. They won't let a stray compete."

Cleo agreed. "We need a human, someone kind, clueless, and willing."

Max let out a dry laugh. "Right. Volunteers? Because the only humans we know want to dissect us."

Silence. Then Tao began pacing. "It has to be a stranger. Someone gentle. Someone we can... adopt."

Titan tilted his head. "Adopt?"

Cleo's golden eyes gleamed. "Like strays choosing their owner. We find the right human in Raleigh, play the part, and see if they take the bait."

Titan considered it, cautious but intrigued. "So... we pretend to belong to them. Just for a day."

"Exactly," Cleo said.

Max chuckled. "Funny world when dogs are hunting for humans instead of the other way around." His grin softened into something almost wistful. "Never thought I'd be chasing dog food prizes, either."

Tao nudged him. "Better than dumpster beans." Her voice softened. "And cats eat dog food too, when it comes down to it."

Titan pushed the door open with his muzzle. A shaft of moonlight sliced into the dusty shed, illuminating the weary but determined faces around him. "So, it's decided?"

Cleo tucked the flyer back under the blanket like a secret treasure. "Raleigh's half a day's journey if we follow the woods. We leave tomorrow night."

Tao leapt back to his perch, tail flicking. "If we're doing this, we do it smart. Recon first. No surprises."

Titan grinned faintly. "Since when do we ever avoid surprises?"

Tao snorted. "Fair point. But still, one mistake, and it's game over."

The group exchanged glances and subtle nods, each of them silently weighing the gamble. The risk was enormous, but so was the reward. Hunger had a way of forcing decisions none of them would have considered otherwise. As Titan finally curled up on the dusty floorboards to try to catch a few hours of rest, his mind refused to slow. Already, it was racing ahead to what the dog show might look like. He imagined the arena: bright lights, an audience clapping, and rows of obstacles waiting for him. He could almost feel the rush of diving through narrow tunnels, bounding over ramps, and weaving in and out of poles. A strange mixture of excitement and nerves coursed through him. He was really going to do this, compete in a canine obstacle course, the kind of spectacle he'd only ever watched on TV back when he was human.

Across the shed, Max's snores rumbled in steady bursts. The French Bulldog had the uncanny ability to fall asleep almost at will, as though he'd trained himself to shut out worry whenever exhaustion demanded. Tao, by contrast, kneaded the cushion a few times before curling herself into a sleek ball. One emerald eye, however, remained half-lidded and vigilant. Cleo didn't even bother with pretense; she dissolved into the darkness of a corner, her sleek body nearly indistinguishable from the darkness he loved.

Titan rested his chin on his forepaws, staring at the cracked shed door. Through the narrow gap, stars twinkled faintly in the humid sky, remote and untouchable yet oddly reassuring. He let his thoughts form into a quiet vow, as if sending it both to his rumbling stomach and to the restless hearts of his friends. *Hang tight. Tomorrow, we find our human. Tomorrow, we win that prize. Tomorrow, everything changes.*

Recruiting a Human Ally

By the following evening, twilight wrapped the world in muted purples and blues. The fugitives slipped away from their ramshackle shed, leaving behind the dusty backroads that had hidden them for weeks. Their destination was Raleigh, and the lure of adventure waiting at the dog talent show. The journey was long but uneventful, a silent, cautious trek across dew-laden fields, past shuttered farmhouses, and along quiet suburban streets where porch lights flickered to life like fireflies.

They kept far from main roads, darting between wooded buffers and skirting neighborhood fences. A pack of stray dogs and cats traveling together was unusual enough to raise eyebrows, and possibly earn them a quick trip in the back of an animal control van. Titan, as always, led the way, guiding them through alleys and half-hidden paths with an instinct for stealth.

When at last the skyline of downtown Raleigh loomed against the pre-dawn glow, Titan's heart tightened with both relief and unease. The city was a barrage of scents and sounds unlike anything in the countryside: exhaust fumes tangled with the aroma of food carts; the musk of other people's pets blended with the stench of overstuffed dumpsters. Compared to the silence of their rural hideout, it was overwhelming, a chaotic palette that made Titan's nose twitch nonstop.

They finally took refuge in a sprawling public park on the city's outskirts, tucking themselves into a hedge-thickened corner overgrown with weeds. There, in the cool damp grass, they caught a few hours of restless sleep, pressed together like an odd little family of strays.

Sunrise brought no rest but urgency. They had only a single day to secure what they needed most: a human ally. Without one, the plan to enter the show collapsed before it could even begin.

The park, by then, was waking up. Joggers padded along the winding trails. Dog walkers chattered into phones while their pets sniffed the air. Children threw frisbees. From their vantage point behind a clump of azalea bushes, the fugitives began their quiet scouting, eyes sharp, weighing every passerby with the precision of undercover matchmakers.

Max flicked his ears toward a man practicing tai chi on the lawn. The man moved gracefully, each gesture deliberate,"What about him?" Max whispered. "Animal lover for sure."

Tao studied the man, then shook his head with a twitch of Tao. "Too put-together. He looks like the kind of guy who'd *notice* things. We need someone a little more... malleable."

"Clueless?" Cleo murmured dryly.

"Open-minded," Tao corrected with a sly smirk. "We want someone who won't question a strange situation."

Titan scanned the paths. A woman wrangling three hyper chihuahuas marched past, too busy. A boy no older than twelve laughed while throwing a ball to his golden retriever, too young. Then Titan's gaze fell on a young woman seated alone on a wooden bench beneath a maple tree. She sipped coffee from a thermos while reading, her ponytail loose and casual. Every so often, she tossed a crumb to the pudgy squirrel that scurried eagerly at her feet, gathering what looked like bits of granola bar.

"What about her?" Titan asked softly.

The others peered out. She wore a T-shirt decorated with cartoon cats, and when a stray ginger tabby crept from a bush to approach her, she didn't shoo it away. Instead, she smiled, dug into her pocket, and offered it a treat. The cat accepted happily, circling her legs with affection. She laughed, an unguarded, genuine sound.

"Perfect," Max breathed, tail thumping softly. "She's exactly the type."

Tao's tail flicked with finality. "Titan, time to turn on the charm."

Titan felt a nervous jolt. Talking about it was one thing. Walking up to a stranger, trying to win her trust, was another. What if she panicked, or worse, called animal control?

"Confidence," Cleo whispered, nudging him gently with his head. "Just be yourself."

"Yeah," Max added with a grin. "Puppy eyes. Weaponized."

Steadying himself, Titan stepped out from the cover of the azaleas. He kept his posture friendly and non-threatening, head low, tail wagging slowly, ears pulled back in cautious humility. He trotted onto the path toward the bench.

The ginger cat was still basking in head scratches when Titan let out a short bark to announce himself. The squirrel bolted for the safety of the tree, and the woman's hazel eyes lifted in surprise.

"Oh! Hello there," she said warmly, pocketing her snack so both hands were free. The ginger cat slipped away, leaving Titan the center of her attention.

Up close, Titan saw she was in her mid-twenties, her expression open and gentle. She held out a hand tentatively. "Hey, buddy... You lost? Where's your owner?"

Titan dipped his head to sniff politely, fighting the urge to wag too hard. She smelled faintly of vanilla lotion and coffee. Her voice carried no suspicion, only concern.

"No collar," she murmured, noting the bare fur at his neck. Titan's stomach tightened, without a collar, he screamed *stray*. But instead of reaching for her phone, she reached out and stroked gently behind his ears.

The sensation was bliss. His tail thumped uncontrollably against the ground. *Focus!* he scolded himself.

"You're friendly," she murmured. "Someone must be missing you."

Hidden in the shrubs, Tao prowled toward the nearby community board. A bright poster they'd spotted earlier still hung there, announcing the Raleigh Pet Expo & Talent Show, Tomorrow 10 AM! With a quick leap and a swipe of his paw, Tao sent it fluttering to the ground at the woman's feet.

She bent down, picked it up, and scanned it. "Dog Talent Show... agility competition..." She grinned as her eyes flicked back to Titan. "You wouldn't happen to be a talented dog, would you?"

On impulse, Titan barked once and lifted his head proudly.

Her laughter rang out, bright and delighted. "No way. That almost sounded like a yes!"

Titan tilted his head to one side, ears uneven, perfecting his look of endearing curiosity. She clasped her chest. "Oh my gosh. Okay, you are officially too cute."

Reading over the flyer again, she bit her lip. "If you were an agility dog, maybe your owner would be at this show tomorrow... Or maybe..." She hesitated, then laughed at herself. "Maybe *I* could take you? Just for fun?"

Titan barked again, bouncing in a circle, his joy impossible to contain.

The woman giggled, shaking her head. "Either I'm dreaming or this dog understands every word." She ruffled his fur. "You want to come with me, boy? I can give you a bath and some dinner. You must be starving."

As if on cue, Titan's stomach growled loudly. They both froze, then she laughed until tears came to her eyes. "I'll take that as a yes."

Behind the shrubs, Max whispered, "It's working. He's actually pulling it off."

Cleo purred with quiet pride. "Titan has always been the charmer."

Tao returned, flyer in his mouth, and set it down. "Step one complete. We've got our human."

The woman slung a tote bag over her shoulder and picked up her thermos. "Alright, buddy. Let's get you home. My name's Ellie, by the way. You look like you could use a friend. Honestly... so could I."

She whistled softly, patting her leg. Titan glanced toward the azaleas. To anyone else, it was a dog pausing to notice a rustle in the bushes. To him, it was one last check with his friends. From the Cleos, three pairs of eyes gleamed back, and Cleo gave the faintest of nods.

Titan barked lightly, a soft sound that, in his mind, meant *See you soon*, and trotted after Ellie as she led him out of the park. His heart pounded with a mix of excitement and relief. He had done it. Against all odds, he had found them the perfect temporary human ally: kind hearted, trusting, and blissfully unaware that the lanky Dobermann prancing at her heels was anything more than a clever stray.

As Titan left with Ellie, the others kept to the bush and cover in the darkest shadows, trailing just far enough behind to remain unseen. Tao slunk from hedge to hedge, tail low, his paws barely making a sound on the asphalt. Cleo, true to his name, was nearly invisible, melting behind parked cars and dark corners. Max, far too bulky for subtlety, lingered further back, but his loyalty anchored him to their path. Their mission was clear, track Ellie's movements, ensure Titan's safety, and be ready to intervene if anything turned suspicious.

Ellie chatted freely as they walked, her voice carrying the ease of someone who had been waiting to share her thoughts with a listening ear. "You know, I always wanted a dog growing up," she confessed, tugging at her cartoon cat T-shirt with a sheepish grin. "But we had cats, lots of them. My mom always said dogs were too much work, too high-energy. But me? I love both. Honestly, I still sneak into the shelter on weekends just to get my puppy fix." She reached down to pat Titan's shoulder warmly. "So, this, walking home with you, is kind of a dream come true."

Titan wagged his tail to show he was listening. Her words touched him more than he expected. A pang of guilt nipped at his heart, she seemed genuine, and here he was, planning to use her kindness for a free meal and an entry ticket. But another part of him soothed the guilt away. *It's survival,* he told himself. And maybe, just maybe, he could leave her with something real, a memory, a friendship, perhaps even a new dog after he and his friends vanished again.

They arrived at Ellie's bungalow on a quiet suburban street. The small house carried a gentle, lived-in charm: a blue front door with a beautiful flower motif welcome mat, flowerpots of drooping petunias on the steps, and a porch swing that creaked slightly in the breeze. Ellie pushed the door open with a cheerful flourish. "Welcome to Casa de Ellie," she announced. "Ignore the mess, I wasn't expecting canine company tonight."

Inside, the air smelled faintly of cinnamon and... tuna. Titan quickly discovered the reason: a fat orange tabby streaked across the living room, brushing against his legs before bolting into the kitchen.

"Ah, that's Chester," Ellie explained with an affectionate sigh. "Neighborhood cat. He doesn't *live* here, exactly, he freeloads. I gave him treats once, and now I'm basically an all-you-can-eat buffet."

Outside, Tao and Cleo peered in through a window, watching the orange blur demand snacks with shameless meows. Tao smirked and muttered, "Smart cat. Knows a pushover when he sees one."

Ellie bustled toward the kitchen, clapping her hands. "Alright, first things first, food! You must be starving." Titan followed eagerly, trying not to drool or glance too hungrily at Chester, who had claimed the top of the fridge and was glaring down like a smug king.

Ellie rummaged through her fridge, muttering. "Let's see... no dog food, of course... but I've got leftover roast chicken. That should work." She set a plate with a generous chunk on the floor. "Bon appétit, buddy."

Titan's eyes widened. Real, cooked meat, rich, savory, and warm. His stomach growled so loudly it echoed in the small kitchen. Fighting the urge to inhale it in one bite, he forced himself to chew slowly, savoring every generous mouthful.

Ellie watched, her smile tinged with sympathy. "Poor thing. You eat like you haven't seen food in days."

You have no idea, Titan thought between gulps, though outwardly all Ellie heard was happy snuffling.

When he finished, Ellie crouched beside him with a bowl of cool water. "We'll get you sorted tomorrow," she promised. "I'll buy proper dog food. For now, this will do."

As Titan lapped greedily, Ellie studied him, tapping her chin. "We should give you a name, at least for tomorrow. Unless you already have one... but you can't exactly tell me, can you?" She tilted her head. "Hmm... you're quick. What about Bolt? Or Flash?"

Titan nearly sputtered water in amusement. Of all the names, she had landed close to the truth.

Then Ellie's eyes lit up. She snapped her fingers. "Dash. Yes! Because you dashed right up to me at the park, and I bet you'll Dash through that course tomorrow."

Titan barked and nodded, ears flopping comically. Inside, he marveled at the coincidence, fate seemed to be playing along.

Ellie beamed. "Dash it is. Either I'm an amazing trainer, or you really understand me." She tapped his nose, and he responded with a grateful lick, sealing the pact.

"Alright, Dash," she declared, "bath first, then practice. If we're doing this agility thing, I need to see if you've got the chops."

What followed was fifteen minutes of watery chaos. Ellie plopped him into her bathtub and lathered him with lavender-scented shampoo. Water splashed up the walls as Titan wagged furiously whenever her scrubbing tickled. By the time she towel-dried him, both were soaked, she was laughing breathlessly, and Titan sneezed in what sounded suspiciously like a chuckle.

When she finally let him loose in the backyard, he bolted out like a cannonball, shaking water in all directions. Cleo, watching from the fence, had to smother Max's guffaws at the sight of their sleek racer now smelling like a spring bouquet.

Ellie wasn't finished. Gathering odds and ends from her shed, she built a makeshift training course: a broomstick between lawn chairs for a hurdle, an old hula hoop for a hoop jump, and, after some inspiration, a fabric tunnel emptied of gardening tools.

She raised her eyebrows at Dash aka Titan. "Okay, no idea if you'll do any of this. But let's try."

One by one, Titan cleared each challenge, careful to perform with just enough clumsiness to look like a beginner. He added playful spins, exaggerated missteps, and a dramatic tumble out of the tunnel that had Ellie doubled over in laughter.

"You're amazing," she said, hugging him tightly. Her voice softened. "I don't even care if we win tomorrow. Just seeing you run makes me happy. Deal?"

Titan licked her cheek, though privately he thought: *Winning is still the plan.*

That night, while Ellie slept, Titan slipped out to the porch to meet his friends. Max greeted him with an envious grin. "Chicken dinners and bubble baths? You're living the dream."

Titan smirked. "Jealous?"

"Completely," Max admitted.

Tao perched on the railing, tail flicking. "She's buying every second of it. Tomorrow's our shot."

The ten huddled close, whispering their plan for the dog show. Titan would shine in the arena while the others slipped into the grounds, scouting and securing opportunities. Cleo promised to slink near the announcer's tent, unseen. Max vowed to keep a lookout near the prize stand. Tao, as usual, would improvise.

Tomorrow, everything depended on Titan's performance, and Ellie's unwitting role as their cover.

Morning came quickly. The sun rose over Ellie's neighborhood in a wash of gold, and Titan stretched on her porch, the scent of dew and freshly cut grass in the air. His stomach fluttered, not just with nerves, but with purpose. Today wasn't just about running and jumping for cheers. Today was about survival, strategy, and securing what they needed.

Ellie bustled out the door with a backpack slung over her shoulder, her hair tied in a hurried ponytail. "Alright, Dash, big day! I packed snacks, water, and, oh, I even brought my lucky charm." She dangled a keychain shaped like a tiny paw print. "We're going to crush this."

Titan wagged dutifully, but as Ellie locked the door, his eyes flicked toward the Cleos down the street. Max, Cleo, and Tao were already in position. The six other Wolves of New York were just witnesses

The plan had been laid out the night before:

- **Titan** would compete as Ellie's dog, stealing the spotlight. His charm, speed, and agility would be their distraction.

Every set of eyes would be on him, not on what the others were doing.

- **Tao** would slip into the judges' prep tent, snooping for information, entry lists, prize storage locations, anything useful.

- **Cleo** would haunt the perimeter, watching for security and sniffing out threats before they closed in.

- **Max** would hang near the prize stand, his sheer size enough to discourage curious humans if things went sideways.

The stakes were clear: if Titan could win, they'd have access to the prize pool, which meant resources, food, money, and maybe even connections to bigger opportunities.

At the fairgrounds, the dog show was already buzzing with life. Tents were pitched in neat rows, banners flapped in the breeze, and the air was thick with the smell of popcorn, hot dogs, and wet fur. Dozens of dogs barked and whined, their owners fussing over them with brushes, bows, and treats.

Ellie's eyes went wide. "Wow... this is huge. I thought it was just a local thing!" She clutched Titan's leash a little tighter. "Don't worry, Titan, we'll just have fun. Winning doesn't matter."

It does to me, Titan thought grimly, though outwardly he gave a cheerful bark.

As Ellie signed them in, Titan's friends melted into the chaos. Tao darted under a flap of the judges' tent. Inside, clipboards and ribbons lined the tables. The cat's sharp eyes scanned every detail: prize crates at the back, locked but not closely guarded; papers listing the top competitors and their routines. He committed it all to memory.

Outside, Cleo kept low, slipping behind benches and trash cans. His gaze tracked two security guards strolling lazily near the prize stand. They weren't paying much attention, yet.

Max settled near the prize table, pretending to gnaw on a discarded bone. From there, he could keep an eye on the trophies gleaming in the sunlight, silver cups, medals, and an envelope that looked suspiciously like it contained cash. His chest swelled with determination. *That's what we need. That's our way forward.*

Meanwhile, Ellie led Dash toward the staging area. Nervous handlers whispered about the competition: a sleek border collie named Juno, a German shepherd with military precision, and a golden retriever whose fur practically glowed.

Ellie crouched beside Dash, her hand trembling slightly as she stroked his head. "Don't worry, buddy. No pressure. Just have fun."

But Titan felt the weight of all their hopes pressing on him. His friends, their hunger, their survival, it all depended on his speed, his charm, and his ability to make Ellie believe this was just a game.

When the announcer's voice boomed over the speakers, calling the competitors to the ring, Dash trotted forward with his tail high. The crowd cheered, Ellie smiled, and from the corners of the grounds, three pairs of eyes watched intently.

The infiltration had begun.

Max thumped his tail against the porch floor. "I might be able to pass as a stray wandering around, or maybe as some spectator's off-leash pet. If needed, I can cause a distraction. You know I'm good at the ol' 'oops, I knocked over a trash can' routine."

Tao kneaded the wooden railing, his green eyes narrowing as he thought aloud. "Our biggest concern is the competition. We need to ensure Titan wins. That likely means some... subtle interference with the other top dogs."

"Sabotage, you mean," Titan said, ears perking uneasily.

"Clever sabotage," Tao corrected, flashing a wicked little grin. "We can't exactly guarantee the competition, nothing violent or obvious that would get humans pointing fingers at you or Ellie. But distractions? Those, we can do."

His gaze glinted with mischief as he went on. "Picture this: a well-timed laser dot to misdirect a dog mid-run, or the sound of a phantom squirrel to make one dart off course."

From beneath the table, Cleo extended a paw and delicately revealed a small red laser pointer between two claws. Titan blinked in astonishment. "Where did you...?"

Cleo's smile was sly and enigmatic. "Ellie has plenty of cat toys lying around. Chester's a spoiled guest. I borrowed one from a shelf."

Max snorted with laughter. "Never underestimate a cat's ability to sniff out the laser pointer stash."

Tao, tail curling in satisfaction, laid out the plan. "I'll handle the laser. I'm quick on my feet and can stay out of sight. Cleo, you might topple something, say, a food bowl, to throw off another dog. Max, a convincing bark or a sudden appearance could be enough to make a high-strung competitor falter."

Titan listened, conflicted. On one paw, his chest warmed with gratitude, they had his back, willing to bend rules for his sake. On the other, unease prickled at him. This wasn't exactly fair play. But then again, neither was life these days. Their survival depended on this.

"I just don't want anyone getting hurt," he murmured. "No dogs, no humans."

"Of course," Tao said softly, his usual sharpness dimmed for a moment. "Distract, not harm. We only want the odds tilted in our favor."

Cleo nodded. "And ideally, no one should even suspect sabotage. It has to look like ordinary slip-ups."

All three exchanged glances and silently agreed, committing to their roles.

As Titan turned to slip back inside, Max whispered after him, "Good luck tomorrow, Titan. Show them what a former track star can do."

Titan wagged his tail humbly. "Couldn't do it without you guys."

Tao rested a paw on his for a heartbeat. "Be careful, all of you. And Titan, enjoy it, okay? How often does a guy like you get to run in a dog show? Crazy world, huh?"

Titan allowed himself a small smile. "Crazy indeed."

With that, he slipped back through the loose screen into the quiet house. Inside, the living room glowed faintly from a streetlamp filtering through the curtains. Ellie's soft snores drifted from her bedroom, steady and comforting. Titan curled up beside the couch, his mind racing even as his eyes grew heavy. He pictured the obstacle course again, rehearsing each leap and sprint. Tomorrow, he would be running not just for himself, but for all of them. For once, he had the chance to win something that truly mattered.

He only hoped their gambit wouldn't come crashing down around them.

Showtime in Raleigh

The sun was barely up when Ellie loaded Titan into her little hatchback. She was practically buzzing with excitement, helped, no doubt, by one too many cups of coffee, while humming tunelessly under her breath. Titan sat in the backseat, tongue lolling, projecting the perfect image of a carefree dog. In truth, his heart hammered with nerves and anticipation.

As they neared the Raleigh Pet Expo, Titan pressed his nose to the glass. The fairgrounds stretched out in front of them: a wide field beside a community center, already bustling with people and dogs. Cars funneled into a makeshift grass lot, while tents and booths lined the perimeter, hawking everything from pet food brands to local groomers and veterinary clinics.

At the center stood the real prize: the obstacle course. Bright blue and red tunnels glinted under the morning sun, an A-frame ramp towered like a miniature mountain, and rows of upright weave poles promised a tricky test of speed and precision. Several jumps of varying heights dotted the ring. Wooden bleachers lined one side for spectators, while a massive banner flapped overhead:

"Raleigh Pet Expo – Talent Show & Agility Championship Today!"

Ellie rolled down the window at a volunteer's direction and was guided into a parking spot. "This is so cool," she chattered, pulling out the keys. She glanced back at Titan. "You ready, boy?"

Titan answered with an enthusiastic bark that made her laugh. "I'll take that as a yes!"

She clipped a simple green nylon leash onto his new collar, the one she'd bought that very morning. It wasn't fancy, but

Titan felt an unexpected pride in wearing it, almost as if it were a badge of belonging.

"Let's get you signed up."

At the registration table, Ellie filled out the form, writing "Dash" with a flourish. An older woman handed her a tag with the number **13** to pin onto his collar. "Lucky thirteen," Ellie remarked with a grin. "Hope you're not superstitious, Dash."

Titan gave a soft woof. If anything, the number felt perfect. He could practically hear Tao making some dry remark about them being the stealthiest, most unlucky-lucky team in the ring.

The fairgrounds bustled like a carnival of canines. Big dogs, small dogs, fluffy and sleek, tails wagged, paws scrambled, owners barked commands or offered treats. Some dogs strained against leashes in excitement, others sat patiently, focused on their handlers. Titan soaked it all in. After weeks of skulking in shadows and bushes, being surrounded by so many humans who weren't chasing him felt... liberating.

Ellie guided him toward the warm-up area. Along the way, Titan's sharp eyes spotted a familiar figure. Max lounged near a hot dog stand, his stocky body relaxed, mouth open in a convincing pant. A vendor laughed and tossed him bits of bun, which Max caught with practiced ease. When their eyes met, Max gave the faintest wag of his tail, everything was under control, and yes, the hot dog was delicious.

Tao and Cleo were unseen, but Titan trusted their skills. They'd be nearby, perhaps under the bleachers or weaving through equipment trailers, waiting for the right moment.

At the warm-up ring, Ellie crouched beside Dash, whispering conspiratorially, "Just like last night, okay? Over!" She pointed at a low hurdle. Titan bounded over with ease, earning extended applause from Ellie.

"Good boy!" she said proudly. A few handlers glanced over, nodding appreciatively. "That dog's got springs," one murmured.

After a few more warm-up runs, a voice boomed over the loudspeaker:

"All participants in the agility contest, please report to the main ring. Repeat, all agility contestants, please gather at the main ring. The event will begin shortly."

Ellie exhaled, smoothing her shirt. "This is it. Ready to be a star?"

Titan licked a smudge of powdered sugar off her cheek, leftovers from her breakfast donut. Ellie giggled, taking it as an enthusiastic yes.

At the main ring, about fifteen contestants gathered. Some pairs were seasoned and sharp, border collies practically vibrating with energy, a Belgian Malinois standing like a soldier, a Jack Russell bouncing with anticipation. Others were casual entrants, like a droopy basset hound more interested in treats than trophies, or a nervous poodle whose owner fussed endlessly with its sequined bandana.

Ellie smiled nervously at a family with a golden retriever ahead of them. "Quite the turnout, huh?" she said, half to herself.

The atmosphere buzzed with tension and excitement, dogs yipping, owners murmuring strategies, the scent of anticipation thick in the air.

Then, a ripple passed through the crowd. Heads turned.

A late arrival was approaching the ring.

"Oh, look who it is," one handler muttered.

"That's the one to watch," whispered another.

Ellie and Titan turned. A woman strode forward with crisp confidence, designer sunglasses flashing, a sporty jacket emblazoned with sponsor logos. At her side trotted a border collie so impeccably groomed it seemed to shine. The dog's gait was elegant, its eyes sharp and calculating.

The famed rival had arrived.

The woman slid her sunglasses to the top of her head and flashed a competitive smile at the group.

"Morning, everyone," she said brightly, though there was a razor-edge to her friendliness. "Hope you're all ready for a good run. Lightning here is feeling fast today." She gave the border collie a confident pat.

Lightning, for his part, surveyed the other dogs with what could only be described as a smug expression. If dogs could smirk, Lightning was doing it. When his sharp gaze landed on Titan, Titan offered a polite wag of the tail. Lightning sniffed dismissively and turned away, as if none of the others were worth his notice.

Ellie leaned down and whispered, "Yikes. That's some big competition. Lightning... even his name sounds speedy."

Titan chuffed softly. Up close, he could see that Lightning was all muscle and precision, the product of long hours of training. This dog had probably been bred and groomed for agility from day one. *Well,* Titan thought, *so have I, just in a different way.* A spark of determination lit inside him. He might be the underdog (literally), but he had something Lightning didn't: an entire crew working behind the scenes.

The loudspeaker squealed, then the announcer, a jovial man in a straw hat, welcomed the crowd with infectious enthusiasm.

"Ladies and gentlemen, dog lovers of all ages, welcome to the Raleigh Pet Expo Agility Championship! We've got a fantastic lineup of talented canines and their handlers today. Get ready for some high-flying, tail-wagging action!"

A cheer rolled through the bleachers as families settled in with popcorn and programs. Children leaned over the rails, craning for a better look at the competitors. The announcer explained the rules: each dog would tackle the obstacle course one at a time, racing against the clock. Mistakes meant time penalties, knocking down bars, skipping an obstacle, or missing contact zones. The fastest clean run would win the grand prize. He rattled off the list of challenges: the starting jump, tire hoop, the A-frame climb and descent, weave poles, tunnel, seesaw, and finally a high jump to finish.

Ellie let out a shaky breath. "Oh boy," she muttered under her breath. "We didn't practice half of that, Dash." Her worried eyes searched his face.

Titan gave her calf a reassuring nuzzles. True, they hadn't rehearsed the weave poles or the seesaw, but he felt confident he could improvise. He had watched enough agility meets on TV back in his human days, a guilty pleasure on lazy Sunday mornings. Now, in this body, his instincts seemed sharper than memory. His muscles *knew* what to do, even if his human brain hadn't rehearsed it before.

A volunteer ushered the contestants to a holding area beside the gate and called the first competitor to the start line.

Tricks, Traps, and Tunnel Titans

The golden retriever Ellie had greeted earlier, contestant #1, was up first, cheered on by her sign-waving family. "Go Red !" a child shouted, hoisting a glitter-covered poster with the dog's name.

Red bounded onto the course, tongue lolling, clearly having the time of her life. She clipped one bar and lost focus halfway through, nose to the turf in search of some fascinating scent. Her young handler had to dance and clap wildly to pull her back on course, sending the audience into laughter. Red eventually finished to raucous applause. The announcer gave her time, not the fastest, but the crowd loved her joyful spirit.

One by one, more dogs took their turns. A serious German shepherd stormed through the obstacles with precision, setting an early benchmark. Then a wiry terrier stunned everyone, zipping through the weave poles like a needle through fabric, the crowd "oooh"-ing at each lightning-fast pivot.

Ellie kept glancing at Titan, murmuring encouragements like a mantra. "We can do this. Just have fun. We can do this."

Titan stayed composed, though his heart was pounding harder with each run. His number was coming, lucky #13. He could already feel adrenaline tingling through his paws.

And then, the commotions began. Subtle, controlled, exactly as planned.

- The German shepherd, on what might have been a record-setting pace, suddenly lunged after a food bowl that rolled mysteriously onto the course. The handler dragged him back with effort, losing precious seconds as the audience chuckled at the unplanned "snack break."

- The Jack Russell terrier was blitzing through the weave poles until a tiny red dot danced across the grass. The terrier yipped, pounced, and spun in circles after it, much to the bafflement of the owner. The dot vanished quickly, and the terrier was steered back into the course, but not before the distraction cost him time.

The audience murmured about the odd mishaps but brushed them off as the unpredictable chaos of any pet event.

Ellie furrowed her brow. "Weird, huh?" she whispered to Titan. "Maybe it's the sun reflecting off a watch or phone screen?"

Titan whined softly, licking her hand to calm her. Inside, though, he was impressed. The team was executing their roles flawlessly, and no one seemed suspicious.

Finally, the volunteer at the gate called: "Number 13, Titan and Ellie!"

Ellie stiffened. "That's us. Oh gosh." She wiped her palms on her jeans and led Titan forward.

From the corner of his eye, Titan spotted movement under the bleachers, a faint glint of green cat eyes. Tao was in position, laser ready for Lightning's run. Cleo crouched behind hay bales near the far end of the course, poised to make noise at the perfect moment. Max had drifted near the finish, dragging a spare leash for camouflage, looking every bit like a dog whose owner had just stepped away.

At the start line, Ellie unclipped Titan's leash as per the rules and knelt, her hands trembling slightly. She smiled bravely, eyes glassy with nerves.

"Okay, Titan," she whispered, voice shaking. "Showtime. No matter what happens, you're my hero for getting us this far."

Titan rested a paw on her knee, meeting her gaze with unflinching confidence. *I've got this,* his eyes said.

Ellie nodded, took a deep breath, and stood. The judge signaled, the announcer's voice boomed, and the timer buzzed.

"Go, Titan!" Ellie cried.

Titan exploded forward.

First obstacle: the jump. He soared over it with room to spare, ears streaming back, tail flagging. The crowd whooped at his energy.

"Tunnel, tunnel!" Ellie shouted as she jogged behind. Titan was already halfway through the dark blue tube, bursting out like a rocket. Ahead loomed the A-frame ramp.

Claws clattering against the wooden slats, Titan sprinted upward. At the apex, the entire scene stretched below him, the crowd roaring, Ellie flushed and running, tents scattered across the fairgrounds, and beyond, the city skyline. For one heartbeat, time froze. He was racing as a dog in a human world, absurd and wonderful, and it felt *freeing.*

Then gravity pulled him down the far side, paws landing perfectly in the yellow zone.

Ellie was gasping but keeping up. "Weave, Titan! Weave!" she cried as he approached the poles.

Titan hesitated for only a moment, recalling TV runs: left shoulder against the first pole, snake through tight. His body found the rhythm, left, right, left, right, like he'd been born for it. He cleared the last pole without fault. Ellie squealed, the crowd applauded, and his confidence surged.

Next: the seesaw. Titan braced himself as it tilted beneath him, the sudden slam making his stomach lurch. For a second his paws scrambled, and gasps rose from the stands.

"Easy... easy..." Ellie murmured, hands half-raised.

Titan steadied, riding it down like a surfer, then leapt off clean. The audience clapped with relief.

The tire jump came next, set high, but nothing he couldn't handle. Titan tucked and sailed cleanly through. The announcer's voice spiked with excitement: "This dog is on a mission, folks!"

Last obstacle: the high jump.

Ellie shouted, "Go, Titan! Jump!" Her voice cracked with both fear and exhilaration.

Titan drove forward, gathering every ounce of strength. He launched himself, soaring high above the bars. For a generous moment, he felt weightless, flying. He cleared them effortlessly, landing with power as the timer beeped.

The steward whistled. A clean run.

The crowd erupted.

Ellie rushed in, throwing her arms around Titan in a joyful tackle. She nearly tripped over the last hurdle, but laughter rippled through the stands at her exuberance. Titan barked, wagging furiously, tail thumping so hard it shook his entire body.

For one shining moment, everything was perfect.

The announcer's voice boomed through the loudspeakers:

"What a run! Let's get a time on that... Wow! Titan and Ellie have taken the lead with a blistering 39.4 seconds and no faults! That is the time to beat, folks!"

Ellie gasped, both hands flying to cover her mouth as happy tears prickled her eyes. "Under forty seconds? Oh my gosh, Titan!" Her words came out in a rush, followed by a stream of breathless baby-talk praise. Titan tolerated the embarrassing gush, barely. His tongue lolled out in a huge, goofy grin as he basked in her joy. He was as proud of himself as she was of him.

From the sidelines, Max was silently bouncing in place like an over excited pup, unable to contain himself. Cleo, still in his hidden post, gave a satisfied swish of his tail. And under the bleachers, Luna flicked an ear in quiet triumph, though his green eyes immediately fixed on the one competitor left: Lightning.

Yes, only one dog remained. Lightning, the reigning champion, and his handler, Vanessa Harding, stepped confidently toward the start line. The crowd hushed with anticipation, the air thick with the promise of a showdown. Everyone knew Lightning's reputation: two-time winner, fan favorite, the dog to beat.

As Ellie clipped Titan's leash back on and guided him off the course, they passed close to Vanessa and Lightning. Vanessa gave Ellie a professional but tight smile.

"That was a fantastic run," she admitted, though there was an edge of surprise in her voice. "Especially for a newcomer."

"Th-thanks!" Ellie stammered, still giddy and flushed with adrenaline. "He's... he's really something, isn't he? I'm so proud of him." She scratched Titan between the ears with glowing affection. Titan panted innocently, as if none of this meant anything more than a fun game.

Vanessa's eyes narrowed slightly as she took in Titan's appearance, the lack of specialized gear, the lolling tongue, the casual air. "Rescue dog, I take it?" she asked.

Ellie laughed nervously. "Found him yesterday, actually." The words sounded absurd even to her own ears, and she almost wanted to apologize for how ridiculous it sounded.

"Yesterday?" Vanessa's eyebrows shot upward. For once, the champion handler seemed at a loss. But then Lightning gave an impatient tug on the leash, pulling her back into focus. The professional mask slid neatly into place again. "Well, good luck to you," she said, her tone polite but tinged with the certainty that luck was about to favor her.

Ellie and Titan moved to the fence line to watch. Ellie absently stroked Titan's fur, her earlier nerves returning in full force. "If he's as good as they say… I mean, I won't mind if we get second. But oh wow, Titan, you might actually win this," she whispered, voice trembling with hope.

Titan leaned against her legs, eyes fixed on Lightning. His ears, though, were tuned elsewhere. A faint *mrrp* sounded from under the bleachers, Tao' signal. The sabotage plan was a go.

The announcer's tone shifted to reverence. "Last but certainly not least, our returning champion! Give a warm welcome to Lightning, handled by Vanessa Harding! Can they defend their title?"

The audience erupted in cheers. Lightning stood at the start line like a coiled spring, eyes locked on the course. Vanessa unclipped his leash, posture confident and composed.

"Ready… set… GO!"

Lightning launched like a bullet, a black-and-white blur over the first jump. He tore through the tunnel in a heartbeat, emerging so quickly the crowd gasped in unison. Even Titan had to admit, the dog was fast. His stomach tightened as Lightning attacked the A-frame with breathtaking speed, scaling and descending like a panther.

Then came the first intervention.

At the weave poles, a small red dot flickered on the grass at the far end. Tao' laser danced just enough to catch Lightning's eye. The collie froze for a fraction of a second, paw hovering mid-air, attention snagged by the strange, skittering light. He recovered almost instantly, weaving flawlessly through the poles, but the hesitation was there. Vanessa clapped sharply. "Focus, boy! Go, go!"

Tao flicked the laser off. Mission accomplished.

The seesaw loomed. Lightning bounded onto it with unshakable confidence, too much confidence. At that exact moment, Cleo tipped a precarious stack of plastic bowls behind the concession stand. The crash rang out like a gunshot, followed by the clatter of kibble bouncing across concrete.

Lightning's head snapped toward the noise, just a quick glance, but enough to throw him off. The seesaw slammed down, and his paws slipped for the briefest moment. He caught himself and sprang off, but that half-second stumble had cost him.

The announcer, quick to narrate, remarked, "He seems a bit distracted today, tiny blips in an otherwise polished run."

Ellie gripped the fence so tightly her knuckles turned white. Titan stayed steady, watching with quiet calculation.

Ellie's jaw clenched, her smile gone. "Come on, Lightning!" she urged, her voice sharp with tension.

The Dobermann leapt through the tire jump cleanly, sailing with elegance. One obstacle remained: the high jump.

Max tensed for the final move. Positioned near the edge of the ring, he waited until Lightning was airborne, mid-leap over the final bars. Then he let out a commanding bark, a sound that split the air like a whipcrack:

"BAAARRRK!"

To Lightning, it was everything, a command, an order. Years of rigorous training conditioned him to respond instantly to such cues. In mid-air, confusion hit. Was Vanessa calling him? Was he doing something wrong? Instinct overrode momentum, and he twitched, trying to adjust in flight.

The result: his back paw clipped the top bar. The pole clattered to the ground.

The crowd groaned as one. "Ohhh!" A fault.

Lightning still bolted across the finish, ears pinned back, but the damage was done. Vanessa's face was like stone, every muscle in her jaw locked as she calculated the math in her head. Could their blazing speed still save them?

The announcer drew out the suspense. "Lightning's raw time is... 37.2 seconds! But with the 5-second fault for the bar down... that brings it to 42.2 seconds."

Gasps, murmurs, then cheers erupted. Forty-two point two. Slower than Titan's 39.4.

"That means our winner is Titan, with 39.4 seconds!" the announcer crowed. "The newcomer has unseated the reigning champion!"

The bleachers thundered with applause. The crowd loved an underdog story, and this one was literal. Ellie stood frozen, stunned. "We... we won?" she whispered, as if speaking it might shatter the moment.

Titan barked triumphantly, chest swelling with pride. That was all the confirmation Ellie needed. She squealed, scooped him into a hug, and bounced in circles, laughing and crying all at once. Titan licked her face with joyous abandon, her ponytail whipping as she jumped. They probably looked ridiculous, but to the audience, they looked like champions.

Nearby, fellow competitors and spectators offered congratulations. The man with Luna, the Weimaraner, patted Titan on the head. "Heck of a run, buddy!" he said warmly. Luna herself play-bowed with wagging tail, inviting Titan to join in. Still high on Titany, Titan bowed back with a cheerful *woof,* the perfect picture of a champion who knew he'd earned his win.

Vanessa, meanwhile, took Lightning's leash from a volunteer with a stiff smile. To her credit, she managed to plaster on sportsmanship even though disappointment Cleoed her features. She gave a polite clap for the winners, then turned to pat Lightning. The border collie sat, tail thumping faintly, gazing up at her with apologetic eyes. Vanessa sighed and scratched behind his ears, a silent message: *It's okay. Not your fault.*

Lightning, for his part, was still puzzling over that phantom command he could have sworn he'd heard mid-jump.

The Prize and the Pursuit

The announcer invited Ellie and Titan to the winners' podium at the side of the ring. It was a cheerful, low platform decorated with paw-print decals and balloons. Ellie, cheeks flushed with excitement, guided Titan up the tiny ramp onto the podium marked "1st."

A bubbly representative from Pet Paradise, dressed in a half-dog, half-superhero costume complete with a flowing cape, bounded up to join them, clutching a giant golden trophy shaped like a dog bone.

"Congratulations to our champions!" the emcee boomed into a microphone, his voice carrying over the cheering crowd. He handed Ellie the oversized bone trophy while a second staffer rolled out an enormous bag of dog food, taller than Titan himself, stamped with the words "Lifetime Supply!" For spectacle's sake it looked impressive, though everyone knew the real prize would come as vouchers or deliveries.

Ellie awkwardly balanced the trophy in one arm while keeping her other hand firmly on Titan's collar. She was radiant, grinning ear to ear. Titan sat proudly at her feet, chest puffed out, looking for all the world like a dog who knew he'd just conquered destiny. If ever a mutt had smiled for the cameras, it was Titan at that moment.

"Ladies and gentlemen, let's hear it one more time for Titan and Ellie!" the announcer hollered.

The crowd erupted. Flashbulbs popped. Local press snapped photos of the grinning young woman and her scruffy champion.

After the applause began to taper off, the Pet Paradise rep leaned in with the mic and prompted Ellie: "Would you like to say a few words, ma'am?"

Ellie blinked, startled to find herself suddenly in the spotlight. But the adrenaline still buzzing in her veins gave her courage.

"I, I just want to say, this is such a surprise!" she began, her voice trembling with joy. "I actually only met Titan yesterday. He... well, he sort of found me, and we just clicked." She laughed in disbelief at her own words. "He's an amazing dog. I can't take much credit, he's clearly very special and talented on his own. I'm just lucky he picked me as his partner."

The crowd *awwwed* appreciatively. The local news crew zoomed in close, catching every heartfelt word, while Titan's panting grin and wagging tail stole the frame.

A reporter stepped forward, holding out a mic of her own. "Found him yesterday? That's incredible! What a heartwarming story, folks, a stray dog finds a loving owner and wins it all!"

Ellie nodded, scratching Titan behind the ears as he soaked up the applause. "Yeah, I guess we were meant to be!" she said brightly. "Thank you to Pet Paradise and the event organizers. Titan is going to be eating like a king, that's for sure." She lifted the novelty check, made out to "Titan the Dog – 1 Lifetime Supply of Kibble", and flashed another broad smile for the cameras.

On the sidelines, Tao observed the hoopla from beneath the bleachers, safely tucked out of sight. "Adorable," he muttered, half-sarcastic, though his twitching Tao betrayed a begrudging warmth. Against all odds, one of their own stood center stage, in the spotlight for something good.

Cleo, perched in the shade of the announcer's stand, wasn't as charmed. His yellow eyes swept the periphery. With the contest over, people were drifting away toward the rest of the expo, but his instincts prickled. "We should be moving soon," he murmured in Tao' direction. His tone was cautious, the thrill of Titan's victory already giving way to old vigilance. "Too many eyes on them... on us."

Tao nodded. The black cat knew he was right. The longer Titan remained in front of cameras, the more likely someone unfriendly would take notice. "Let's retrieve Max and get to the rendezvous point," he said.

Max was nearby, still close to the prize display. The pit bull mix had taken it upon himself to "liberate" part of their winnings. In the confusion, he'd dragged two hefty bags of Top

Dawg kibble into a shaded spot behind a banner. *Might as well stock up while the humans are distracted,* he thought, licking his lips.

Ellie eventually stepped down from the podium with Titan, making way for the runners-up. The Pet Paradise rep followed, clipboard in hand.

"Congrats again!" he said cheerfully. "Now, about that lifetime supply, we can arrange monthly deliveries to your address, or, if you prefer, you can take some of it now. Totally your call!"

Ellie laughed nervously, still dazed from the attention. "I don't think all that will fit in my car! Maybe just one or two bags to start? I can come by the store to work out the rest."

"Absolutely!" the rep said, signaling another staffer. Together they hefted two fifty-pound bags into Ellie's arms, bags that were suspiciously lighter than expected. Max, having hollowed one out for a secret stash, trotted innocently nearby, cheeks bulging with smuggled kibble.

Ellie staggered under the weight until a volunteer kindly took them from her. "Let's load these into your car, ma'am," the volunteer offered.

"Oh, thank you so much," Ellie replied, leading the way to the parking lot. Titan strutted at her side, the novelty check tucked under her arm and the oversized bone trophy clutched under the other. Overburdened but glowing with joy, she looked utterly endearing.

Reporters followed, peppering her with questions. "What kind of mix is he?" "Where did you say you found him?" "Will you enter him in more competitions?"

Ellie answered as best she could, though her story of "found him yesterday" left many wide-eyed. "Honestly, I think someone must have trained him before... or he's just naturally brilliant," she admitted, smiling down at Titan. At that very moment, Titan clamped the golden bone trophy in his teeth and paraded along, making photographers burst with delight at the image.

Titan's friends faded into the night and carefully gathered away from the crowd. Cleo slinked along fences, Tao slipped behind parked cars, and Max alone blended into a departing cluster of dogs. He shed his borrowed leash near a trash bin, walking free once more.

Then Cleo froze under the Cleo of a pickup. His fur bristled. At the far end of the lot, a black van had pulled in, its side panel marked with a subtle geometric logo, something that looked like a brain made of interlocking nodes. Pet-link.

His heart dropped.

Two men stood by the van, scanning the dispersing crowd. They looked casual in navy windbreakers and caps, but the earpieces and stiff postures told another story. One was tall and broad-shouldered, Cleo recognized him instantly as the security officer who had nearly caught him during their escape weeks ago. The other, lean with glasses, was unmistakable: Dr. Clayburn, one of the scientists.

Both men looked tense. The taller one spoke quickly into a phone, then pointed toward Ellie and Titan at the edge of the crowd.

Cleo's blood ran cold. *They've been found.*

He darted back and intercepted Tao beneath a parked SUV. His eyes were wide. "Pet-link van. North side of the lot. Two agents. I think they've spotted Titan."

Tao felt as though ice water had been dumped in his stomach. "Already? How," He cut himself short. No time to speculate. "We have to get Titan out. Now."

Max joined them, his teeth bared as soon as he caught sight of the van. "Those lab rats... how did they track us here?"

"Later," Tao hissed. His brain was already spinning through contingencies. "Cleo, warn Titan. Max and I will stall the agents."

The team split without hesitation. Cleo melted into the rows of cars, racing toward Ellie's vehicle. Tao and Max veered toward the Pet-link men, who had started walking briskly, closing in on their target.

Ellie had just reached her car, where the volunteer was hefting the second giant bag of dog food into her trunk beside the first.

"There you go!" he said cheerily, dusting his hands. "All set. And congrats again."

"Thank you so much!" Ellie responded brightly. She tucked the trophy and oversized check into the trunk as well, then wiped her brow, still buzzing on adrenaline. "What a day, huh, Titan?"

She bent down to ruffle Titan's fur, only to realize her dog's attention had locked elsewhere. His ears pricked forward, his body stiffening at something behind them.

In a blur, Cleo burst out from under a nearby car and nearly collided with Titan's front paws. The sleek black cat skidded to a halt, green eyes blazing with urgency as he looked up at the shepherd mix.

Titan froze, muscles rigid. *"Cleo? What?"*

The cat wasted no time. He yowled loud and sharp, an urgent *MRAOW!* that to Ellie sounded like nothing more than the start of a parking lot catfight.

Ellie startled backward. A puffed-up black cat was practically at her feet, fur bristling and eyes wild. "Oh! Hey, little guy,"

But Cleo ignored her completely. He yowled again, the sound more layered and desperate this time. To Titan's ears it translated with crystal clarity: *"Trouble! Pet-link! RUN!"*

That was all Titan needed. Out of the corner of his eye he caught movement, two figures in navy uniforms closing in fast between the parked cars. One of them met his gaze directly, locking onto him like a predator.

It felt like lightning struck through Titan's veins. Instinct overrode everything. Without hesitation, he lunged forward, yanking so hard against the leash that it ripped free of Ellie's grip.

"Titan?!" Ellie cried, her fingers stinging as the leash tore through them. She stumbled forward, stunned. In the next heartbeat her champion dog bolted across the lot at full speed. "Titan! Stop!" she shouted, her heart dropping into her stomach.

Guilt twisted in Titan's chest at her voice. *I'm sorry, Ellie!* he thought desperately, wishing he could explain. Instead, he barked twice, a sharp, apologetic cry, and kept running.

Cleo darted ahead, guiding him toward the gap in the chain-link fence they had scouted earlier. Titan galloped after him, leash flapping and bouncing behind. In seconds, the two slipped through the fence and vanished into the brush.

Behind them, Ellie was in tears, sprinting toward the gap. "Titan! Titan, come back!" Her voice cracked with panic, confusion, heartbreak. Only moments ago, he had been calm, triumphant, what had changed?

She was about to push through the fence when the volunteer caught up, alarmed. "What happened?"

"He just... he just bolted!" Ellie stammered, her voice wobbling. "Something spooked him, a cat, I think? I have to get him!"

The volunteer widened the wires for her. "Careful, those edges, I'll help you look!"

Neither of them noticed the two men in navy had nearly reached them, only to halt when their target escaped into the woods. The taller officer, Mills, muttered a curse and spoke sharply into his wrist radio:

"Subject Titan in motion. Heading east into wooded area. Possible accomplice cat in sight. Pursuing on foot."

Ellie *did* notice when one of the men suddenly seized her arm just as she ducked through the fence.

"Ma'am, step aside," Mills barked. His grip was firm his eyes fixed on the fence gap. He flashed a badge, though in Ellie's confusion, she barely registered it. "We'll handle this. Please step back."

Handle what? Ellie's pulse spiked. She yanked her arm free, fear and anger colliding. "Who are you? That's my dog! Let me go!"

Dr. Clayburn raised his hands in a placating gesture. "Miss, that dog is property of Pet-Link, "

"Property?!" Ellie repeated, bewildered, fury rising.

The volunteer immediately stepped in, protective. "Hey, what's going on here?"

Before anyone could answer, chaos exploded. Max barreled into view from the far side of the lot, a snarling brown blur. He lunged straight at Dr. Clayburn and clamped down hard on the man's pant leg with bone-crunching force.

"GAH!" Clayburn howled, tumbling backward as his trousers ripped wide open, leaving his pale legs flailing in the open air.

Mills yanked a taser from his belt and trained it on the German Shepard mix. "Back off!"

But Max released the pant leg only to growl low and dangerous, planting himself squarely between the men and the fence gap.

Ellie's mind reeled. First her dog bolts, then strangers with badges appear, and now a stray German Shepard was attacking the, wasn't that the large dog she'd seen earlier? Who now was apparently defending *her?* Or attacking them? The world had gone mad.

At that exact moment, Luna struck. With perfect feline timing, the gray tabby leapt onto Mills from behind and raked claws across the man's backside.

Mills let out a yelp, convulsing forward as the taser discharged with a sharp *Pop!* The prongs shot wide, crackling harmlessly in a bush.

Max didn't hesitate. He lunged upward, teeth snapping around the taser, and ripped it from Mills' grip. He flung it across the asphalt where it skittered under a parked car.

Dr. Clayburn, still sprawled on the ground, could only gape as the Shepard seemed to *wink* at him before bounding away, Tao close at his heels. Both animals disappeared into the tree line in seconds.

Mills cursed, spinning around, his rear end bleeding from claw marks.

By now, bystanders were gathering. "Is everything okay?!" someone called. They saw Ellie distraught, Clayburn on the ground half-exposed, and Mills swearing as he clutched his butt. Confusion rippled across the lot.

Their cover blown, Mills hauled Clayburn upright.

"We have to go after them!" Clayburn sputtered, his face red with fury.

"Not here," Mills snapped. "Too many civilians." He yanked the scientist toward their van, growling at Ellie and the volunteer: "Federal business. Stay out of it."

The van screeched away, tires squealing as they tried to cut off the animals from another angle.

Ellie stood trembling, confusion swirling with fear. *Federal business? Property?* None of it made sense. "I–I have to find my dog," she whispered, more to herself than anyone else. Without waiting, she ducked through the fence and sprinted into the woods, tears streaming.

Deeper in the woods, Titan ran like a streak of gold, Cleo a black blur just ahead. They crashed through underbrush and leapt over logs, panic propelling them forward. After several hundred yards, Cleo angled them into a dry creek bed, hoping to break the trail.

Moments later, Max and Tao appeared from a side path. Max panted hard, shoulder sore from body-slamming Clayburn, while Tao shook a burr from his fur, tail still puffed.

They regrouped in a hidden clearing shielded by briars and pine. Titan skidded to a halt, sides heaving. Max flopped down, exhausted but alert. Cleo climbed a stump, scanning the back trail for pursuit. Tao barely caught his breath before exploding in frustration.

"They found us! I can't believe they found us so fast!" His fur bristled twice its size. "That was them, right? You saw the logo?"

Titan nodded grimly. "It was them. Cleo warned me just in time."

Max tried to lighten the moment, though his voice still shook. "You should've seen their faces when I tore into 'em. Gave 'em a good scare." He let out a short, nervous laugh. "But they'll be back on us soon. We gotta keep moving."

Titan finally let the reality sink in: they had won their prize, but Pet-link was already on their heels again. Then another pain, sharper than fear, cut through him, Ellie. He had left her behind without explanation, without protection. He pictured her frightened and confused, calling his name in desperation. The thought made his throat tighten and his chest ache.

"Ellie…" he murmured, ears drooping low.

Through the trees, faint but clear, her voice still echoed. *"Daaash!, please!"* The sound carried heartbreak, tearing at him with every syllable.

Tao padded close and rested a paw gently on Titan's leg. His own ears tilted back with sympathy. "I'm sorry, Titan. But you saved her from being pulled into this. If we'd stayed, those men would've cornered her too. Maybe even hurt her. It's better she thinks you just… ran."

Titan squeezed his eyes shut, the guilt like a heavy stone pressing down. "Better for her, maybe," he whispered. "But she's probably broken hearted. She really cared about me, and I…" His voice cracked. "I cared about her too."

Max rose and leaned against him, offering the steady weight of his shoulder. "I know, bud. I know you liked her. She was a good human."

"She would have been a great owner," Titan admitted, his tail limp. He allowed himself a moment to grieve, to mourn the hopes of curling at Ellie's feet, of sharing quiet evenings together, of not having to say goodbye so soon.

Cleo hopped down from his lookout stump, eyes sharp as ever. "The coast looks clear for now. But we can't linger. The van went east, we'll cut south."

Tao forced a brightness into his tone, his Tao twitching. "Come on. We didn't come out empty-pawed." He nodded toward the object Max still clutched stubbornly: one hefty bag of *Top Dawg Kibble*, soggy with slobber, dusted with pine needles, but intact.

Despite everything, Titan let out a huff of laughter. "You actually dragged that all the way here?"

Max wagged his tail, trying to play off the soreness in his shoulder. "No dog left behind. And by dog, I mean dog food." He flashed a grin around the bag.

Even Cleo cracked a smile. "Our prize, at least in part. Not a lifetime supply, but enough to keep us fed for a while."

Titan mustered a determined nod. "We paid dearly for that bag. It'll taste all the sweeter."

Ellie's cries grew fainter, drifting westward as she searched the wrong trail. Titan's heart clenched. He pictured her stumbling through the brush, tears in her eyes, calling his name into the emptiness. He prayed the volunteer, or anyone, would help her back to safety. Perhaps, in time, she would heal. Maybe she'd even walk into a shelter one day and give another lonely pup the love she had shown him. The thought, bittersweet as it was, gave him the tiniest sliver of solace.

He looked at the three pairs of eyes fixed on him, eyes that held trust, loyalty, and concern. They had risked everything for him today. And he for them.

Titan straightened, lifting his head, shoulders squaring with resolve. "Alright," he said, voice steadier now. "We stick together. Always. At least we have food this time." He managed a weak smile. "Not a lifetime's worth, but we'll make it stretch."

Max hefted the kibble bag proudly like a hunter with his prize. Cleo slipped ahead, melting into the underbrush. Tao fell into step beside Titan, brushing his flank with his tail-tip in silent reassurance.

"You know," Tao said after a beat, glancing sideways, "if Pet-link thinks they can haul us back, they've got another thing coming. We're a savvy crew now."

Titan's lips twitched into a smile. "Pulled off a dog show heist and bagged ourselves dinner. That's not exactly on most résumés."

Max grumbled through the bag, "Next time, let's aim for a lifetime supply of steak."

Cleo chuckled softly. "One mission at a time, big guy."

The ten of them pressed deeper into the woods. Sunlight slanted through the trees in fading golden stripes, painting the ground in shifting patterns of light and Cleo. From somewhere near the fairgrounds, sirens wailed faintly, maybe animal control, maybe more Pet-link agents. Either way, the noise urged them onward.

Titan cast one last look over his shoulder. Through the trees, the city's outline shimmered against the horizon. For a fleeting instant, he imagined Ellie on a park bench, scanning every dog that passed, wondering why the best one she'd ever met had vanished.

"Thank you, Ellie," he whispered, hoping the breeze might somehow carry the words to her. She had given him kindness. A glimpse of a normal life. That would have to be enough.

Then he turned forward, into whatever waited ahead. The Cleos of evening gathered, but Titan's heart burned with a new steadiness.

Tao poked him lightly. "Hey. Next hideout? Something without spiders this time."

"An abandoned barn," Cleo suggested. "I could live with hay."

"Anywhere is fine," Titan said, picking up the pace. His voice carried a weight of finality and hope. "As long as we're free."

Max rumbled agreement through his mouthful of kibble.

Step by weary step, they left Raleigh behind. They had survived the impossible once more. Their prize might have dragged them into trouble, but they were still standing. Still free. And together, they were stronger than Pet-link could ever imagine, a scrappy, stubborn family forged in escape and survival.

As the last rays of sun dipped below the North Carolina horizon, the four figures melted into dusk. The forest swallowed their tracks. Whatever tomorrow brought, they would meet it side by side, swift paws, sharp claws, quick wits, humor intact, and, for once, bellies not entirely empty.

Their adventure was far from over. Tomorrow was a new day. And every dog, every cat, too, would have its day.

Chapter 6

CARNIVAL OF ANIMALS

Strange Sights and Scents

A chorus of crickets sang through the North Carolina woods as seven dogs and three cats padded quietly beneath the pines. The night air was thick with the scent of damp leaves and distant honeysuckle, but another aroma had the group's collective noses twitching: something oily, sweet, and utterly foreign to the wild.

Max lifted his snout and sniffed hard, his ears tilting forward. "You smell that?" he whispered.

Daisy, a golden retriever with gentle eyes, inhaled deeply and let out a slow canine grin. "Funnel cake… and corn dogs, if I'm not mistaken," she murmured.

The cats trailing behind cocked their heads with intrigue. Titan the Dobermann who used to be a Marine, squinted into the distance. Sure enough, a faint glow flickered against the star-scattered sky ahead.

Peeking out from behind a stand of rhododendrons, the group beheld a sight that felt like stumbling into a fever dream:

neon lights twinkling beyond the treeline, accompanied by faint, tinny carnival music carried on the breeze.

"Is that... a carnival?" Winston whispered. He wore a perpetually worried look. "Smells like a deep-fried heart attack waiting to happen. My cholesterol's rising just sniffing it." Despite his grumble, Winston's nose quivered eagerly at the greasy perfume of funnel cakes and popcorn.

Chai, stepped forward with cautious authority. "Could be trouble," he growled softly. "Where there's a carnival, there are humans. And where there are humans..." His warning trailed off, but everyone knew how it ended: Pet-link could be anywhere, hunting for the ten mysteriously missing people who now wore fur and padded on four legs. Chai's eyes scanned the woods behind them, every muscle taut with vigilance.

Still, hunger and curiosity were powerful forces. Peanut, actually drooled at the medley of scents swirling in the night air. "Trouble? It smells like heaven, man," he whispered. "I swear I can already taste the corn dogs."

Cleo, flicked her tail in restrained annoyance. "We should be careful," she cautioned, her voice hushed and melodic. But even Tao's stomach betrayed her with a low rumble.

In the end, temptation won. Moving as a unit, the ten former humans crept through the underbrush toward the lights. Their paws and claws moved silently over pine needles, a skill they had honed since their strange transformation. The closer they drew, the louder the music and the sharper the scents, until their instincts burned with anticipation.

Picasso, let out an excited yip before clamping his jaws shut. she ducked her head sheepishly. Even on the run, it was hard to contain excitement.

Under the Big Top Lights

The carnival was mostly deserted at this late hour. Colored bulbs traced the outlines of rides and booths, casting long shadows over trampled grass. In the center loomed a Ferris wheel, its lights blinking in hypnotic patterns and reflecting off a low bank of clouds.

The group skirted the perimeter fence until Max found a gap big enough to squeeze through. One by one, they wriggled under the chain-link.

Luna, quipped as Max nudged his hindquarters through: "Breaking into a carnival after hours. Just when I thought my Friday nights couldn't get any weirder."

Inside, they huddled behind a row of parked bumper cars, drinking in the strange world. The smells were intoxicating: grease, sugar, popcorn, and the tang of spilled soda mixed into a dizzying bouquet. Titan's stomach growled so loudly Luna shot him a look.

"Sorry," he whispered. "Hard to stay dignified when funnel cakes on the line."

Luna noted, "Fun fact: under perfect conditions, dogs can smell things from twenty kilometers away."

Titan twitched his Tao. "So, about twelve and a half miles."

Picasso whistled low through his jowls. "No wonder we followed it straight here."

They slinked deeper, weaving past booths. A ring toss counter stood to their left, strewn with abandoned plastic rings. Stuffed-animal prizes dangled lifelessly from hooks. A grinning clown face, painted on plywood, caught the shifting light. Luna's fur puffed, his tail bottle-brushing. "C-creepy," she muttered, trying to disguise her unease with a grooming swipe.

Next came a cotton candy stand. The air was thick and pink with sugar. A paper cone of candy floss had melted into a fluffy blob on the ground. Luna sniffed it longingly. "Haven't had cotton candy since I was a kid," she said softly. She dared a lick, only to end up with a bright pink nose. Daisy and Titan stifled barks of laughter as she pawed at her snout, muttering, "Great. I'm a marshmallow mutt now."

Moments later, Daisy struck gold under a fried food stall: a whole corn dog abandoned in a trash bin. He emerged triumphantly, grease glistening on his Tao. "Sacrilege to throw this away!" she declared, devouring it in two bites.

Luna wrinkled her nose. "That can't be sanitary."

"Five-second rule," Daisy mumbled. "Give or take a few thousand seconds."

Soon the others scavenged their own treasures: Max gnawed a caramel apple, Titan nibbled cold fries on a picnic table, Daisy tore at a turkey leg, and Luna proudly dragged out a nacho tray. For a while, they feasted like kings at a banquet of junk food, tails wagging, Tao twitching, muzzles sticky. Peanut and Picasso wrestled over a Double Cheese Burger. They conceded one patty to each in the end. Still amazed at the senses they possessed as dogs.

Titan licked mustard off his muzzle and sighed happily. "I've never enjoyed corporate catering half as much as this."

Raccoon Ruckus

Titan's joke was still lingering when Cleo froze, eyes narrowing. "Guys... we're not alone," she whispered.

From behind a garbage can waddled a chunky raccoon clutching a pretzel, with a smaller one beside it chewing funnel cake. The raccoons froze. The ten ex-humans froze. For a second, it was a Tense standoff, predators on one side, scavengers on the other, the night air heavy with tension.

The big raccoon narrowed its eyes. Titan, unable to resist curiosity, took one step forward. That was enough.

With a furious chitter, the raccoon hurled its pretzel. It bounced off Titan's forehead with a dull thud.

"Hey!" Titan yelped, stunned.

The raccoons bolted.

Daisie's instincts kicked in. "Oh no you don't!" he barked, charging after them.

Chaos erupted. Dogs thundered across the midway, cats streaked after them, claws clicking on the asphalt. The raccoons zigzagged expertly, knocking over tin cans at a shooting gallery, scampering over booth roofs, even scattering prize racks in their wake.

Luna bounded after one, hissing, "We just want to talk, you little bandits!", which, predictably, persuaded no one.

Max barreled through the clanging cans muttering, "Sorry, sorry!" as if apologizing to pedestrians. Titan and Luna in hot pursuit. Daisy growled for quiet, but his order was drowned in the ruckus.

At last, the raccoons slipped through a plywood gap beyond the food court and vanished into the woods, leaving the panting, disheveled band of fugitives surrounded by toppled booths and the echo of carousel music.

Daisy skidded to a halt beside an upturned cotton candy cart, chest heaving and tongue lolling. "Well... that happened," he puffed, still catching his breath.

Tao gave him a withering look; her fur dusted with popcorn kernels and bits of paper. "Chasing raccoons? Really? We're supposed to be laying low," she scolded.

Daisy drooped, ears sagging. "Sorry. Reflex."

Winston shook his head, still listening for signs that their racket had drawn unwanted attention. Luna, perched dramatically on a barrel as though it were a stage, groomed his ruffled fur and sighed. "I can't believe we just debuted as our own circus act... starring us."

As if on cue, a new sound sliced through the night, the squeal of a metal door and a distant voice.

Daisy's ears swiveled. A man's gruff call echoed across the empty midway: "Hello? Anyone there?"

Wide-eyed glances shot around the group. Their supersensitive ears picked up the jingle of keys and the crunch of gravel long before the guard appeared.

"Scatter and hide!" Daisy breathed.

In an instant, the pack melted into the shadows. Titan and Luna slipped under a painted concession trailer, while Tao and Cleo tucked themselves behind a teetering stack of folding chairs. and Tom pressed flat against the side of the carousel ticket booth. Daisy herded Picasso and Peanut into a dark alley between tents. Tao, her Siamese coat blending effortlessly with Cleo and light, slunk behind a humming generator at the fence line.

A flashlight beam swept across the midway. The security guard, a burly man in a ball cap, walked slowly, boots crunching, light dancing over the knocked-over cotton candy cart and scattered cans. He frowned, scratching his head. "Darn raccoons," he muttered. With a grunt, he righted the cart and nudged a can aside with his boot.

None of the twenty watchful eyes peering from the darkness so much as blinked.

After a tense moment, the guard shrugged and turned back. "Ain't worth my time." The metal door clanged shut behind him, leaving the carnival in silence once more.

One by one, the Wolves of New York crept from their hiding spots. Heartbeats slowed, tails un-tucked.

"Everyone okay?" Max whispered.

Soft affirmatives answered him. Lisa pawed the last bit of pretzel from Titan's head. Daisy exhaled in relief, though his protective instinct made her add sternly, "We're extremely lucky he blamed the raccoons and didn't look harder."

Luna hopped down from his barrel, stretching with deliberate nonchalance. "On the bright side," he said breezily, "we gave the raccoons a run for their money. If this whole evading capture thing doesn't work out, we could have a future in carnival entertainment. Coming soon to a town near you: *The Amazing Talking Animal Escapees!*" His green eyes sparkled. "We do our own stunts."

Titan smiled as happy as he could be, and even Daisy allowed herself a reluctant grin.

The Fortune-Telling Goat

Still catching their breath, the group edged toward the far side of the carnival, aiming for the tree line. Slipping between a garish carousel and the faded "Haunted House" trailer, they stumbled upon a smaller tent draped with mystic symbols and strings of twinkling Christmas lights.

A weathered sign announced:

Madame Orla's Mystifying Menagerie, Fortunes Told by the Amazing Psychic Goat!

And there it was, a goat. A real, live goat, white with black patches, horns curling back, standing lazily behind a low fence. It was chewing on a torn strip of poster paper, utterly unbothered by the late hour or the unlikely company of seven dogs and three cats.

Luna, naturally, broke the silence first. He hopped to the fence and addressed the goat in a mock-serious tone. "Oh, wise and mystical goat, we beseech thee. Tell us our fortunes!"

The goat paused its chewing, blinked once, then let out a long, phlegmy bleaaaat.

Titan snorted. "What'd it say, Luna? I don't speak goat."

Luna cleared his throat with dignity. "Obviously, it said: *'Strangers, your future is... unclear.'*"

The goat bleated again, shorter this time, and tore another bite of poster. Emily tilted her head, golden ears flopping. "Sounded like a no to me."

Titan, ever pragmatic, checked for wandering staff. Seeing none, he joined in the bit. "Great Goat of Destiny," he said in mock reverence, "do we stand a chance against the big bad Pet-link team?"

The goat stopped chewing, staring with unsettlingly square pupils. It lifted a hoof and stomped once. *Thump.* Then it raised its head and bleated loudly into the night.

"Mbaaa!"

Titan blinked. "Was that... a yes? Or a battle cry?"

Daisy chuckled. "Could be goat for *'you betcha.'*"

Tao allowed herself a soft purr of amusement. "I'll take that as a good omen."

Max trotted forward, ears perked. "Oh, mystical one, will I ever get a warm bed and a real meal cooked just for me again?" His voice wavered between humor and genuine yearning.

The goat tilted its head at him, then released a long, almost sympathetic bleat, before bending down to nibble at a discarded popcorn box.

"That sounded like a yes," Lisa said with a wag of her tail.

Titan managed a sheepish grin. "Guess the goat thinks our luck will turn around."

For a moment, the group was quiet, the silly oracle's "answer" striking a tender chord. Safety, warmth, food, it was all any of them really wanted.

The goat, prophecy dispensed, tore down the rest of its poster in a shower of paper scraps.

"I think that's our cue," Emily whispered.

Titan gave a polite nod. "Thank you for your... guidance."

The goat belched. Titan barely stifled his laugh as they slipped past the tent.

One by one, they wriggled through the fence and back into the woods. As Henry crawled out last, he glanced back. The fortune-teller's lights glimmered faintly, the goat's silhouette still calmly chewing. For an absurd second, it looked like the old creature was watching them go.

Henry huffed at himself. Since when did he believe in signs? And yet, a small flicker of hope stirred inside him.

Campfire Comedy in the Woods

Half an hour later, the group had put safe distance between themselves and the carnival. Deep in the woods, they settled in a mossy clearing. The adrenaline of the night gave way to exhaustion, but also to an odd giddiness. They had eaten their fill of junk food, outwitted humans, and even consulted a fortune-telling goat.

In the silver glow of moonlight, the ten companions formed a loose circle.

Luna, tail high, strutted to the center like it was a stage. "Ladies and gentlemen, welcome to Comedy Night at Camp Chaos, featuring... us!" He bowed low. Dogs woofed, cats tapped their tails in applause.

"In all seriousness," Luna continued, dropping into a warmer tone, "I think we could all use a laugh. It's been a weird, wild day. So... who's up for some stand-up comedy? Emphasis on *stand,* since, well..." He gestured to his four legs and earned chuckles. "We're all technically stand-up comics now."

Max sat back on his haunches, grinning. "You want us to... tell jokes?" The idea was so absurd it made perfect sense.

"Exactly!" Luna's eyes gleamed. "We've got material for days. New perspectives on old lives." He cleared his throat and launched in: "Hi, I'm Luna, and I'm a workaholic-turned-housecat."

Laughter rippled around the circle.

"I used to think I was climbing the corporate ladder. Now I climb trees. Turns out the view's better." More laughter. "Back in marketing, I had to sell products like they were the best thing since sliced bread. Now my strategy is giving sad kitty eyes whenever I want food. And let me tell you , it's fool-proof."

He mimed a pitiful kitten face, making the whole group break down. Even Daisy barked out a rare laugh.

Luna bowed. "Thank you, thank you. I'll be here all night. Literally. Max, care to take the bone? Or the mic?"

Max trotted forward. Speaking in court had been second nature to him, but telling jokes as a dog to his friends under moonlight? That was new.

"Hi, I'm Max," he began. "I used to be a Marine. Now I'm just a dog without a boat that nobody cares about." Groans of laughter rippled through the group.

"I used to sing the wrong song during drills. Now I just say *'Woof!'* And honestly? People take me more seriously this way." He puffed up his chest, gave a sharp bark, and the others clapped paws against the earth.

He continued, warming to his theme. "As a marine, I spent years chasing bad guys. Now I just chase my own tail. Far less effort and paperwork." That line earned appreciative barks and meows. He added, "Oh, and those jokes about marines? Totally true in my case. Except now I actually do chase the siren when I hear one. Can't help it." Max finished with a toothy grin, tail wagging in time with his humor. His friends whooped (or yowled, in the cats' case), cheering him on with genuine delight.

Next up was Daisy. The golden retriever trotted forward, tail swishing behind her, and positioned herself in the circle's center. "I'm Daisy, and I'm a student, or, well, used to be. Now I guess I'm technically an unlicensed animal." She winked, earning an immediate ripple of laughter. "Which is fine, because all my partners these days are mostly animals, present company included."

Chai let out a chuckle. Titan exaggerated a cough; paw pressed dramatically to his chest as though demanding medical attention.

Daisy rolled with it. "In my human life, I worked many shifts that went all night. Now I'm pulling an all-nighter roaming the woods. The pay's a lot worse, but at least the professors bite less… usually." She flicked her gaze toward Daisy, recalling how he nearly clamped down on a Pet-link scientist's leg during their daring escape last month.

"I was provoked!" Daisy blurted, holding his paws up defensively. The circle broke into laughter again.

Daisy grinned and leaned into her finale. "Seriously, though, I used to stress over everything in my life and dealing exams and course work. These days? No paperwork!" She swiped a paw through the air in mock triumph. I can literally lick everything in school. Don't recommend that for human, by the way." Dogs panted with laughter; cats flicked tails in amusement.

Then came Peanut's turn. The Pug shuffled forward, his belly dragging ever so slightly as he planted himself in the spotlight. "I'm Peanut," he sighed in an exaggerated drawl, "and I survived years in middle management. Now I'm enjoying my demotion to stray dog." A chorus of giggles rose from the circle. Peanut straightened his posture and tugged at an imaginary tie knotted around his furry neck.

"Every morning, I used to take a crowded bus to a tiny cubicle and dream of escaping to nature. Well... wish granted! Except now my cubicle is a bush, and the only buzzing fluorescent light is the fireflies." Right on cue, a few fireflies drifted across the clearing, their glow punctuating his line. "Also, I had a boss who was always breathing down my neck. These days, the only thing breathing down my neck is Daisy when he thinks I've got a snack I'm not sharing."

"Hey!" Daisy protested, and the group erupted in laughter. Picasso wagged his stubby tail with satisfaction.

"I wrote so many reports and emails that nobody read. Now when I bark, at least someone pays attention, even if it's just to tell me to shush. Honestly, running for our lives aside, I don't miss the Monday meetings at all."

A collective cheer rose. Clearly, no one missed meetings.

Chai padded forward next, coat gleaming in the moonlight. She sat as if at the front of a classroom, posture precise, tail curled neatly around her paws. "Hello, I'm Chai. Software engineer." A respectful hush fell. Several dogs even dipped their heads slightly, instinctively recognizing the patience and grit it took to manage technology projects.

Chai smiled warmly. "Thank you, thank you. Honestly, managing a pack of animals in the woods isn't so different from managing my team. Lots of running, occasional biting, nobody wants to sit still... The main difference is that now I'm the one licking myself to stay clean."

Titan nearly toppled over laughing.

Chai pressed on, eyes sparkling with mischief. "Programmer conferences used to terrify me. But facing down an angry mama bear over territory? Way less scary, trust me. At least out here if someone has a bad day, I don't have to clean it up" The dogs exchanged guilty side glances, sparking another round of laughter.

Finally, she softened her tone. "In all seriousness, I think I prefer this. She stepped back, earning approving chuffs and meows.

Titan padded forward after her, habitually pushing an invisible pair of glasses up his nose. "I'm Titan. Marine. Now full-time dog, putting out fires for our merry band." He gave a mock bow. "You wouldn't believe it, but listening to a drill Sargeant was actually more confusing than chasing raccoons at 3 AM." The group howled with laughter.

"I used to complain about dinner being lousy. Now my biggest is stealing *dinner because* I can't mentally connect with the squirrel I'm trying to catch for dinner. The guy just doesn't respond to my input."

"Have you tried turning it off and on again?" Luna quipped.

Titan snapped his paw in mock revelation. "That's it! Next time I catch a squirrel, I'll control-alt-delete him." Groans and chuckles blended together.

Titan grinned, pressing on. "Seriously, I spent most of my human life training to be a soldier, living on energy drinks. Now I've got night vision and endless energy after dark. It's like I got upgraded to the ultimate night-owl operating system. And the graphics out here in nature? Unreal, and I don't mean the engine." Max smiled at the gamer reference while the others tilted their heads, half-clueless. Titan exited with paw-stomping applause.

Cleo bounded forward next, tail wagging. "I'm Cleo, and I used to be a doctor. Now I specialize in marking my territory, she lifted a leg in mock demonstration ", We now have problems of a different kind!" The circle howled with laughter.

"Back in the office, my job was to make medicine sound exciting. Now my patients pay me in Kibble. I don't even have to advertise, one howl and the whole forest will know I'm here." She winked. "At work I obsessed over bandages. Now I'm more worried about branding in the literal sense, please, no microchips, thank you." The group groaned knowingly at the reminder of Pet-link's obsession with tagging them.

Chloe wagged on. "I also used to schedule endless meetings. Now my daily agenda is: wake up under a bush, run for our lives, forage for food, share a heartfelt chat, sleep on leaves. Repeat. Honestly, it's simpler than Outlook and way more fun than team-building retreats!" Several dogs barked approvingly; even the cats agreed silently that a trust fund could never beata freedom. Cleo gave a playful curtsey and hopped back.

Winston hesitated before stepping forward. Normally stern and vigilant, the French Bulldog surprised the group with a shy smile. "Uh, I'm Winston. I was a lawyer, for a military contractor. I used to handle criminal cases in the service. Funny twist, huh? Now I am the K9.and I think the humans believe I am the criminal the way they are acting"

The crowd rumbled with appreciation.

Winston continued. "And I'll admit, I've got way more sympathy for the police dogs now. I used to bark orders like, 'Quiet!

Sit still! Chase that suspects!' Now if someone told me to sit still… well, okay, I still would, because I'm a good boy, His deadpan delivery shattered the circle into laughter. Even Daisy broke into a grin.

"I want to patrol high-security zones. Now I patrol the woods, keeping you all out of trouble." He shot a mock stern glance at Titan and Max, their raccoon-chasing spree still fresh. Another wave of laughter. "Honestly, the stakes feel higher now. But at least if I smell something suspicious, I don't need a warrant. I just go check it out." He sniffed theatrically. "Yep, smells like… no paperwork and zero bureaucracy. Works for me." Applause met his bow, and Winston retreated, tail wagging proudly.

At last, Picasso bounded forward, energy practically spilling out of his wiry frame. "Hi, I'm Picasso, and I used to be a college intern and artist. Which basically meant I fetched coffee and got paid in experience. Now I fetch sticks and don't get paid at all." He beamed, tongue lolling.

"I thought being at the bottom of the corporate ladder was rough. But that was nothing compared to literally rolling in mud every day. And you know what? I prefer the mud." Cheers erupted. "No student loans, no finals, no rent, and definitely no pants."

"Pants are overrated!" Titan called, setting off giggles.

Picasso nodded furiously. "Exactly! I used to pull all-nighters gaming or cramming for exams. Now I'm up all-night dodging tranquilizer darts. And let me tell you, that's way more adrenaline-pumping than pop quizzes." He shook his head with mock solemnity. "But seriously, I always wanted to go off-grid, live in the wilderness. Careful what you wish for, right?"

His laughter was infectious as he bounded back to his spot, where Tao gave him a reassuring pat.

Luna reclaimed the center, bowing grandly. "Let's give a round of appaws," she clapped his front paws ", for all our brave comedians tonight!" Tao isn't feeling it tonight so she is up first in the next event...

The clearing roared with howls, barks, and meows. Their sides ached from laughter. For one shining moment, they weren't fugitives or experiments. They were simply friends, gathered in a circle under the stars, rediscovering what it meant to laugh together.

As the noise subsided, the forest's chorus crept back: crickets chirping, an owl hooting, leaves whispering in the breeze. One by one, the animals settled into the cool moss and leaves. A few stretched out on their backs, paws skyward, gazing at the endless sprawl of constellations.

Titan broke the comfortable silence, his voice softening as if he were confessing something long buried. "You know... we really did used to worry about the silliest things." He let out a deep sigh, the kind that seemed to carry years of traffic jams, endless email chains, and pointless meetings. "I'd give anything to have one of those trivial days again, even for just a minute," he admitted. Then he tilted his head thoughtfully. "But also... I don't miss it as much as I thought I would."

Tao nodded slowly, her fur shimmering under the silver wash of moonlight. "I used to complain about eighteen-hour shifts just staring at files and evidence," she said, her tone caught between fondness and regret. "But after all this... if I ever get back, I'll never take a hot shower or a coffee break for granted again." Her lips curved into a small, sad smile. "Still, I definitely don't miss filling out legal documents at three in the morning."

Max gazed upward, his dark canine eyes catching reflections of the stars above. His voice was low, almost reverent. "I used to measure life battles won," he murmured. "Now I measure it in sunrises and how long it's been since we last ran into a search team." A faint chuckle escaped him, though it was tinged with bittersweetness. "It's a simpler life, in a way. Maybe not as hard physically... but simpler in the soul." Several heads nodded, some eyes closing as if savoring the truth of that statement.

"I used to be afraid of getting old," Luna said quietly from where he lay sprawled, his tabby form half covered by the trees. "Now I'm... actually kind of free." Her voice held genuine surprise, like she was hearing it for the first time herself. "No mortgage, no deadlines. The only deadline is, well, staying alive." He gave a self-deprecating laugh. "Puts things in perspective."

Cleo curled her tail neatly around her, sitting sphinx-like as if addressing a classroom that only she could see. "I catch myself worrying about my students sometimes," she admitted softly. "Whether they're okay, if they wonder where I went." Her ears dipped slightly, then rose again. "But then I remind myself I have to worry about us now. About keeping us safe." She pressed her nose gently into her paws before lifting her gaze again. "It's funny... I never imagined I'd literally turn into a mama cat herding kitten's." She flicked her eyes toward Max and Titan, who were busy nudging each other like mischievous schoolboys. The two dogs froze under her stare, then had the grace to look mildly guilty before settling down.

A comfortable lull fell over the clearing. The group was tired, but unexpectedly content. The absurd carnival escapade and their shared jokes had left behind a warmth that lingered in their chests.

It was Chai who finally broke the quiet, his voice softer than usual, almost hesitant. "Do you think… do you think we'll ever have normal lives again?" He didn't clarify whether "normal" meant regaining their human forms or simply finding stability as animals, but the unspoken meaning was clear enough. The Corgi's usually cheerful face was pensive now, his short snout resting heavily on his paws.

For a moment no one spoke. Then Daisy answered, his deep voice carrying both steadiness and empathy. "I think we'll make a new kind of normal, whatever that ends up being." He swept his gaze across the circle, his friends, his pack. "We have each other. And as long as we stick together, we have a chance. Whether that's finding a way to reverse this or…" He trailed off, and in that pause each of them faced the silent truth: that this might be permanent. "…or making the best of it," he finished quietly.

Winston rose and padded over to Chai, giving the Corgi a reassuring nudge with his nose. "One day at a time, buddy," he said gently. Then, with a grin that felt almost mischievous, he added, "And hey, if that goat is to be believed, there's a cozy bed and a meal waiting in our future." His tail wagged in encouragement.

Chai managed a small smile, ears perking slightly. "That goat better not be a fraud. I'm holding him to that prophecy."

A ripple of chuckles moved through the group. Luna stretched out luxuriously, already drifting toward sleep. "If not, we'll go back and demand a refund," he muttered with a lazy grin, eyes sliding shut.

Titan circled three times before curling snugly against Cleo's side, his usual routine. "Next time, maybe we consult a fortune-telling owl," he yawned. "Goats are so 19th-century carnival."

Daisy snorted at that, a soft doggish laugh. "Goodnight, guys," she whispered, her voice already thick with drowsiness. One by one, the others echoed her. "Goodnight." "Sweet dreams." "'Night." Above them, the stars peered through the canopy while a crescent moon laid silver light across the clearing. Slowly their breathing synchronized, rising and falling like the rhythm of a single heart. Despite the absurdity, the danger, and the loss of their human lives, they had found something that resembled family here. And in the quiet honesty of the night, perhaps that mattered more than anything else.

Max lifted his head one last time before sleep claimed him. His ears twitched at the night's symphony, the chirp of crickets, the distant hoot of an owl, the soft rustle of leaves. No engines. No footsteps. Just the forest, alive and unbothered by human concerns. Far off, faint as memory, came a drifting tune from the carnival carousel, or maybe it was only his imagination. Henry let out a soft, contented huff and lowered his head. Absurd as it all was, this was their life now. Tomorrow would bring whatever tomorrow would bring.

As the first blush of dawn touched the eastern horizon, ten former humans slept soundly in a tangled heap of seven dogs and three cats. For this one night, at least, they were safe, they were together, and they were at peace in their strange, makeshift carnival of animals.

Chapter 7

HUNTERS AND HUNTED

Night had settled gently over the pine woods. The sky above scattered with stars like sugar spilled on dark velvet. In a small clearing sheltered by towering oaks, a camp had taken shape: a circle of ten unlikely travelers, seven dogs and three cats, huddled together in the hush of the late hour. The air was cool but not biting, softened by the warmth of early summer as they journeyed south from New York.

For hours they had moved quietly under the cover of dusk, weaving through brush and Cleo. Now they had finally found a safe wooded spot far from any road or wandering human eyes. The clearing smelled of pine needles and damp earth, the scent strong but oddly comforting. A fallen log and a ring of stones hinted that others had once camped here long ago. In the center, glowing embers crackled softly under a makeshift fire. It had taken no small amount of ingenuity, striking matches with teeth and claws had been a near-comedic ordeal, but at last they had managed to coax a flickering flame into life. Its orange glow danced over fur and Tao, painting long Cleos that reached into the dark beyond.

On one side of the fire, Daisy the golden-furred retriever lay with his head on his paws, amber eyes reflecting the flames. Titan, though he wore a canine body, his human mind and name remained, let out a tired, content sigh. Beside him, Max, sat with a soldier's posture, his broad chest slowly rising and falling as he let himself relax. A few feet away, Cleo perched on a flat rock, tail curled neatly around her paws, the fire light shimmering in her green eyes. She paused to groom an errant tuft of fur behind one ear before settling, her ears swaying to the night's chorus.

Not far from Cleo, a sandy-colored mutt named Picasso lay curled like a doughnut on a worn blanket they'd "borrowed" from a shed earlier that day. Her ears twitched at every rustle in the undergrowth, but her posture was easy, comfortable among friends. On the fringe of the clearing, Peanut and Luna paced the perimeter with watchful precision. After one last check for hidden threats, she padded back into the circle and lay down, letting the warmth of the fire seep into her paws.

One by one, the others also settled, some stretching out on their sides, others sitting upright with noses tilted toward the breeze. In total, ten pairs of eyes gazed into the fire light or looked upward to the jeweled sprawl of the stars.

For the first time in days, there was no sign of pursuit. No helicopters droning overhead. No black vans with tinted windows. No alarms or shouting scientists. Only silence and the steady chorus of crickets. The group exhaled as one. This place, at least for tonight, was safe.

A gentle quiet settled over them, a silence filled with thought. With the adrenaline of escape fading, memories crept closer fragments of families left behind, homes that seemed impossibly far away, lives that no longer fit.

Tao broke the stillness in her own way. The gray cat began to hum, almost shyly. It was a delicate, lilting melody, a lullaby so faint it nearly vanished beneath the fire's crackle. One of her ears remained perked, as if embarrassed, but she hummed on, eyes distant in the flames.

"That's a pretty tune, Tao," Titan said softly, lifting his head. "What is it?"

Tao froze as though caught in something private. Her tail-tip flicked. "Oh… it's just a lullaby," she murmured. "Something my mom used to sing to me when I was little."

Cleo uncurled slightly on her blanket, her brown eyes warm. "It's lovely," she said. "I've never heard it before."

Tao offered a small, bashful smile, flashing the tiniest hint of fang. "I haven't sung it in a long time."

Luna padded closer, lowering herself onto her belly with her paws stretched toward the fire. "You miss her," she said softly. It wasn't a question. Whether it came from instinct or empathy, Luna had a way of sensing feelings.

Cleo's eyes dropped to the flames. "I do. I miss… everything. My parents, our house… even my old piano." Her voice was so quiet it nearly disappeared in the crackle of pine logs.

Silence followed, heavier now. Ears drooped. Gazes drifted. Each of them felt the tug of their past, the people they loved, the homes that might never be theirs again, at least not in the present way. A log popped, sending sparks upward, while somewhere in the dark a night bird trilled.

Titan cleared his throat. "It's hard not to think of home on a night like this," he said. His accent, usually softened by years in America, grew more pronounced when he spoke of it. "Quiet moments... they make you remember things."

Max nodded, staring into the fire. The reflection painted his eyes with flickers of gold. "Yeah. I keep wondering what my family's doing right now. If they're okay. If... if they think I'm okay." His voice was low, weighted with worry.

Cleo rose, stretched, then trotted to Max's side, nudging his shoulder with her nose. "They'll be okay," she said with gentle conviction. "We'll find a way back to them. Somehow."

"We will," Luna agreed, her ears lifting with determination. "But Max is right, they're probably worried sick. None of us got to say goodbye." The truth of it made her voice falter, her tail lowering toward the ground.

The forest filled the silence again, a whispering breeze, an owl's soft hoot, the chorus of insects. Instinctively, the group pressed a little closer, drawing comfort from warmth and fur.

Titan looked around the circle, at this odd patchwork family fate had thrown together. "You know," he said slowly, "we've been through so much together these past weeks. But there's still a lot we don't know about each other... from before."

"Before we became science experiments on the run, you mean?" came a wry voice. Tao, the wiry Siamese cat, flicked his tail with sardonic amusement. "Hard to picture you all having normal lives."

A few chuckles rose. Dark humor, yes, but not untrue. Their old lives already felt like someone else's story.

"I had a normal life," Titan said, smiling faintly. "And an interesting childhood. I bet we all did." He hesitated, then gave a small nod, as though deciding something. "Maybe we should share some of it. Stories from when we were kids. I don't know about you, but I don't want to forget who we were."

Cleo's ears lifted, green eyes thoughtful. "That… actually sounds nice," she said softly. "I'd like to hear your stories. All of them."

Tao's tail thumped once against the blanket. "Me too. A trip down memory lane might be good for us."

Max's dark muzzle stretched into a grin, tongue lolling briefly. "Never thought I'd be doing this at a campfire," he joked. "But alright, as long as no one minds if it gets a little sappy."

Luna let out a quiet laugh. "We're literally a pack of talking dogs and cats sitting around a fire in the woods. I think 'normal' left us behind a while ago. A little sap won't kill us."

Titan sat taller, ears pricking forward. His golden fur glowed in the fire light as he looked around the circle. "Who wants to start?"

For a moment no one spoke, glancing at one another. Then Luna nudged him with her paw, eyes kind. "You should. You brought it up. Tell us about where little puppy Titan came from."

Titan let out a breath that turned into a laugh, a puff of steam in the cool air. "Alright," he said. Sitting straighter, he gazed up at the stars as if pulling words from their patterns. The others quieted, ears tilted toward him, waiting.

"I was born in a small village in Illinois, not too far from the border," Titan began. His voice was steady, but tender. "My childhood was simple, I suppose. We didn't have much, but we had a big family house with a courtyard. On warm nights, my cousins and I would sneak onto the roof to fly kites under the moonlight. We'd stay there for hours, telling stories, chasing the night breeze. Below us, my mother and aunties cooked dinner, the smell of spices drifting up and mixing with the cool air."

Luna sighed dreamily, eyes half-closed. "That sounds beautiful."

Titan smiled gently at her, then continued. "It was. My father was a schoolteacher, my mother stitched clothes. We weren't rich, but I never felt poor. I had my little sister, Amrita, and a whole gang of friends from school. Every afternoon we'd rush to a dusty field to play soccer." A chuckle escaped him. "I was the smallest, so they always stuck me in the goal, where no balls ever got stopped. I'd spend half the game daydreaming, kicking dirt, until someone finally kicked one my way."

Max grinned. "I used to hate being picked last for basketball. I feel you."

Titan's tail gave a small wag. "Eventually they let me play forward I wasn't half bad once I had the chance. Once, I even kicked the ball hard enough to smash a neighbor's window." Her eyes gleamed at the memory. "I got in so much trouble, had to apologize a hundred times. But the next day, my father surprised me. He brought home a new-cleats. He told me, 'Practice. Just try not to break any more windows son.'" Titan's voice softened, heavy with love. "He believed in me, even when I was just a scrawny kid."

Cloe leaned forward on her rock, her eyes soft. "Your father sounds kind," she said gently.

"He is," Titan corrected with quiet emphasis. "I mean... I hope he still is, wherever he is." For a moment his voice faltered, heavy with uncertainty, but he steadied herself and continued. "Around the time I was ten, my parents made a big decision. My auntie had already moved to America and kept telling us there were better opportunities there. So... we left. We uprooted our whole lives to come to New York."

She drew in a slow breath, his ears tilting back as he pictured it again. "I remember landing at JFK, holding my sister's hand. Everything was so loud, so fast. New York felt like another planet. We went from our quiet little village to this sprawling city of skyscrapers and honking taxis and people everywhere."

Luna gave a knowing nod. She understood that feeling all too well but stayed silent, letting Titan's memories flow.

"I didn't speak much English yet. I'd learned a little in school, but not enough to keep up. In fifth grade I was the weird new kid who could barely talk to anyone." Titan gave a sheepish laugh, her amber eyes crinkling. "On my very first day, a girl asked if I played football, I was so proud of my football skills that I answered, 'Yes, I'm a very good forward.'" She shook his head at the memory, half amused, half embarrassed. "They all stared at me like I was from another galaxy. I didn't know 'football' wasn't a word they used here. They teased me about it for weeks."

Daisy covered her muzzle with a paw, muffling a giggle. "Aww, poor Titan. Kids can be brutal."

Titan shrugged lightly, still smiling. "It was rough at first, but it got better. I made a friend eventually Jensen, from my class. Turns out he lived right upstairs from us. He'd come down to help me with homework sometimes. Curly red hair, freckles everywhere, and the patience of a saint. Every day he'd teach me new American phrases so I could understand the jokes the other kids made." Her ears tilted bashfully, and he grinned. He made me feel like I belonged."

Luna's tail gave a happy thump. "That's adorable. Did he ever know?"

Titan let out an amused whine. "No clue. I was way too shy to say anything. I was eleven and clueless." She groaned dramatically. "But I do remember trying to impress him at a middle school dance a couple years later. I'd been practicing hip-hop moves I saw on TV, thought I was slick. Instead, I tripped, crashed into the punch table, and spilled the whole bowl all over his new suit."

The circle erupted with laughter. Even Max, usually stoic, let out a hearty bark. "Oh man, Titan!"

Titan hid his face behind a paw. "Mortifying doesn't even cover it. I must have apologized a thousand times. Jensen just laughed and said it was only punch. But I swore off dancing for a good long while."

Tao quivered in amusement, her green eyes gleaming. "I bet you were still cute, though."

Titan chuckled, his tail wagging faintly. "Not sure about that." Then his tone softened, more reflective. "Those first years in New York were hard, but moments like that made them brighter. My sister and I slowly adjusted. My parents... they worked constantly. My dad started driving a cab, my mom found a job in a tailor shop. I had to grow up fast. By twelve I was translating at parent-teacher conferences because they couldn't manage the English yet."

He fell quiet, gaze distant as the fire light flickered in his eyes. A log shifted in the embers, breaking with a soft pop. The others waited, knowing he wasn't finished.

Titan's next words came lower, weighted. "The moment I knew my childhood was over was about a year after we arrived. We were still struggling. One night I woke up to voices in the kitchen – my mom and dad. I peeked in... and saw my father with his head in his hands, crying." Titan's ears drooped. "I had never seen him like that. He kept saying he was sorry – sorry for bringing us there, sorry for how hard it was. My dad had always been this strong, steady man. But that night I realized he was just... human. And afraid. Everything shifted for me in that moment. I felt like I had to step up, to be strong for him, for all of us. The next day I started looking for odd jobs after school. Babysitting, delivering newspapers, anything I could manage. I stopped being just a kid. I became another adult in the house."

Silence felt heavy around the fire. The crickets filled the space with their steady rhythm.

Cleo had edged closer; her small body pressed to Titan's side for comfort. She rested her head gently against him. Max reached out, laying one broad paw over Titan's in quiet solidarity.

Titan exhaled, the weight of the memory softening into a grin "Things improved. My dad got steady work as a clerk, my mom saved enough to start a little home business. We found our footing. But I never forgot that night. It was like one day I was just a kid chasing soccer balls and spilling punch on guys... and the next, I understood what real worry was."

The group sat hushed, the fire light glinting in their eyes.

Finally, Titan gave a rueful half-smile. "Sorry. That was heavier than I meant."

Luna shook her head, her voice tender. "Don't apologize. Thank you for sharing that." Her eyes glistened in the glow.

"Yeah, girl," Max rumbled softly. "I get it. Having to grow up fast... I really get it." He didn't elaborate, but his tone said enough.

Cloe nuzzled Titan's neck affectionately. "Your family's lucky to have you," she said warmly. "And so are we." Then she brightened, her voice playful again. "And I'm sure you became a much better dancer later."

Titan barked a laugh, ears perking up. "Actually, I did! College cured me of two left feet. Emily would've been proud."

That earned cheers and giggles, breaking the somber spell. Titan looked around at his friends – this odd, precious family – and felt lighter for sharing. "Thanks for listening," he said sincerely, curling his tail around his paws. "So... who's next?"

"I'll go," Luna announced brightly, her sandy fur catching the fire light. Her tail wagged with eager energy. "Little Luna's turn."

A few playful whoops and barks rose in encouragement. Titan dipped his head gratefully, relieved she had picked up the thread so smoothly.

Luna cleared her throat with a dramatic little flourish, as if preparing to take the stage. "Alright," she said with a grin. "But fair warning – my story might make you all hungry. Most of my memories involve food."

Max groaned, his stomach rumbling audibly. "You're telling us this after we ate the last sandwich?"

Tao smirked. "We'll survive. Go on, Luna"

The Tabby's eyes gleamed with affection as she began. "I grew up by the ocean. A little town on the coast of the

Dominican Republic. If I close my eyes, I can still smell the Peanut oil in the air – and the garlic and onions drifting through the neighborhood at dinnertime." She smiled, lost in the memory. "My mamá ran a small food stand, so half my childhood was spent on a stool beside her, munching sweet fried plantains or fresh empanadas while she chatted up customers."

Max's stomach growled again, loud enough to make a couple of them laugh. Tao giggled. "See? I warned you. But it's true – food was everything for us. We didn't have much money, but Mamá could turn the simplest ingredients into a feast. Our house always smelled of oregano, cilantro... a kitchen that never rested."

Her tail wagged as she went on. "I lived with Mamá, Abuita, and my two little brothers. Papá... well, he left for New York when I was six to work and send money back. So, it was really us women raising the boys. Being the oldest – and the only girl – meant helping all the time. Stirring pots, washing dishes, minding my brothers. But it wasn't all chores. We had a big family all around – aunts, uncles, cousins – the door was never closed. Everyone was family."

Maria as Luna sighed softly, her expression glowing with second hand warmth.

"Every Sunday after church," Luna continued, "we threw a backyard party. Someone always brought a guitar or a radio, and soon the whole place filled with music and dancing. I'd run between the grown-ups, sneaking sips of soda, trying to snatch bites of roast chicken before anyone caught me." She chuckled, eyes sparkling. "Mom taught me to dance merengue as soon as

I could walk. I'd stand on her feet, she'd hum a tune, and we'd spin around. I loved it."

Her ears twitched with delight. "Music, dancing, baseball – oh, baseball was huge. My brothers and I played in the alley so much we broke windows left and right. Neighbors used to groan whenever they saw us coming with a ball."

Titan chuckled knowingly. "Sounds familiar."

Luna winked. "Hey, what can I say? Latinos and baseball – it's a cliché, but it's true. My first glove was a hand-me-down, way too big, but I refused to let it go. I insisted on playing with the boys, and by ten I could throw farther than most of them."

A few impressed murmurs rippled through the circle.

Luna smirked. "Remind me never to challenge you in a snowball fight."

Luna laughed. "Trust me, you'd lose." Then her tone softened with longing. "Those were good days – hot sun, ocean breeze, music on every corner… and people who knew me everywhere I went. Sometimes I miss that the most – how everyone back home felt like family."

Her expression softened as she continued. "I had a best friend, Isabela. We did everything together, school, chores, sneaking mangoes from the neighbor's tree." Sofia's grin turned sly. "We also had our eyes on the cute boy for a while, Miguel, the baker's son. He was a couple of years older and thought he was the town's big baseball star." She laughed, shaking her head. "Isa and I would sit on the curb eating shaved ice, making up silly songs about how dreamy Miguel's eyes were. Total, total puppy love."

At the word *puppy,* she paused and snorted. "Heh, little did I know I'd literally become a puppy later in life."

The others cracked up, a chorus of barks and meows echoing among the trees. Luna gave a melodramatic bow. "Thank you, thank you, I'll be here all week."

"Don't quit your day job, comedian," Picasso quipped, flicking his tail. "Oh wait, our day job is what, exactly? Running and hiding?"

Luna stuck out her tongue at him, then went on. "Anyway… Miguel. My first crush, I guess. Once, at a big street festival, I got all dressed up, I mean, I was maybe eleven, but I put on my prettiest blue dress and borrowed Mamá's lipstick, thinking I looked very grown-up." She rolled her eyes at the memory. "That night I actually got to dance with Miguel during a merengue song. Well, he mostly spun me around, and I nearly fell over because I was so nervous. My face must have been as red as a tomato." She gave a soft laugh. "When the song was over, he patted my head like I was still a little kid and said, *'Buen baile, niñita.'*, *Good dance, little girl.* I was mortified that he still saw me as a child… but also over the moon that I'd danced with him at all."

"Sounds pretty cute to me," Tao commented.

"It was, in its silly way." Luna smiled faintly. "I never told him I had a crush. A year or so later he had a girlfriend his own age anyway. But I still wrote his name in my diary with little hearts for a while." She shrugged lightly. "By the time I turned twelve, though, I had other things on my mind."

Her voice grew more serious now, and the group sensed the turn in her story. "See, that was the year Papá finally sent for us to join him in New York. He'd been gone almost six years at that point. We missed him like crazy, and he missed us. He finally saved enough to buy plane tickets. It was exciting… but also terrifying. I'd never been on a plane. I'd never left my town, let alone the country."

She took a slow breath, letting the fire light flicker across her face. "I remember the day we left. The whole neighborhood came to see us off, it was like a big party, but everyone was crying. Mamá tried to be strong, but she cried too, hugging my aunts and my uncles. My brothers were too young to understand how huge it all was; they were just excited about the airplane. But I understood. I was leaving behind everything, my friends, my school, the mango trees, the sound of waves at night."

Luna's brown eyes glistened. "My aunt pressed a rosary into my hand at the airport and told me God would watch over us. I didn't want to let her go. I was her favorite, you know," she added with a trembling smile. "She whispered to me, *'Take care of your mamá and hermanos, okay?'* Because suddenly, I was going to be the responsible one in America, since I was the eldest."

A few tears slipped down her cheeks, and she pawed at her face quickly. "That moment, when I hugged Auntie for the last time at the airport, I think that's when my childhood ended. I felt something in my heart... kind of break and grow at the time. I was leaving behind being a kid in that little town and becoming... something else. I had to be brave for my brothers and Mamá. I remember on the plane, my youngest brother got scared and started bawling during takeoff. I held him and sang the lullaby Auntie always sang to us. Even though I was scared too, I tried not to show it. That was the first time I really acted like a little mom."

By now, Cleo had silently moved to Luna's side, the gray cat pressing close in solidarity. Cleo rested her chin on Luna's back comfortingly. Cleo exhaled, a mix of sorrow and grief at having said it aloud. "New York was a whole new world. Papá was practically a stranger to us at first, and life got busy and hard in new ways. But we managed. Still," she gave a watery chuckle, "there's a part of me that's still that island girl chasing boys with a baseball mitt and dancing barefoot to a tambora drum."

Titan leaned over and licked Luna's ear in a brotherly gesture, making her giggle and scrunch up her shoulder. "Thank you, Luna," he said warmly. "You paint a beautiful picture."

"It really was," Luna murmured. "I'm glad I got to grow up there, even if I had to leave it behind." She sniffed and then smiled more strongly, looking around at her friends. "And now here I am, I can't dance on two feet anymore, but..." She stood on all fours and did a little comical twirl, her tail wagging. "I can certainly wag with the rhythm! Maybe one day I'll show you guys a proper merengue, doggy style."

The group burst into laughter and applause, some stomping their paws in appreciation.

"I'd pay to see that," Picasso joked.

"Better than your dancing, Picasso," Luna shot back, sticking out her tongue.

Luna gave another mock bow before settling back down. The laughter faded into a comfortable hush. Her eyes found Max. "Your turn?" she asked gently.

Max's smile had thinned during Luna's last part. He sat a little straighter now, a flicker of nerves showing in his eyes at being in the spotlight. "Alright," he said, clearing his throat. His deep voice rumbled, "Guess it's my turn to spill."

"I grew up in New York City," he began. "Not the fancy part or anything, a pretty rough neighborhood in the Staten Island. For me, there was no idyllic village or ocean breeze," he added with a small smirk, nodding to Titan and Chai. "But we had our own kind of community on our block. Loud, tough, sometimes chaotic, but it was home."

He glanced into the fire, then up at the stars as Titan had done. "I was raised by a single mom. My dad took off before I can even remember. Never met him. So, it was just Mom, my older brother Jamal, my baby sister Tisha, and me. Mom worked two jobs; she was a home health aide by day and a cashier at a bodega at night. Basically, my brother and I raised Tisha, and in a way, Jamal raised me."

A soft smile touched Max's face. "Jamal was four years older than me. He was my hero. He taught me how to ride a bike, well, actually it was his bike, way too big for me, and I ended up crashing into a mailbox. Still have a scar on my knee from that." He chuckled warmly. "We used to play basketball at the park whenever we could. I was this scrawny kid but quick on my feet, and Jamal was tall and could shoot from anywhere. We pretended we were a two-man NBA team, putting on a show. He'd commentate our moves in this booming voice and make my sister and her little friends cheer for us as an 'audience.'"

Picasso grinned. "Sounds like you had your own personal hype man."

"Exactly." Max's tail wagged slightly. "Those were good times. We didn't have much money, but Jamal would always find a way to bring joy, day-old pastries from the bakery, or bootleg DVDs of the latest movies. On summer nights, we'd all sit on the fire escape, me, Jamal, and Tisha, sharing a dollar pizza slice and listening to the radio. Sometimes, when Mom wasn't dead-tired, she'd join us and tell stories about her childhood in Georgia." He chuckled. "She came to New York from the South when she was eighteen, so I guess in a way that was our family's little immigration story, just moving north instead of across oceans."

Titan dipped his head, recognizing the parallel in Max's words.

Max's voice grew quieter. "The thing about my neighborhood... you grow up fast. By middle school, I'd seen fights, seen people get hurt... even saw a kid pull a knife once." The others exchanged uneasy glances; some of their sheltered upbringings stood in stark contrast to what Max described. "My mom tried her best to keep us straight. Church every Sunday, dinner together when we could, strict rules about school. But Jamal... he started slipping when he turned sixteen. Fell in with some guys on the corner." Max's ears drooped. "I was twelve then, and I could tell he was changing, coming home late, bruises on his face sometimes, lying to Mom. I was scared for him, but also kind of angry, you know? He was my big brother, my protector, and suddenly he was out doing who knows what."

He paused, clawing absently at the dirt as old frustration bubbled up. Tao purred gently, and Luna leaned closer, lending him quiet strength.

"One night," Max said at last, "we were all woken up by banging on the door. Police. They arrested Jamal right there in our living room. He'd been caught stealing electronics from a store, running with those so-called friends of his." His voice was thick with remembered pain. "I'll never forget my mom's face as they put him in handcuffs. She was crying, begging them, *'He's a good boy, please.'* And Jamal… he wouldn't even look at us. He just hung his head."

The circle fell into heavy silence. The fire crackled, and somewhere in the distance, a car horn echoed faintly.

Max spoke softly. "Jamal was sent to juvenile detention upstate. He was gone. And Mom, she just… broke for a while. She still went to work, still put food on the table, but I'd catch her crying at church, or staring off instead of scolding Tisha when she misbehaved. She'd lost hope, I think." He swallowed hard. "That was when I knew I had to step up. I was the man of the house now, at twelve years old. Overnight."

He glanced at Titan. "You mentioned seeing your dad cry, for me it was seeing my mom stop crying. When she went quiet, I knew childhood was over. I couldn't be a dumb kid anymore; I had to make sure Mom and Tisha would be okay."

Max drew a long breath, his voice shaky despite his effort to keep it even. "I started picking up whatever hustles I could. I'd carry groceries for the lady down the block for tips, or clean the barbershop after school. I'd take Tisha to daycare, then school, then home every day, make her do her homework, tuck her in. I tried to keep her from realizing how bad things were. When I was fifteen, I even lied about my age to get a real part-time job washing dishes at a diner. That meant I had to quit the basketball team I'd joined freshman year. That… that hurt. But it wasn't really a choice. Mom needed the extra money, and I wasn't about to let her lose the apartment or something."

A couple of tears glinted in Max's eyes now, and he blinked them away quickly. "I remember one evening, I was passing by the park and saw some guys I used to play ball with. They were just goofing off, being teenagers, yah know? Flirting with girls, talking about some new video game. I realized I hadn't done any of that in a long time. While they were out having fun, I was scrubbing pans in a kitchen or putting my sister to bed. That moment, watching them, I knew my childhood had ended back when Jamal left. I was jealous of them... and then I felt guilty for being jealous. Life wasn't fair, but it was what it was."

Tao hopped down from her rock and walked over to gently press her head against Max's foreleg. He gave a sad smile and lowered his head to nuzzle the top of the cat's head in thanks.

"I'm happy to say," Max continued, his tone brightening just a little, "Jamal got out when I was about seventeen. He'd wised up in juvie, came back, and actually got a job at a mechanic's shop. He's doing okay now. We mended things between us, slowly. I think seeing me holding it together at home made him want to be better. But by that time, I was already basically an adult. I graduated high school and went straight to working full-time, no college or anything. Needed to keep helping out." He shrugged his broad shoulders. "No regrets, really. My mom and sister, they're everything to me. I'd do it all again."

Daisy wiped her eyes with a corner of the blanket. "They must be so proud of you, Max," she said softly.

"I don't know," Max replied, voice thick. "Maybe. I just hope they're okay... I hate that right now they probably think I'm missing or worse." He sighed, a low whine in his throat, and quickly tried to steer away from that thought. "Anyway, uh, you wanted a first crush in there, right?" He attempted a grin to lighten the mood. "Let's see... Her name was Danielle. We sang in the church choir together when I was like thirteen."

Luna's ears perked. "You sing, Max?" she interjected, pleasantly surprised.

Max gave a bashful laugh. "Don't look so shocked. I used to. Tenor section. I mostly joined because, well, Danielle joined. She had this amazing voice." His tail tapped the ground as he remembered. "We'd walk home from choir practice together, and sometimes I'd carry her music books for her. I thought I was really smooth." He chuckled. "One time, I worked up the nerve to buy her a single rose for Valentine's Day. Left it in her choir robe locker with a little anonymous note that just said, 'From a secret admirer.' I was too chicken to sign my name. I'm pretty sure she knew it was me, though, because she gave me the sweetest smile when she found it."

"Aww!" came the collective chorus from the group. Even Picasso pretended to gag but was clearly listening intently, his tail curled around his paws.

Encouraged, Max continued, "Yeah, well... that was as far as it went. I never asked her out or anything. Not long after, I had to stop going to choir to work more hours. So, that was that. Just a tiny chapter in my life." He gave a little shrug, but there was a note of regret in his voice.

Titan reached over and squeezed Max's shoulder with a paw. "Maybe not as tiny as you think. It's a good memory."

"Yeah," Max conceded, smiling softly. "It is. I wonder if she stayed in choir, if she kept singing... She wanted to audition for one of those TV talent shows, I remember. Who knows, maybe she did."

A silence settled, full of empathy for the life Max had lived. In the quiet, Max straightened up and added, "I will say this: taking care of my sister all those years taught me patience. And how to braid hair." He chuckled, and the others smiled with him. "Now, as a dog, I don't have hair to braid and I definitely don't trust any of you with my fur."

This earned the desired laugh. Serena held up a paw. "Don't worry, we won't try any makeovers on you… yet."

Max rolled his eyes with a grin. "My point is, looking out for people is kind of what I do. I guess now you guys are my people. Or my pack." He looked around at the ring of furry faces illuminated by fire light. "I've only known y'all a short time, but… I care about you. And I promise, I'm going to do everything I can to protect you. That's what my mom raised me to do for family."

For a moment, no one spoke, moved by the earnest pledge in his deep voice. Sofia broke the hush gently. "We know you will, Max. And we've got your back, too."

A round of grateful nods and vocal agreements followed. Max ducked his head, a little embarrassed by all the attention, but clearly touched.

To rescue him from the spotlight, Serena cleared her throat. "Well, since we're doing this like a middle school classroom," she teased lightly, "I nominate Tao to go next. If she's up for it."

Tao gazed at Max with gentle sympathy as he finished, and when Serena suggested her name, the Siamese cat sat up a little straighter. Her green eyes reflected the fire as she nodded. "O-okay," she said softly. "I'll go."

She took a moment, kneading the rock beneath her with her paws, an unconscious cat-like motion that made a couple of the dog's smile. Tao noticed and huffed a shy laugh. "Sorry, cat instincts," she murmured, then cleared her throat. "I was born in Beijing, China," she began. "But we moved to the U.S. when I was really little, like four years old. So, I don't remember much of living there except bits and pieces: my grandma taking me to a big park with a lake, feeding ducks... stuff like that. My parents moved here for grad school and a new life. We ended up in Ohio of all places."

"Ohio?" Picasso echoed, tail twitching. "I always thought you were a New Yorker through and through, like Max."

Tao shook her head. "Nope. I grew up in a suburban town in Ohio. We were one of the only Asian families around. My parents are both scientists, pretty brilliant ones, actually. They set very high expectations for me from the start. I think, being immigrants, they felt a lot of pressure to succeed, and for their kids to succeed." She gave a tiny shrug. "I was an only child until I was ten, then my little brother came along. But for a long time, it was just me, and they put all their hopes into me."

Her tail curled around her paws as she continued. "Don't get me wrong, they loved me a lot. They just... showed it in different ways. When I was five, my mom started teaching me piano. She's a pianist, she had dreams of being a concert pianist when she was younger. Every day after kindergarten, it was an hour of piano practice. By age six I was in lessons with a teacher who would rap my knuckles whenever I missed a note."

"Ouch," Daisy muttered.

Tao smiled wryly. "At first, I actually enjoyed it. I had a knack for it and I loved music. Playing little songs with my mom, getting gold stars from my teacher, it felt good. And my parents were so proud when I performed well. So, I kept practicing, and the better I got, the more they expected."

She glanced up at the stars. "My world kind of revolved around two things: school and piano. I didn't really mind not having much free time when I was small. But when I hit middle school, I started noticing other kids hanging out after class, going to the mall or movies, having sleepovers... and I was always either at home doing homework, at piano lessons, or at competitions on weekends. It started to bug me."

Tao's head drooped a little as she recalled her frustration. "I remember this one time, I got invited to a friend's birthday party, it was a classmate I really liked. Actually, he might've been my first true cush," she admitted, a slight blush in her voice. "His name was Aaron. He was funny and sweet, and he loved rock music. Anyway, he invited me to his twelfth birthday, which was going to be at an arcade and then pizza. I was over the moon to go. But... I had a piano recital the next morning that my mom said was too important. She forbade me to go to the party; said I needed to practice and rest." Tao sighed. "We fought about it. It was probably the first big argument I ever had with my mom. In the end, I didn't go to the party. I remember sitting at the piano that night, supposedly practicing, but I was crying so hard I couldn't see the sheet music."

"That's rough," Max said softly.

"Yeah." Tao shrugged faintly. "I mean, I understand why she did it, she thought she was protecting my future or whatever, but at the time, it just felt so unfair. Aaron drifted away after that, and any silly hopes I had that he liked me back drifted away too. I buried myself in music even more after that, maybe out of spite or maybe because I felt I had nothing else."

Tao drew a deep breath. "By the time I was fourteen, I was entering these statewide competitions. Big pressure. My parents would invite all their friends to my recitals. It's like… I was their trophy. I didn't mind completely, because I still loved music, but it was also scary. I developed horrible stage fright. Every time I stepped on stage, my hands would shake." Her tail flicked anxiously just thinking about it.

Max spoke up kindly. "Hard for me to picture you afraid of anything. You're one of the bravest among us, Tao."

She gave him a grateful little nod. "Thanks, Max. But back then, I was terrified of failing. And then… one day, I did fail." Tao's voice grew quieter, her ears dipping. "It was a regional piano competition. My whole family came to watch. I was playing a really difficult piece, Mozart. I had practiced it for months, pouring every ounce of myself into it. But halfway through, I blanked. My mind just… went dark, and my fingers froze. I missed an entire section, then tried to cover it up and stumbled through the rest. It was a disaster."

Tao swallowed hard. "I didn't win anything. In fact, I placed near the bottom. Afterwards, my parents were… not unkind, but painfully silent. My dad gave me a quick pat on the shoulder and said, 'We'll do better next time,' but my mom… she didn't say a word the whole ride home." Tao's eyes glistened. "That silence was worse than yelling. I remember getting home, going straight to my room, and just… breaking down. I cried harder than I had since I was a little kid. Because

I realized I wasn't their perfect prodigy anymore. And without that... I didn't know who I was supposed to be."

A couple of tears slipped down her furry cheeks despite her efforts to blink them away. Titan reached over gently, using the edge of his paw to brush one from her face. She gave him a trembling smile in thanks.

"That night," Tao continued softly, "my mom eventually came in and found me still crying. I'll never forget it. She sat on the edge of my bed... and then she started crying too. She apologized, said she was sorry for pushing me so hard, that she only wanted to give me opportunities. It was the first time I'd ever seen her doubt herself." Tao's ears flattened. "In that moment, I realized my parents weren't infallible. They were just people, doing their best, maybe even trying to live out their own dreams through me. That was the day my childhood ended, I think. Because for the first time, Mom didn't treat me like her little girl or her star pianist, she treated me like a person who had her own feelings. Our relationship changed that night."

Daisy dabbed at her eyes with a paw. "That's heavy, Tao. But also... kind of beautiful, that she apologized."

"It was," Tao agreed. "After that, she eased up a little. I mean, she didn't suddenly let me quit playing piano or anything," she added with a small laugh. "But she let me have more of a say. I even went to a couple of high school dances later on. And when I got a B in math once, they didn't flip out the way I thought they would." She gave a self-effacing grin.

"What about music? Do you still play?" asked Daisy gently.

Tao looked down at her paws. "I did, up until... well, up until this happened." She lifted one paw and flexed her soft pads and tiny claws. "Hard to play piano with these." She tried to make it a joke, but the sadness in her voice lingered.

"I'll bet you'd play a mean keyboard with those if you tried," Picasso joked to lighten the mood. "Cats walk on pianos all the time making crazy sounds."

Tao actually giggled, wiping her tears. "You know, I've fantasized about sneaking into some house with a piano just to plonk around. The funny part is, I can probably hear music better now than I ever did." She tapped one of her large pointed ears. "These ears, this brain, I pick up every cricket chirp and owl hoot. It's like the whole forest is a symphony if you just listen."

The others smiled at that thought, some even tilting their heads to catch the night sounds.

"I still hum sometimes, obviously," Tao continued, her voice carrying more hope now. "And I remember all the songs I learned. I'm not going to forget them. Maybe one day, if, no, when, we get back to normal, I'll play for you all properly. I'd like that."

"We'd like that too," Titan said warmly. "And even now, your music is still inside you, Tao. We all heard you humming earlier. It was beautiful."

Tao's eyes shone, reflecting the first night as she looked around at her friends. "Thanks. I'm lucky to have you guys. I lost some things from my old life, but... I gained a new family, in the strangest way." She let out a soft purr of contentment as Sofia stroked her back with a paw.

After a peaceful pause, Daisy gave a little stretch. Her collie-mix tail wagged as she realized all eyes were turning toward her. "I guess that leaves me," she said with a playful smile.

"Alright, gather round, kiddos, it's story time with Auntie Daisy."

All eyes turned toward her now, the lean Golden Retriever with a spark always dancing in her gaze. She gave a mock-serious sniff. "Call me the wandering wolf," she began. "Because I didn't have a hometown like you guys. I had about a dozen. We moved so much I barely stayed anywhere more than a couple years."

"Military family?" Titan guessed.

Daisy shook her head. "Diplomats. My mom works for the Foreign Service, and my dad's a journalist. They're both American, but they've lived overseas since before I was born. So, I was literally born abroad, Brazil, actually. By the time I was ten, I'd already lived in six different countries."

"Wow," Peanut murmured, trying to imagine that kind of life.

Daisy smiled, her eyes distant as memories surfaced. "It sounds glamorous, but it was a mixed bag. I mean, I've stood on the Great Wall of China at sunrise, and I've ridden a camel by the pyramids in Egypt. By age twelve, I could swear in four languages, useful when kids tried to pick on me." She winked. "But it also meant I was always the new kid, always saying goodbye. I learned not to unpack my heart too deeply, if that makes sense."

The fire popped, and Serena poked at it with a twig. "Some places we stayed a year, some two or three. I was basically a professional new-girl-in-class. My mom used to joke I should write a guidebook about it. I got good at making friends fast. Soccer helped, no matter the country, kids always play soccer. I'd show up at a park with a ball, and before long we'd be laughing and playing, even if we couldn't understand a word of each other's language."

Max grinned. "Smart. Sports as the universal language."

"Exactly," Daisy said. "When I lived in Kenya for a year, I barely spoke Swahili beyond greetings. But every evening I'd join some girls in the neighborhood to kick around a beat-up soccer ball. We'd end up rolling in the dirt, giggling. They taught me clapping games and songs. I still remember one of their lullabies." She hummed a few gentle notes, her smile softening. "Then a year later, we were in Russia, snow instead of sun, frozen ponds instead of dirt fields. I learned to ice skate with kids who thought my accent was hilarious."

She laughed lightly. "I have a million snippets like that, street food in Asia, trying dances in India, getting lost in a market in Spain. My childhood was an adventure, no doubt. And my parents... they loved me, but they were busy. A lot of the time, I was a free-range kid. They trusted me to handle myself early."

His tone shifted, softening. "The downside was, I learned not to get too attached. I had to. Because just as soon as I'd start to really care about a friend or... or a girl," he added with a chuckle, "it'd be time to pack up again."

"You poor thing," Tao said gently.

Daisy gave a half-shrug. "It wasn't all bad. I got good at keeping in touch, emails, letters, pen pals on every continent. But there's one goodbye that really broke me." He took a steadying breath. "I was fifteen, back in Brazil, in Rio. That's where I met the most beautiful girl." A wistful smile crossed Daisies face. "If my life were a movie, he'd have walked on the ocean in slow motion."

Cleo and Tao teasingly taunted the last statement, making Daisy laugh.

"She taught me how to surf," he said. "We'd sneak to the beach early, before my parents even woke up. She was patient, kind. We just clicked. My Portuguese was awful, but he teased me in English while I helped him with her dream of applying to U.S. colleges." Daisie's eyes grew misty. "Marina was my first love, though maybe I was too young to call it that. We were inseparable that year. For the first time, I felt truly at home with someone."

The group listened quietly, picturing Daisy as a sun-kissed teen on a Brazilian beach.

Her voice wavered. "But the next summer, Mom was reassigned, to the Philippines. Just like that, it ended. We tried long-distance, emails, video calls, but we were fifteen, sixteen. Long-distance is hard even when you're grown. The calls got fewer. He got busy, I got busy. By the time I heard she had a new boyfriend at college, I wasn't surprised. Just... sad." Daisy swallowed. "Watching Rio fade from the airplane window that day, I felt something lock up inside me. I knew then life wasn't beaches and waves, it was airports, luggage, and promises that didn't always last."

Titan gave a low, sympathetic whine. "Daisy... that's hard."

Daisy smiled softly, eyes shining but calm. "It's okay. That's life. I didn't have one hometown, but I have pieces of many. And each place, each person, taught me something." She stretched out her front legs and gestured at her canine body with a wry grin. "I think all that moving around made me adaptable. Maybe that's why I haven't completely lost my marbles in this crazy situation."

Picasso joined the conversation. "True, you do seem oddly at ease being a big old mutt on the run."

Daisy smirked, her eyes glinting with humor. "Hey, at least I finally get to do a road trip across the U.S., right? Always wanted to, though I imagined it with fewer fleas." She scratched behind her ear in exaggerated fashion, drawing laughter from the circle.

"But seriously," she continued after the chuckles died down, her tone softening, "all that moving around taught me to value the people who stick by you. And right now, that's you guys. This is actually the longest I've ever stayed with one group of friends without someone moving away." She looked around at them, her tail wagging slowly, almost shyly. "I know we've got a lot ahead of us, and it's scary. But I'm really grateful I'm facing it with all of you. Losing my old life was awful... but finding you has been kind of amazing."

For a moment, silence lingered in the circle, filled with the warmth of her words and the crackle of fire. A few noses sniffled, though later, every single one of them would insist it was just the cold night air, not tears.

Daisy finally broke the stillness in a gentle voice. "To new families, then."

"To new families," Titan echoed, dipping his head solemnly.

Tao's soft purr joined the affirmation, blending with Max's low bark of agreement. Picasso raised his head dramatically and gave a theatrical, "Hear, hear!" Even those who hadn't spoken much contributed, tails thumped against the ground, ears twitched in quiet assent, and a few heads dipped in silent solidarity.

Above them, the stars glittered brighter, as if bearing witness to the bond forged among this unusual band of seven dogs and three cats. The little campfire popped and sighed, keeping them warm as they leaned closer together, shoulder to shoulder, fur to fur.

They lingered in that golden moment, then drifted into lighter stories. Someone pressed Serena for her wildest travel mishap, and she sheepishly admitted to once eating fried crickets in Thailand without realizing what they were. The group howled with laughter. Then they turned their teasing on Titan, coaxing him into describing his questionable dance moves, and even Tao got roped into playacting as a famous concert pianist, tossing paw-scribbled "autographs" to imaginary fans. Each shared joke, each burst of laughter, felt like another stitch in the fabric that bound them.

As midnight deepened, the weight of the day began to catch up with them. Yawns spread through the group, punctuated by soft doggy snuffles and the occasional stretch of fine limbs. One by one, they curled or sprawled around the dimming fire. Max kept his usual place on the perimeter, head lifted in a half-watchful, half-drowsy way. Daisy nestled between Titan and Tao for warmth, while Max circled three times, as if following some ancestral instinct, before plopping down with a contented sigh.

In the hush that followed, a rare and fragile peace descended. They could all feel it, that sense of home, fragile yet real, blooming in the middle of nowhere. Yes, they had lost one life, their human lives. But in exchange, they had found each other. A ragtag family stitched together not by blood, but by trust, struggle, and the stubborn spark of hope.

The fire burned down into glowing coals, their red light pulsing softly like the last heartbeat of the day. Around them, the forest rustled and whispered with hidden life. And under the patient stars above, ten former humans, now seven dogs and three cats, drifted into sleep. Tomorrow, the journey south would continue with the dawn. But tonight, for this one precious night, they were simply a family around a campfire, dreaming of the past, holding on to the present, and step by step, learning how to embrace this strange new life together.

Chapter 8

THE RECKONING

Open Mic Night

The abandoned community center auditorium was dimly lit by a jerry-rigged string of holiday lights and a couple of flickering candles, their weak glow struggling against the darkness and shadows that clung to the walls. Scattered around the makeshift stage sat an unlikely audience: seven dogs and three cats, each carrying a human mind behind their curious, watchful eyes. The air smelled faintly of aged wood layered with dust, and beneath that lingered the sharper musk of nervous animals waiting their turn. Tonight was no ordinary gathering. It was their improvised open mic night – a brief, much-needed respite from the chaos of their strange new existence – and every tail, big and small, thumped or swished with a mix of anticipation and anxiety.

On stage, Daisy adjusted the microphone stand with a paw, doing his best to tighten the screw that kept letting the mic droop. As the de facto organizer of this ragtag event, Daisy's tail wagged in a slow, steady rhythm – the canine equivalent of a reassuring smile to keep everyone calm.

"Testing, one, two, woof… is this thing on?" he said, his voice coming out in a slightly rough-but-clear timbre. A ripple of snickers erupted from the front row, where Max, Picasso, Winston, sat side by side. Daisy flashed them an amused look, his eyes bright with humor. "Welcome, ladies, gentlemen, and furballs of all ages, to our first – and probably only – open mic night!"

A soft chorus of whoops, barks, and one sarcastic meow answered him. In the second row, Luna – a Plump Tabby cat with one torn ear – lifted a paw in polite encouragement. Her Tao twitched with a tentative smile; she was still learning to find humor in their predicament. Nearby, Chai, a the Corgi, practically vibrated with excitement, his tongue lolling in a goofy grin. He lived for moments like this, the chance to make others laugh.

Daisy continued, "We've been through a lot, to put it mildly. I figure we deserve a little laughter and maybe a few tears. So, the stage is open. Who's brave enough to go first?" She scanned the semicircle of his friends. For a moment, no one moved – it was unclear whether fear of public speaking or simply the logistics of getting on stage as a four-legged creature held them back.

Then Chai could contain herself no longer. "Oh, move aside, I've got this!" the Corgi barked eagerly. He trotted up to the stage, nails clicking against the wooden floor, and Daisy relinquished the spotlight with a playful bow of his head.

Chai hopped onto a stool placed at center stage. He almost slipped – balancing on a stool as a dog was no small feat – but caught himself by digging his front paws into the cushion. The sight alone drew a round of encouraging applause, which in this case was a mix of tail thumps against the floor and a couple of supportive yips.

The Corgi puffed out his chest comically. "Thank you, thank you," Chai began, swiping a pretend tear from his eye with a paw. "It's great to be here. You know, as a stand-up dog median."

A groan mixed with laughter rolled through the audience. "Boo, bad pun!" called Luna, an elderly tabby cat lounging in the front. Her tail flicked, though a ghost of a smile betrayed her enjoyment.

Chai wagged his tail. "Tough crowd. Hey, what do you expect? All my material is ruff draft." He paused, eyes shining mischievously, waiting for the reaction.

Daisy lowered his head, covering his snout with a paw in mock despair, while laughter and groans spread among the group. Then Winston, let out an amused whine that sounded suspiciously like a chuckle. Even Luna, usually reserved, purred softly in amusement.

Encouraged, Chai pressed on, pacing as much as his small stool would allow. "So, ever since I became a dog, I've been learning a lot. For example: mailmen. I finally get it. Chasing them is like Black Friday shopping – you don't really know what you'll do once you catch up, but the thrill of the hunt is everything."

A round of genuine laughter erupted. The bulldog, Winston, barked out an especially loud laugh, nearly toppling over. Once a high-powered lawyer in her human life, Winston had discovered as a dog the joy of simple things – like sharing a belly laugh with friends.

Emboldened, Chai continued. "And squirrels – don't get me started. I used to just watch those little guys from my office window, but now?" She leaned forward as if confiding a great secret. "Now I know they're the true puppet masters of the universe. Oh yeah. They tease us on purpose. It's a conspiracy." She nodded sagely, ears bobbing.

Luna chimed in dryly from the front, "Maybe they're unionizing. Squirrels Local 101: messing with canine minds since time immemorial."

Chai pointed a paw at Luna. "Exactly! Thank you, Luna – she gets it! The squirrels are unionizing, and frankly, I respect their hustle."

The group dissolved into laughter. For a moment, the tension of their bizarre situation melted away. In their laughter, they sounded less like animals and more like what they truly were at heart: friends sharing a funny story, never mind the barks, yips, or purrs that colored their chuckles.

Chai finished with a final bit. "I do have one serious observation, though," she said, her tone shifting to faux-seriousness. "Dog life has taught me something profound." He paused dramatically, letting a hush fall. "It taught me that... sniffing each other's butts is a completely valid form of greeting, and we humans have been doing it wrong all along!"

A cacophony of groans, barks, and meows exploded. Peanut, sitting next to Luna, covered his face with a paw in embarrassment and laughter. "Oh my god, Chai!" he cried between giggles. "Too far!"

Chai hopped off the stool, bowing in unabashed pride as laughter and playful heckles rained down. "Thank you, thank you, tip your waitresses – oh wait," he glanced around dramatically, "no waitresses. Just tip your pet-sitters, folks. I'll be here all week!" With that, he bounded off stage, tail wagging furiously as Daisy returned to the mic.

Daisy's eyes crinkled with warmth as he watched Chai rejoin the others. "Give it up for Chai, everyone – proving that comedy isn't dead, it's just gone to the dogs!" The crowd (small as it was) clapped and barked appreciatively. A few tossed in more gentle ribbing, and Chai took an exaggerated bow, nearly sweeping Daisy into a hug in the process. The old tabby pretended to claw Daisy for show, which only fueled another round of laughter.

As the mirth died down, Daisy cleared her throat. "Alright. Who's next? Don't make me start picking volunteers."

After a brief hesitation, Peanut the Pug rose to his paws, his tail wagging hesitantly. His soulful brown eyes darted nervously around the circle. Public speaking wasn't his forte; in his human life, he had preferred writing code in a quiet office to standing under a spotlight. But something about the supportive gazes of his companions – and perhaps the lingering giddiness from Chai's act – nudged him forward.

"I... I'll go," Peanut said softly. Daisy gave her an encouraging nod as they swapped places. The microphone was set too high for her, and seeing this, Daisy quickly stepped back to adjust it down, earning a thankful smile.

Peanut took a deep breath. "So, um, I wanted to share a song. Well, part of one." He cleared his throat nervously. "Bear with me – this is my first time singing as a dog."

A friendly chuckle rose from the audience. "We love you, Peanut!" Luna called gently, and a few others yipped in agreement. Peanut visibly relaxed at the show of support.

He hummed a few tentative notes, testing her pitch. Then, in a surprisingly clear voice – a warm mezzo-soprano that only occasionally wavered when her canine tongue stumbled on a word – Peanut began singing an old folk tune the group had often listened to on the radio during their travels.

His voice floated through the room, soft and earnest:

"Come gather 'round people wherever you roam..."

The opening line, half-sung and half-spoken through canine jaws, drew smiles of recognition. It was Bob Dylan's *The Times They Are A-Changin'* – an on-the-nose choice that nonetheless sent a shiver through more than one listener. Peanut pressed on, her confidence growing:

"...and admit that the waters around you have grown..."

Her tail swayed gently in time with the rhythm. One by one, the others joined in, quietly at first. Winston closed his eyes and hummed along in a low rumble. Daisy mouthed the words, his retriever ears pricking forward. The cats added their voices too – Luna with a sweet, soft alto hum, and even Luna, who couldn't carry a tune to save her nine lives, offering a gravelly purr of harmony.

For a few magical minutes, the empty auditorium resonated with an unlikely choir: ten animals singing (and humming) a human song about change and hope. The absurdity of it – and the beauty – tightened throats and made a couple of them blink back tears. Peanut's voice cracked with emotion on the lyric *for the loser now will be later to win,* and a supportive whine from Winston encouraged him onward.

They ended the song together on a slightly shaky but heartfelt note. Silence followed, heavy and reverent, until Luna padded down from her seat and head-bumped Peanut's leg in lieu of a hug. "That was beautiful," she whispered.

"Absolutely," Daisy agreed, stepping forward. His voice was a little thick with emotion; he quickly blinked and forced a grin to lighten the mood. "Who knew we had *American Idol: Canine Edition* right here?"

Peanut laughed self-consciously and returned to his seat amid wagging tails and nodding heads.

Daisy took center stage once again. "Anyone else want to share? A poem, a story, interpretive dance?" he teased, glancing at Winston, who had been known to sprint in wide circles when excited – a dance of sorts. She stuck her long pink tongue out at him playfully but didn't rise.

A soft voice rose from the side. "I'll go next," said Tao.

The agile Siamese cat moved gracefully to the stage, her tan, black, and deep brown patches glowing faintly under the string lights. Unlike the others, she didn't bother with the microphone – it loomed comically high above her small head. Instead, she settled at the very edge of the stage, paws tucked neatly together like folded hands.

"I don't have a song or jokes," Tao began quietly. "But I wanted to share something." Her green eyes flicked downward, fastening on a knot in the wood floor as if anchoring her nerves. "This is a story… about the last day I was human."

The room stilled. Even Chai, who had been wagging and panting with residual comedy energy, sank onto his haunches and wrapped his tail around his paws, ears pricked forward.

Daisy's ears tilted back in empathy, his gaze steady, as he gave Luna the space she needed.

"I never told you all this," Tao continued, her voice strengthening. "The day of the experiment – the day we all became… like this – I almost didn't come. I was supposed to be at a play that afternoon." Her ears flattened with guilt. "But I had volunteered for this Pet-link trial months earlier. When they moved up the schedule, I thought… I thought I could do it quickly and still make it in time. I told myself it was important, that I was helping advance science. She swallowed hard, her tail tip twitching with the weight of memory.

Daisy instinctively stepped forward, but Luna caught his eyes and gave the smallest shake of her head. She could carry this.

"Well, I never made it to that play," he said, her voice thick. "None of us made it to where we were supposed to go next. And I just… I wanted to say I'm sorry. To all of you." His gaze swept across the circle – this strange, new family she had forged in accident and necessity. "Some of you were part of the Pet-link team, some were volunteers like me. We all took a leap of faith that day. And when things went wrong…" Her voice caught; she drew in a steadying breath. "I felt responsible. If I hadn't come, maybe the chain reaction wouldn't have started. Or maybe I'm just searching for meaning in the mess."

Winston rose silently and padded forward, sitting at the foot of the stage, her steady gaze urging Chai to go on.

"I miss my family every single day," Chai whispered. "I wonder if they've given up hope, or if they're still looking for me. When I sing to myself at night, I sing my mom's favourite song. She gave a fragile laugh. "Silly, I know. But thinking that way... it keeps me going."

From the audience, Peanut's gentle voice cut through the quiet. "It's not silly. Not at all."

Chai's eyes softened. "Thank you." She looked around at the others. "And thank you – all of you. We've been each other's family through this. I couldn't have survived this past month without your friendship and... and your craziness." His gaze flicked to Peanut, who responded with an exaggerated wink, then to Daisy, who nodded firmly.

A beat of shared understanding passed among them. They weren't just survivors anymore – they were a pack, a clowder, a pride. United by accident, held together by choice.

Luna cleared his throat into the hush. "Since we're sharing regrets..."

The old tabby uncoiled himself slowly and padded to join Tao on the stage. She settled beside her, her cloudy cataract eye glinting faintly in the candle light, his one good eye sharp as ever. "I have one too."

Murmurs rippled – Luna had been the most guarded about her life before. He'd embraced the cat role so completely that sometimes it was easy to forget he had ever been human.

"I was pretty much a loner before all this," Luna admitted, ears flicking uneasily. "Not exactly a people person. I worked as a school teacher but that was my existence. My social life outside of that was a book club I rarely attended. I signed up for Pet-link because I was curious and, to be blunt, because they paid a stipend." A rueful smile curved her mouth. "I figured, why not? Nothing ever happens to girl like me anyway."

She drew a deep breath. "But something did happen. And it turned my life upside down. At first, I was furious. Trapped in this body, everything too loud, too bright. I was angry at myself, at all of you, at the universe. I thought it was the end of my life." Her claws flexed into the stage wood, as if grounding himself against that memory.

A few heads nodded – they knew that despair.

"But," Luna continued, his tone softening, "somehow it wasn't the end. Against my very cranky nature, I ended up with nine new friends." A chuckle escaped him. "Me – the girl who couldn't stand office parties – now curling up to sleep in a pile with a bunch of dogs and two other cats every night."

Affectionate laughter rippled through the room. Chai pantomimed dabbing at a tear, which earned him a smirk from Luna.

"I guess what I'm trying to say," Luna went on, "is that I regret not appreciating people… companionship… before. It took becoming a cat to teach me the value of human connection." He shook his head at the absurdity. "If – no, when – we get through this, I'd like to think I'll be a better person if I ever get back. Maybe one who won't hide so much from the world." A pause, then a dry addendum: "That's all. No jokes from me – Chai already used them all up."

Chai raised a paw in mock protest, drawing chuckles.

Luna leaned against Tao's shoulder with a soft bump. "Thank you, Luna." Together, the two cats descended, Luna lending her a gentle lady assist that drew a few warm "aww"s – and one playful wolf-whistle from Chai.

Daisy returned to the mic, her chest brimming with pride and affection for this strange family. What had begun as an open mic had become something far deeper. His gaze swept across them: Ava, the once-workaholic bulldog who now lingered over life's simple joys; Peanut, who had discovered his voice in more ways than one; Titan, the quiet Dobermann at the back, who hadn't spoken tonight but gave a shy wag with shining eyes; and of course, Chai, Luna – and all the rest.

Daisy stepped closer to the mic. "Anyone else?" he asked gently. The silence said enough: every heart that wanted to speak had spoken.

"In that case..." Cleo drew a breath, shoulders rising with the subtle weight of the message. "I have a little something to say. I know I pushed for this open mic because I thought we needed a morale boost. But truthfully... I think I needed it the most." His golden-brown eyes swept across them, soft and steady.

"You all know I worked on the Pet-link project," he said. A few ears flicked; this wasn't news, but Cleo rarely spoke of his own feelings. "Since that day, I've been carrying guilt. Wondering what I could've done differently to stop this. I was so focused on proving the tech could help people, linking minds for the better... I never imagined it could cause this. But seeing you all here, hearing you tonight – it reminds me that even from disaster, something good can grow. You are incredible. The strength, the humor, the heart you've shown... If I had to be stuck as a cat or dog with anyone, I'm glad it's you." He grinned, breaking the heaviness just enough for a few chuckles.

His tone grew firm, heartfelt. "No matter what happens tomorrow, or next week, or whenever – whether we get back to our old lives or continue like this – this family we've found is real. And it's ours. Nothing can take that away."

Winston padded up and leaned against his leg, tail brushing him in solidarity. One by one, the others joined – Luna climbing onto Winston's broad back for a perch, Peanut pressing his nose into Luna's fur, Chai snug against Daisie's other side. Soon, they were a cluster of fur and warmth, a pack held tight by instinct and choice.

For a long, quiet moment, no one spoke. They simply breathed each other in, comfort and belonging anchoring them.

It was, inevitably, Chai who broke the silence. "Group hug, everyone. Or as I call it – a snuggle puddle." He wriggled himself into the center of the heap with theatrical exaggeration. "Ahhh, life goals."

Laughter bubbled out, and it snowballed into sound – barks, purrs, a clumsy howl from Picasso. Peanut giggled and gave his own shy attempt, setting off Winston, whose clear, high howl carried like music. Not to be outdone, Chai tilted his muzzle skyward and unleashed a string of ridiculous "awooga" siren-howls, sending everyone into helpless fits.

The others piled in, howling, yowling, and barking until the old rafters trembled. Outside, startled birds took flight, and some stray cat answered with a confused yowl. Inside, though, the racket melted back into laughter, leaving the group panting, tails wagging, purrs humming, hearts lighter.

Luna's eyes shimmered with the trace of a tear. "Now that," she murmured, voice soft but steady, "was a howl to remember."

Winston, ever the performer, tossed her head back with mock grandeur. "The howl heard 'round the world, right here," she quipped, then bent in a theatrical bow to an imaginary audience.

Daisy chuckled, warmth still in his chest from the shared moment, but before he could reply a sudden metallic clatter erupted at the back of the auditorium. His ears snapped upright, every muscle tensing. The others froze, heads swivelling as one toward the darkened rear doors.

The Reckoning had come.

For an instant, time seemed to hold its breath. Daisy's gut clenched; he recognized that sound all too well, the careless kick of a boot against a folding chair. It was the sound of an ambush slipping out of stealth.

"Run!" he barked, sharp and commanding.

The cozy intimacy of moments before shattered. In a heartbeat, instinct took over. Ten figures scattered in every direction. Peanut and Titan bolted for the side door, claws scraping. Luna leapt onto Daisy's back in a practiced move, gripping his fur tight as he bounded off the stage. Chai and Winston sprinted for the opposite end of the hall, desperate to find an exit not already blocked.

But before they could escape, the rear doors slammed open with a thunderous bang. Blinding beams of flashlight speared into the gloom.

"There they are!" a harsh voice rang out.

Silhouetted against the light stood a team in black tactical gear, their chest rigs stamped with the neon-green insignia of Pet-link. They moved with mechanical precision, fanning into the room. One carried a long animal-control snare pole; another hefted a tranquilizer rifle, the dart-tip gleaming menacingly.

Winston skidded to a halt, her bulldog frame trembling with fury, a growl rolling from deep in his chest. Luna, the aging tabby, arched and hissed, fur bristling.

"Don't hurt them!" a sharp female voice cut across the chaos.

A figure strode forward into the light: Dr. Katrina Silva, lead neuroscientist at Pet-link, and once Cleo's colleague. Rain plastered her trench coat to her frame, and worry etched deep lines across her face. She looked less like the cold bureaucrat of his nightmares and more like someone dragged here by urgency.

The agents hesitated at her command. Daisy's pulse hammered in his ears. He remembered Silva as brilliant, pragmatic... maybe even compassionate. But could she be trusted now?

That moment of hesitation was all Winston needed. She lunged for a gap between two agents, a tawny blur of speed. "This way!" she barked. Chai darted after her, Peanut and Titan close behind.

"There's an exit!" Peanut yelped, spotting the glowing red sign at the end of a side hallway.

"Go, go!" Kevin urged, bounding after them with Luna clinging tight until she jumped down to race alongside him.

The pack thundered into the corridor, claws scrabbling on cracked linoleum. Behind them, shouts exploded. "Cut them off!" "Circle around front!"

But they were too late. Winston barreled through the exit bar with a shoulder slam, and the heavy door burst open into the cool night air. One by one, the others spilled into the parking lot behind the community center.

For a moment, the world seemed suspended. A siren moaned somewhere far away. A car stereo thumped faintly down a distant street. Overhead, a lonely streetlamp cast the group in a harsh circle of white. Ten animals stood panting on the cracked asphalt, sides heaving.

Then Daisy's stomach dropped. Ahead of them, parked crooked across the lot, were two black vans and a sleek sedan, all branded with Pet-link's logo. More operatives were already pouring out, fanning wide to cut off any retreat.

They were surrounded.

Behind them, Dr. Silva and her first squad spilled from the doorway, closing the trap. Instinct drove the group closer together, a trembling cluster of fur and breath. Titan planted himself at the front, teeth flashing, Chai at his shoulder. Luna and Tao pressed against Kevin's flanks. Peanut shrank low, a trembling laser dot from a tranquilizer rifle dancing just inches from her paws.

"Don't move!" a deep voice thundered.

A tall man in a navy suit emerged from the operatives' ranks, his presence radiating authority. Gregory Hampton, COO of Pet-link. Two burly guards flanked him, though he raised his own hands in a pacifying gesture. "Easy now," he said smoothly, as though soothing skittish livestock. "Let's not make this harder than it needs to be."

Winston snarled, stepping forward protectively. "We'll make it as hard as we need to." Her breath came in hot bursts, her eyes flashing with defiance.

Hampton's eyes widened slightly at her clear speech but recovered almost instantly. He must have been briefed. "We're not here to harm you. We're here to fix this," he insisted. His gaze locked on Daisy. "Kevin, referring to his human name...you understand. This has to be contained."

Daisy stepped forward, tail stiff, hackles raised. Over Hampton's shoulder, headlights swung onto the narrow side street. A car slowed, the driver clearly catching sight of the surreal tableau. They had seconds before this exploded into something Pet-link couldn't contain.

"Greg," Kevin talking now as Daisy said, voice steady though his chest roared with fear, "we're not just 'a situation.' We're people. We'll go, but on our terms."

A murmur rippled through the Pet-link operatives, uncertainty cracking their polished professionalism. Dr. Silva edged closer, hands raised in entreaty. "Kevin, listen to me. The neural implants, the only reason you can even speak, they're unstable. If they fail, reversal might become impossible." Her voice carried genuine urgency.

"Convenient timing," Chai muttered under his breath, earning a sharp look from Luna.

Hampton jumped on Silva's words. "Your original bodies are alive, but time is against us. The sooner we attempt reversion, the better the odds."

Luna gasped, stepping forward, trembling with hope and dread. "Our bodies... they're, okay? My body's, okay? And my family?"

Silva nodded, voice tight. "Stable. All of you. In comas, but alive. We've done everything to preserve them." She hesitated, guilt flickering. "Your families know little. Only that you were in an accident. We thought it best"

"Best to cover it up," Luna spat, her tail lashing.

Hampton cut in smoothly, "To prevent panic. Imagine if the public knew"

A sharp flash split the air.

A cellphone camera.

Off to the left, in the alley, two young onlookers stood frozen, one filming with wide-eyed disbelief. "Oh my god," the man whispered to his partner. "They're talking."

More heads appeared at the edges of the lot, curious passersby, a cyclist who'd stopped mid-ride, patrons spilling from a café across the street. Smartphones rose like a forest of glowing eyes. The parking lot was no longer private. The secret was out.

Hampton swore under his breath, jerking his chin to his guards. "Hold the perimeter. Keep civilians back!"

But it was already too late. Murmurs rose from the crowd: "Are those dogs?" "I swear I heard one talk!" "Is this a movie shoot?"

Winston's eyes locked on Daisy's. What now?

Daisy as Kevin's decision crystallized. This was their leverage. This was their freedom. He lifted his head, golden fur aglow in the harsh light, and raised his voice for all to hear.

"We're done hiding."

Gasps echoed from the civilians. A woman clutched her chest, whispering, "Oh my god."

A Pet-link agent tried to step forward. "Sir, let's take this conversation inside"

"No." Daisy barked, sharp as a whipcrack. He planted himself between his family and the company. "No more hiding. No more running. We'll come with you, but only if it's out in the open. No black vans. No secrets. Everyone will see."

Hampton's jaw tightened, his voice clipped. "Be reasonable. This isn't a show for the public. This is a critical, delicate operation."

From the back, Chai barked out, his voice cutting through the tense air. "Then perhaps you should've thought of that before turning us into a freak circus!"

A ripple of laughter and gasps spread among the onlookers, and more than one phone was clearly up and recording now. Someone was definitely streaming this live.

Dr. Silva shot Hampton a sharp look, a silent plea for restraint, before stepping forward with her palms out in a calming gesture. "Alright. Alright. Kevin or Daisy… everyone…" Her tone softened, professor to students rather than scientist to subjects. "You're right. You deserve a choice." Her eyes flicked briefly toward Hampton, warning him to let her lead.

"The experiment's failure changed your lives in unimaginable ways," she continued, her voice carrying a note of sorrow. "I take responsibility for that. We all do." She glanced down at the embroidered Pet-link logo on her coat, as though it weighed on her shoulders. "Our goal now is to set things right, if you want us to."

Titan snorted, the sound startlingly human coming from the Dobermann. "If we want. Big of you to ask," he said gruffly, bitterness roughening his tone.

Dr. Silva nodded sadly. "I know. It's late, too late, in many ways. But we have to ask now. There isn't time for a lengthy debate." Her eyes swept slowly across the ten transformed figures, lingering on each one with quiet entreaty. "Those of you who wish to regain your human bodies, please… come with us. We are as prepared as we can be to reverse the mind transfer."

"What about those who don't?" Luna asked, his voice pitched low. The question landed with heavy weight, and the ambient murmur of the crowd died instantly.

Hampton started forward, but Dr. Silva raised a hand. He fell back, fuming silently. She answered instead, her voice steady. "If anyone chooses to remain as they are... I can't force you to come. I hope you'll reconsider, but at the very least, please allow us to give you medical care and monitoring. The implants could still harm you."

A sharp cry rang out from the crowd: "Who are these people?!" It sounded like a reporter. Sure enough, a man with a press badge shoved forward, hoisting a large camera onto his shoulder. Its red light glowed as he shouted, "Channel 8 News! Can someone explain what's happening here?" Security officers tried to block him, but he twisted, angling for a shot of the surreal standoff.

Hampton forced a smile toward the camera, the mask of corporate control snapping into place. "No comment at this time," he said sternly. "Please step back for your own safety."

The reporter didn't budge. "Is it true these animals can talk? People online are saying"

Before Hampton could launch into more PR spin, Luna made the choice for him. She turned toward the reporter and, mustering every ounce of strength in her small but powerful lungs, shouted, "We used to be human!"

The words rang out, sharp and clear, silencing the courtyard. The reporter's camera immediately zoomed in on the calico cat now standing front and center.

Daisy stepped up beside her, adding softly but firmly, "We are human, our minds, anyway."

The crowd erupted, shouts of disbelief, confusion, even a scream or two. The reporter nearly dropped his camera, then scrambled to steady it, eyes wide. "This... this is incredible," he stammered, training the lens on Max, Luna, and the others.

Hampton's face flushed with fury. "Enough!" he snapped. "This spectacle is over." He motioned sharply to his team. "Secure those willing to come, and get the others out of here. Now."

The security team advanced, but hesitantly. None of them looked eager to leash what seemed like ordinary pets, let alone ones speaking English, on live television. One guard approached Peanut with a leash; he recoiled, growling. Another reached for Tao's scruff, but Luna darted in front, hissing and swiping with claws bared.

"Back off!" Winston barked at a third guard who neared Luis. The man froze, caught between training and astonishment. How exactly do you subdue a talking dog in front of witnesses?

Dr. Silva's composure cracked. "Greg, wait! Don't do this here"

"Mom...?"

The voice was small, trembling. It cut through the chaos like a bell.

From the edge of the crowd, a curly-haired girl, no older than ten, had slipped past the adults. Her wide eyes locked onto Luna. "Mommy? Is that you?"

Luna's breath caught. "Lily?" she whispered, her whole-body trembling. She knew that face, her daughter, tears glistening in the lamplight.

Her world tilted. How could Lily be here? And then Luna realized, they were only blocks from her family's neighborhood. Their eerie howling song earlier… it must have carried through the quiet night. Somehow, impossibly, her daughter had followed that thread of sound and hope straight to her.

Before Luna could move, a man rushed forward, her husband, eyes wide with shock. He pulled Lily back protectively. "Lily, no, that's not" He faltered, staring at the cat, his expression crumbling between denial and recognition. His voice cracked. "M-Luna…?"

The crowd went still. Even Hampton froze, his hand halfway to a command signal. The spectacle had become something raw, something achingly human.

Luna stepped forward on trembling paws, torn between surging toward her family and the fear of frightening them. Lily clung to her father, eyes never leaving the cat.

Daisy's chest tightened painfully at the sight. This was the cost. This was what was truly at stake. She turned to the others, voice low but urgent. "We need to decide. Now."

Silence hung, heavy and absolute. Then, one by one, decisions came.

"I'm going," Luna said first, voice trembling yet resolute. Her gaze was locked on her family. "I need to go back. Take me. Do whatever you have to. Please."

Her husband closed his eyes in relief, hugging Lily tightly as tears spilled down his face. The reporter's camera whirred, catching every second of this reunion.

Daisy stepped forward next, his nod firm. "I'll go too." He caught Winston's gaze. She would understand, he had to see this through, to help repair the damage he had helped cause.

Peanut padded up beside them, her black Lab frame steady. "Me as well." She offered a brave, wavering smile. "I want my old life back. Or at least... the chance at it."

Cleo limped up, his tail flicking. "Count me in. I've got an overdue date with my own reflection." His joke was thin, the emotion in his one good eye impossible to hide.

Titan, the Dobermann, stepped forward without a word. His silence said more than words ever could: the longing for home, for belonging, etched into his spotted face.

From the back, a Mutt finally crept forward, Picasso who hadn't spoken all night. She gave a tiny nod, her soft whine heavy with longing. She didn't need to say it. They all understood.

Six. Daisy counted quickly. Six ready to return. And the others...

Chai broke the silence, his voice ringing with defiance. "Well, I'm not going." The scrappy Corgi trotted apart from the group, planting himself firmly. "No offense, Doc, but I've grown fond of this look." He flicked his ear playfully. "Besides, who'd keep the jokes coming if I left?"

Max lumbered up beside him. "I'm with the kid," he said simply. His gaze softened as it swept the others. "As a man I was tired, worn down. But as a dog..." His voice caught. "I've felt more alive than I had in years. I'm staying."

Winston joined them, bowing her graceful head. "I won't go back either." Her eyes met Daisy's. "My body was broken. I couldn't walk, couldn't run. Here... I can sprint under the sky, feel the wind on my face. I can't give that up."

Daisy's throat ached at her words. He had suspected, but hearing it laid bare cut deeply. Still, he nodded, respect in his gaze.

At last, Tao, stepped forward quietly. She brushed against Luna in farewell, then padded to stand with Chai, Winston, and Max. Her golden eyes glowed softly as she said, "I... I'm staying too." It was perhaps the most she had spoken in weeks. She lifted her chin with resolve. "This is my life. I want to live it as me."

And so, the choice was made. Six choosing to return. Four choosing to remain.

Dr. Silva's expression was a portrait of bittersweet reverence and regret. "Understood," she said quietly. She gestured to two nearby staff. "Prepare the transport crates, gently, please. And get the equipment ready back at the lab."

Hampton opened his mouth, ready to protest the leniency of allowing some to refuse. But then he caught sight of the sea of phone cameras, the distraught family clinging together in the background, and the intensity of the crowd's attention. His jaw clenched. He exhaled sharply through his nose and gave a single curt nod, signaling his men to comply with Silva's orders.

The Pet-link team rolled forward several padded animal carriers, the kind used for large dogs, though these were reinforced and threaded with monitoring wires. Luna didn't hesitate. She trotted straight toward one, anxious to begin the process, but stopped long enough to press against her husband's hand as he knelt before her, tears streaming freely. "I'll bring her back," she whispered, her voice trembling but certain. "I'll be back." Luna's small hand reached through the mesh to stroke her mother's fur. Luna purred softly in reassurance, then forced herself to step inside the carrier.

Nearby, Daisy bent down until his forehead touched Winston's in a tender farewell. "We'll see each other again," he whispered. Her voice shook as she gave him a playful lick on the nose, a tear sliding down her muzzle. "Count on it," she replied with a brave smile.

Peanut threw her paws around Chai in a tangle of fur, tails, and snuffles that was the closest thing to a hug their forms allowed. "Don't get into too much trouble, okay?" she murmured against his scruffy coat. Chai gave a theatrical sigh. "Who, me? Never." But his voice cracked, betraying how deeply he would miss her.

Luna padded up to Max. Words weren't necessary at first, just a solemn nod. But the bulldog surprised him by leaning forward with a quick, affectionate nuzzle. "Stay scrappy, old man," Luis said gruffly, which in their odd friendship was the closest thing to love. Luna's tail twitched faintly. "Stay lazy, you mean," he murmured back.

One by one, Daisy, Peanut, Titan, Luna, Picasso, and cleo allowed themselves to be guided into the open carriers. None resisted; none had to. They went willingly, each pausing only for a final look at those who remained behind.

The others, Chai, Winston, Max, and Tao, gathered off to the side, standing just outside the glow of the vans' lights. The crowd murmured in uncertainty, some people craning to get closer, others hanging back in awe. The Channel 8 reporter kept his distance, voice hushed but urgent as he narrated into his camera about the astonishing scene unfolding.

Hampton glanced at the four with an unreadable expression, caught between frustration and calculation. "We... we will need to follow up with you," he said, forcing his tone into something that resembled diplomacy. "For your own safety. But tonight... I suppose that's all we can do."

Chai gave a lazy wave with one paw, his grin cheeky even now. "Sure thing, boss man. We're not exactly booking flights to Aruba. You know where to find us."

Dr. Silva moved closer to Winston, concern heavy in her voice. "We'll send someone to check on you soon. Please, be careful. The implant"

"I'll be fine," Winston interrupted gently. Her eyes softened. "Take care of them." She nodded toward the vans being loaded. "That's how you can help me."

Across the lot, Daisy had just been secured inside his carrier. Through the mesh he locked eyes with Chai. No words passed, but the meaning was clear: gratitude, worry, brotherhood. Daisy dipped his head once. Chai returned the gesture slowly. It wasn't goodbye, just farewell for now.

Engines rumbled to life, headlights cutting bright beams through the night. Hampton hurriedly ordered the van doors sealed. Luna's family was ushered into a separate vehicle to follow the convoy, her husband never releasing his hold on the carrier that held his wife.

The crowd of spectators parted to let the caravan through. Some clapped awkwardly, some whispered prayers, others simply stared in shock. A few curious souls ventured closer to the four who stayed behind, offering tentative pats or murmurs of amazement. Winston accepted a gentle head scratch from an elderly woman who whispered, "You poor dear." Tao perched on a low wall, her golden eyes fixed on the retreating taillights, her expression an aching mix of hope and sorrow.

In the flurry of departure, no one noticed Chai slipping toward the far end of the lot. Winston nudged Tao down from her perch and quietly smiled at her. Max cast one last look at the dispersing crowd, wagged politely to the kind old woman, and lumbered after his friends.

By the time anyone thought to glance back, the four "loose" animals had vanished into the night, gone as suddenly as they had appeared.

The public was left stunned, the media in a frenzy, and the world teetering on the cusp of an incredible story.

The reckoning had only just begun.

Epilogue

THE HOWL HEARD 'ROUND THE WORLD

Three days after "The Incident" at the community center, a video surfaced online that would soon capture the world's imagination. Shot in a modest living room under the warm glow of lamplight, it opened with a sight that seemed to belong in the realm of fantasy: a golden retriever, a bulldog, a sleek greyhound, and a black cat all seated with surprising poise on a large couch, flanked by several nervous-looking humans.

A man in his early forties stepped into the frame. Though newly restored to his human body, the gentle determination in his eyes betrayed his true identity, it was unmistakably Yusuf. He drew a breath, steadying himself, and addressed the camera.

"My name is Dr. Yusuf Khan. A week ago, I was a dog, a British Shot Hair cat named Cleo, to be exact. Before that, I was a neuroscientist at Pet-link."

He hesitated, clearly weighing how much the audience could handle. Off-camera, one of the dogs, Chai, the irrepressible terrier now back in human form, flashed a no thumb-up, ever the joker. Yusuf gave the faintest smile and pressed on, voice firming.

"This may sound unbelievable, but everything you are about to hear is true. We are the ten people who volunteered for the Pet-link mind trial last month. Due to a freak accident, a lightning strike during the experiment, our consciousnesses were transferred into the bodies of animals... our own pets."

The camera tilted slightly, panning toward the four animals on the couch. Winston, the bulldog, lifted a paw in a polite little wave. Beside him, Max the German Shepard sat with regal composure, tail thumping softly against a cushion. Tao, the Siamese cat, blinked serenely in the lamplight, her tail twitching as though she were savoring the moment. Perched on the arm of the couch Chai the Corgi, Tao who had chosen to appear briefly to corroborate the story.

One by one, each person began to recount their part of the story.

Peanut, restored to her human body, spoke haltingly of the confusion of waking as a Pug and the raw struggle to adjust to paws and fur. Titan, shy but resolute, explained the sequence of events, the experimental mishap, the panic, and the initial attempts to bury the truth.

Maria Sanchez a woman with kind eyes, admitted that inhabiting a cat's body had profoundly shifted his outlook on life. Kevin O'Neill, normally quiet, mustered the courage to describe how he had missed her family every day he remained trapped in an animal body.

Then came the animals' turn.

The camera zoomed in on Winston, who cleared his throat in an oddly formal gesture for a bulldog. His deep, measured voice resonated.

"My name is Ava Brooks I was a Corporate Attorney. I know I may look like just a bulldog to you, but I am very much a person on the inside."

She offered a warm, wrinkled smile. On screen, a split image appeared: Winston as a bulldog alongside an old photograph of her as a woman next to the dog that was talking. Viewers across the world gasped at the proof, this was no hoax.

Next, Ava spoke softly, her elegant French Bulldog face radiant with sincerity.

Her words, intercut with cellphone footage from the community center, where she had stood protectively in front of her friends, barking at armed agents, struck viewers like a thunderbolt.

Tao, curled sphinx-like on the couch, fixed the camera with unwavering golden eyes.

"My name is Serena Li. I'm 29 years old. I... I know this might be hard to believe, but I'm here. I'm real." Her voice trembled, then steadied with conviction. "Mom, Dad, if you're watching, remember how I always did my homework with Mozart playing? I still love that. And the silver locket you gave me... it's on my collar now."

The camera zoomed in on the small heart-shaped pendant dangling from her purple collar. It was a personal detail no actor could fabricate.

Finally, Chai's segment rolled, not as a human, but as his Corgi self. They had filmed it earlier, splicing it in for authenticity. Chai sat in front of the couch, head cocked, eyes dancing with mischief.

"I'm Rahul Patel. Thirty years old. Former Software Engineer, current Corgi extraordinaire." He winked into the lens. "You might've seen my set the other night, twelve shaky phone videos can't be wrong."

A muffled laugh from Jamal King behind the camera broke the tension.

Then Chai's tone softened. "We know what we're saying sounds impossible. But we're not lying. All we want..." His ears drooped, and for a moment the jokester looked achingly human. "...is to be acknowledged. To see our families again. To have the world understand what happened to us."

The video bore the title: *The Howl Heard 'Round the World, Our True Story.* It was no exaggeration. Within hours of uploading, it spread like wildfire across YouTube, Twitter, and every social feed imaginable.

At first, many dismissed it as viral marketing for some upcoming movie. Comment threads exploded with skepticism: CGI experts debated the authenticity of the animals' mouth movements; skeptics insisted the "humans" in the footage were actors reading lines. Hashtags like **#TalkingDogHoax** and **#PetLinkExperiment** trended worldwide.

But then the puzzle pieces began to align. Local Seattle news confirmed Dr. Yusuf Khan name on an indefinite medical leave list from Pet-link. Talk shows replayed bystander footage from the community center, where the distinct voice, Luna's, was clearly heard crying, *"We used to be human!"* The audio matched the testimony perfectly.

For some, proof was unnecessary.

In a Chicago suburb, a man nearly dropped his mug when he saw Max on screen. He recognized his father's dog instantly, despite the German Sheppard's body. "Dad's alive," he cried into the phone, calling his siblings. "He's alive. He's a dog, but he's alive!"

In San Diego, Serna Li's parents wept openly at the sight of her cherished locket. They had refused to accept the official story of their daughter's "lab accident," and now their faith was vindicated.

All across the country, echoes of recognition spread: a coworker recognized Chai's irreverent humor; an elderly couple in Wisconsin realized the Corgis voice belonged unmistakably to their missing Cousin.

The reaction was a tidal wave: disbelief, awe, wonder, and tears.

Memes surfaced, one dubbed the group "The Lab Rats" (a name Chai found hilarious). Fan art flooded the internet. Yet alongside the humor came serious questions: about the ethics of Pet-link's research, the meaning of personhood, and the legal status of the four who chose to remain animals. Were they citizens or property? People or pets? The world suddenly had a moral quandary to wrestle with.

Pet-link scrambled into damage control. An official statement confirmed a "serious incident" but offered little else. The public was not satisfied. Within days, government agencies announced formal inquiries. Lawmakers debated emergency measures regulating neural experimentation.

Meanwhile, the ten who lived it all tried to reclaim some version of normalcy.

Luna, fully human, spent every possible moment with her husband and daughter, soaking in the ordinary joys she had once feared lost forever. Yusuf and Cleo split their time between their own lives and Pet-link, now under tight government oversight, working with scientists to stabilize the link for those who remained in animal form.

Their group bond remained ironclad, daily video calls, endless group chats where jokes bounced back and forth in a mix of human language, emojis, and the occasional typed *woof* or *meow*.

And the four who chose to remain animals? They became unlikely celebrities.

With Kevin's help, and with funds quietly provided by Pet-link in an effort at restitution, a quiet countryside sanctuary was established. It became both refuge and headquarters, a place where Chai, Winston, Tao, and Max could retreat when needed, yet also broadcast livestreams to the world.

They did not stay silent. Instead, they used their new reality as a platform, advocating for transparency in science, calling for empathy across species, and challenging rigid notions of identity. Their message was clear: if humans and animals could share bodies, minds, and friendships, then perhaps the barriers dividing *anyone* were less permanent than society assumed.

The viral video continued to spread, inspiring people across cultures and continents.

Here was proof, unshakable proof, that cats, dogs, and humans could speak together, laugh together, and stand for one another.

If these ten could bridge the impossible gap between species, the world had to ask itself: what else might be possible?

Late one evening, a few weeks after the video's release, Chai sat beneath a clear, starlit sky at the sanctuary. A phone was propped up on a flat rock in front of him, streaming live to millions of fascinated followers across the globe. Winston dozed beside him, his snores low and steady, while Tao lounged like a queen on top of the world. Both listened, their eyes half-lidded but attentive.

Comments poured across the screen in a constant blur, but one stood out, simple and piercing: *Do you regret what happened to you?*

Chai tilted his head thoughtfully, then glanced at his companions before answering. "It's hard to call such a wild journey a 'regret,'" he admitted, his tone equal parts humor and honesty. "We lost a lot, sure… but we also gained things we never imagined. New perspectives. New family."

As he spoke, movement stirred on the porch behind him. Kevin and Maria, visiting for the weekend, stepped into view and waved cheerfully at the camera. Behind them followed Jamal, Taylor, Talia, and Yusuf, their faces glowing in the warm porch light. In that moment, all ten of them, human and animal, were together again, side by side as the family they had become.

Maria leaned over Chai's shoulder to add her voice to the stream. Her expression was radiant, eyes glistening as she spoke. "We're more than an experiment. Our story is about friendship, love, and never giving up, no matter how unbelievable the obstacles."

The livestream erupted with reactions, hearts, emojis, messages flying so quickly the feed seemed to shimmer. Viewers weren't just watching a reunion; they were witnessing a testimony of resilience, spoken in unison by people and animals who had lived the impossible.

That clip of the impromptu gathering spread like wildfire, quickly dubbed by the media as *"The Howl Heard 'Round the World."* The Wolves of New York were back together What had begun as a joking headline cemented itself as the emblem of their shared legacy.

And indeed, it became more than a phrase, it became a call. A call for understanding, for empathy, for boundaries of science to be redrawn with caution and compassion. In the months that followed, families were reunited, lost voices were heard again, laws were challenged and rewritten, and what had once been dismissed as a bizarre lab accident became a global parable.

A parable of wonder. A parable of warning. And above all, a parable of hope.